Blink, and I'm Gone...

Blink, and I'm Gone...

Elizabeth Diamond

The Book Guild Ltd

First published in Great Britain in 2021 by
The Book Guild Ltd
9 Priory Business Park
Wistow Road, Kibworth
Leicestershire, LE8 0RX
Freephone: 0800 999 2982
www.bookguild.co.uk
Email: info@bookguild.co.uk
Twitter: @bookguild

Copyright © 2021 Elizabeth Diamond

The right of Elizabeth Diamond to be identified as the author of this
work has been asserted by her in accordance with the
Copyright, Design and Patents Act 1988.

All rights reserved. No part of this publication may be
reproduced, transmitted, or stored in a retrieval system, in any form or by any means,
without permission in writing from the publisher, nor be otherwise circulated in
any form of binding or cover other than that in which it is published and without
a similar condition being imposed on the subsequent purchaser.

This work is entirely fictitious and bears no resemblance to any persons living or dead.

Typeset in 12pt Minion Pro

Printed on FSC accredited paper
Printed and bound in Great Britain by 4edge Limited

ISBN 978 1913913 328

British Library Cataloguing in Publication Data.
A catalogue record for this book is available from the British Library.

To Hugh, with thanks for everything.

1

Dying doesn't hurt. I need to tell you that, Ben. Not the actual act of dying. What leads up to it might. In my case, there was a sudden firecracker bolt of pain. But not for long. Then no pain. Nothing. I slipped beyond my body as easily as water seeps from a sponge.

What is it like? It's like a child who has turned up at a party but can't get in. She's bearing gifts, has her best party dress on, but she can't get in. The door doesn't give to her weight, no one answers when she rings the bell. She steps between the shrubs to a brightly lit window. She sees children inside, in the room beyond the glass. They are playing some game or other: charades, pass the parcel. Most of them have their back towards her. And if they don't they can't see her anyway. She sees a child she recognises, the birthday child, and opens her mouth to call out. But as soon as the sound leaves her mouth it is snatched away, as if she's shouting into a wind tunnel.

But there are times when it's possible to reach you. Like now, when you're dreaming. I come often into your room *when you sleep. I sit on the side of the bed, the empty side that used to be mine. You push your limbs into the empty space, as if you are looking for me. Right now, your left kneecap is thrust up against my hip. I love the resistance of it; it makes me feel as if I am alive. I fall into your dream-world like a shadow falls into sunlight.*

"It doesn't hurt. Dying doesn't hurt."

Your left kneecap jerks against my hip.

"Rachel, Rachel..."

I reach out and take your hand. Your knee slides from my hip and you slip away from your dream-world to a deeper place. The glass between us hardens again. In the morning you may remember that I came to you in your dream and told you something. Or you may not.

It is like playing ball with a blindfold on.

*

There is someone else here with me sometimes. Pictures manifest themselves to me. He is giving the pictures to me: rain glistening on grass, falling leaves, footprints in the snow.

"All things change. Nothing is forever. Letting go is everything."

"But I can't let go. Where would I go? Who would I be?"

I can't see him clearly. It is as if he is standing in shadows. But I can sense him. He is here, and then he isn't. It is as if my thoughts draw him to me and then just as easily send him away. When he isn't with me I sense he is somewhere warm and brightly lit, like the room where the children play at the party beyond the glass.

There. You see, I have thought of him and now he is here.

"It's time."
"For what?"
"Time for her to remember. You have to help her."
"How can I help her? I don't remember either."
"When you are willing, it will come back to you."

*

In the blink of an eye I am in Molly's room beside her bed. Her dark hair spills upon the white pillow. There is a bubble of moisture in the corner of her mouth and her cheeks are rosy and smooth. I lean over her and touch her cheek gently and, as if a shadow has softly reached into her dreams, she stirs.

"Molly, it's Mummy. Don't be afraid."

After it first happened she would fight her way out of her dreams as if in danger of drowning. She would surface, struggling and threshing and choking for air. You would come into her room and hold her tight.

"What is it, Molly? Tell me. What were you dreaming about?"

But all she knew about that time was only in pictures, dark and hazy, as if submerged under water. And incomplete. She would see a shape that looked like me. But only part of the shape. The way my hair lay in waves on the floor. The rosebud pattern on my dress. The upturned grooved sole of my sandals.

I lean over her now as she sleeps and I peer into her dreams. I can see light, like air held in a fast-flowing stream. And then, a dark shape. Like something lying on the bedrock of a stream, monstrous and drowned.

I reach into her dream, like a hand disturbing water. The shape dislodges itself, floats up to the surface. A body wrapped up in a shroud. The shroud is covered in a pattern of tiny rosebuds. A pool of red under the body's head. Something else, too. A man. The shape of a man. A man with no face. Molly is sitting up in bed now, her eyes are wide open. She starts to scream. I am trying to hold her, trying to comfort her, but I can't reach her. It is like air touching on glass, leaving no imprint. Then you rush in.

"It's all right, Molls. It's all right, darling. Daddy's here."

You push me out of the way without knowing I am there and sit down beside her on the bed. You wrap your arms tightly around her and she clings to you.

I'm the child at the party again. Out on my own in the cold.

2

Ben sat in the kitchen sipping his coffee. He was waiting for Molly to come downstairs. He'd been up to her room earlier and got her up and dressed in her school uniform. But she'd wanted to play for a short while with her Barbies before coming down for breakfast. He'd let her; he knew she was feeling a little nervous. Today was the first day back at school after the half-term break.

He'd set out two breakfast bowls on the table. One for Molly, one for himself. He picked up the cornflakes and half-filled his bowl, quarter-filled the other one with chocolate Frosties. He picked up the cafetière that stood next to the kettle on the work-surface and brought it over to the table. He topped up his coffee. He fetched milk and a carton of orange juice from the fridge. He went out into the hallway and called up the stairs.

"Molly! Breakfast's ready."

"Coming, Daddy!"

In the blink of an eye I was back upstairs in Molly's

room. She was poking about at the bottom of her wardrobe looking for Miss Moffat.

Not there. Toy box, Molly.

She sighed, got up. She went over to the wooden toy box below the window and threw out Paddington Bear, Henry the Hippo and three Barbie dolls, all in various states of undress, and a scruffy little dog named Rufus, and there she was – Miss Moffat, with her round soft face, wide painted-on blue eyes staring up, as if she was relieved to be found and claimed again. Molly picked her up, hugged her to her chest.

"Naughty, Miss Moffat. You been hiding!"

She left the other toys scattered on the floor and ran downstairs.

"Took your time, Molly."

"I was looking for Miss Moffat. She was hiding."

"Ah." Ben knew better than to question Molly about Miss Moffat's habits of hiding. "Okay, poppet. Now eat your breakfast. All of it. And that apple I've cut up for you."

Molly sat on the chair at the table and laid Miss Moffat's face down across her lap. Ben poured milk into her bowl. She waited until the Frosties settled and softened in the bowl, then picked up her spoon and started to eat. Ben started on his cornflakes. Spoons clicked against teeth.

"Daddy?"

"Yes, darling?"

"I had one of my dreams last night. One about Mummy."

The spoon paused halfway to Ben's mouth. It had been months now since Molly had one of her dreams. Those dreams when she'd woken up screaming, tearing him out of his sleep so he had to rush to her bedside to hold her until the screams subsided. Like he did last night. He'd hoped that it wouldn't be mentioned, that she had forgotten about it by the morning.

"This dream was different, Daddy."

His heart skipped a beat. Mine would have, too, had I a heart to beat.

"How different?"

She hesitated. She glanced over towards her father. She was gauging whether or not he could take it.

"Well, I saw Mummy in the dream, Daddy. She was lying on the kitchen floor."

"Was she, sweetheart?" Time was slowing, almost coming to a standstill for him. He wasn't sure he wanted to hear this.

"Not this house. The old one. The floor was black and white. She was wearing a pretty dress, Daddy. It had little pink flowers on it. Like roses."

His hand trembled slightly. He lowered his spoon back down, let it fall softly onto the table. Flecks of milk and mushy cornflakes spilled out.

"There was red under her head. Lots of it. Like blood. She wasn't moving, Daddy. I wanted to run to her but I couldn't. Then I woke up screaming."

"I know, darling. I was there, remember? I held you till you were okay again, until you went back to sleep."

"I remember, Daddy."

He reached across the table and took her hand, the one that wasn't holding on to her spoon. "You're here with me now, Molls. Just you and me. You're safe."

"Something else, Daddy. Mummy comes in my room sometimes. When I'm asleep. Not that mummy on the floor. Another one. She comes in my room and sits on my bed and tells me not to be afraid."

He tried to smile but the smile came out crooked.

"That's good. She's taking care of you."

"Do you think mummies can do that when they've gone to heaven, Daddy?"

"Yes, darling, I do. I really think they can."

*

I followed them out to the car that was parked on the gravel courtyard. I slid into the passenger seat. Ben opened the back seat car door for Molly to clamber in, but suddenly she froze, a look of panic on her face.

"What's up?"

"Miss Moffat. I can't leave her alone, Daddy."

"Don't be silly."

She screwed up her face, shook her head hard so that her long dark hair whipped across her mouth.

"No, Daddy. I can't."

"I don't think I want you taking your own toys to school, sweetheart."

Molly didn't answer. She didn't move either. She had that look of stubborn resistance on her face that Ben recognised only too well. He sighed.

"Okay. Let's go and get her."

I waited in the car. They came back only moments later, a look of satisfaction on Molly's face. Miss Moffat was tucked resolutely under her arm. We drove in silence. All three of us quiet with our thoughts. The early morning sunlight fell unevenly on the distant hills and the moorlands, so that some parts were brightly lit, glowing intensely with colour, whilst other parts were in shadow.

When we arrived at the school I waited with Ben and Molly in the playground for the morning bell. Some of the other little ones were crying, clinging to their mother's legs. Molly stood silently, hugging Miss Moffat. I felt the pain of not being able to hug her. I felt the pain of being in the world but not belonging to it. The bell rang. I followed Ben and Molly into the classroom. A little girl with blonde pigtails stared at me. She could see me; she had the gift. Miss Austin, who was old for her twenty-six years, in her prim blouses and flat lace-up shoes, came to claim Molly.

"That's okay, Mr Vincent. Best to leave quickly. It works better that way."

But he needn't have worried. Molly was already drifting over to the Wendy house corner, shadowed by the little girl with blonde pigtails.

"Bye, sweetheart, have fun. See you later…"

But Molly had already disappeared from sight.

*

Back home in the cottage Ben made himself a cup of coffee – instant this time, as he'd run out of the real stuff. He took the cup upstairs and into the room he used as his office. He sat there for some time, staring out of the low thick-silled window in front of his desk, over the sunlit hills that were dotted with sheep.

He was thinking of our daughter.

When she first started at the school he worried about how she'd get on. The other children were generally local children, rural children. What would they make of her flatter London vowels? She'd be different to them. Would she get bullied?

But she had been there now for several weeks and she seemed to be happy. She was making friends, was being accepted.

He stood up. He stretched himself up to his full height. He went out of the office and back downstairs to the tiny kitchen and made himself another cup of coffee. He stood on a chair and fumbled at the top of the kitchen cupboard for the packet of cigarettes he had left there, just to prove that he didn't need them anymore. But today his will had deserted him. He lit one and drew on it heavily several times. It went straight to his head. He screwed out the barely smoked cigarette in a saucer by the sink, a little disgusted at himself for giving in, and sat down on the chair.

She is remembering. At last she is remembering. What do I do? Should I contact Inspector Gardiner? Should I get in touch with that Searle guy again?

3

I had been there the day Ben had his consultation with Mr Searle, the psychologist. It had been only a few weeks after the murder. The police had arranged it. They had hoped, of course, back in those early days, that if Molly could express what she remembered about that day then she might reveal something significant, something that would help lead them to my killer.

Ben had left Molly at home with Sylvia, my mother, for that first consultation and gone up to Guy's Hospital alone. In Mr Searle's consultation room he sat in a straight-backed black leather chair. He was tense. Very tense. Grief had tightened the muscles of his face, producing a band of pressure over his eyes, an ache in his jaw. He had a perpetual lump in his throat, a difficulty swallowing. He hadn't been sleeping and knew he looked a wreck. He glanced around at the pictures on the wall. In one, a stiff red boat lurched against a giant wave. In another, a little girl in a triangular striped dress stood under a rainbow, her face split by a red gashed smile. Some of the pictures were in simple wooden frames, others were just Blu-tacked to the wall. There were books on shelves for older children, large picture books about giants and Wild Things in low-boxed containers for the smaller ones.

There was a doll's house on the table in front of him. The roof had been removed so that a child could reach like Gulliver himself into the minimalist room and rearrange the furniture. The furniture, which was wooden, had straight uncluttered lines. There was everything the modern nuclear family could want. A dishwasher in the kitchen. A computer in the study. A coffee table with a little pull-out drawer which held a minuscule plastic remote control to operate the tiny flat-screen television mounted on the wall. The family who lived here were lying in a heap on the living room floor. Tiny peg dolls with floppy bodies. The mum had dark hair. She wore a blue skirt, a red jumper.

Mr Searle was middle-aged but still maintained an attractive elegance. He had silvered hair and what looked like an artificial tan. He wore a white shirt and charcoal-grey suit trousers. A dark blue tie lay neatly against his neck.

"How have you and your daughter been since your wife died, Mr Vincent?"

His right leg crossed his left. As he spoke, his foot jerked upwards, punctuating his words. It jerked on the 'daughter' and the 'Vincent'.

"I don't know what you want me to say."

"I just need for you to tell me how it is for you."

"It's fucking awful, that's how it is."

"Yes, of course."

"My world has collapsed. I feel like my life has ended. I

expect you've heard that from people all the time, but until it's happened to yourself you can't imagine what that's like. The sun still rises in the morning and sets at night. I don't know how it manages to do that."

Ben clenched his hands together on his knees, leant forward. He stared at the doll's house on the table. Through the living-room window he could glimpse the mother with her dark hair lying on top of the father on the floor.

"How are you sleeping? Eating? Generally coping with your life on a day-to-day

basis?"

That right foot again, jerking on the 'coping'.

"I'm not."

"Are you getting any support?"

"My mother-in-law is staying with us at the moment. She's helping me with Molly."

"And how is Molly?"

"I think people who do your job would call it 'regressed.'"

"In what way do you mean that?"

Ben told him about the pureed food and the baby's bottles, the bedwetting and the nappies at night. The nightmares when she woke him up screaming.

"That is all to be expected, Mr Vincent, considering the terrible trauma your daughter has suffered."

The foot jerk again, on the 'trauma' and 'suffered'.

"Don't you think I know that?"

"Of course."

"I'm not able to work at the moment. I can't leave her. She can't bear it when I leave her. She screams. She hangs on to my ankle if I just try to walk out the door to put out the fucking rubbish. Even if her granny's in the room with her."

"I see."

What did he see? The dark circles under Ben's eyes. His three-day old beard. The slight tremor of his right hand as it loosened from his other hand and dangled off his knee.

"This is a terrible time for you and Molly, Mr Vincent."

"I suppose you're going to tell me that time is a great healer."

"I wouldn't insult you by telling you that."

"So it isn't?"

"It can be. We need to do the work though, all the same."

"Therapy, you mean?"

"If you want to call it that."

"That's what you want to do with my daughter?"

"Molly needs a safe way to express the feelings she has suppressed about what happened to her mother."

"Did you know that Molly doesn't speak at the moment? She's hardly said a word since the murder."

"She's been through a deeply traumatic experience. With time and patience the language will almost certainly return."

"But how is she supposed to express herself if she's not talking?"

"A young child's memory is very visual. I will use visual means of encouraging her to remember. Paint, clay, play materials."

Ben stared at the doll's house on the table. He leaned forward, reached into the gaping roof of the house, like Gulliver, and fumbled amongst the heap of bodies on the living room floor. He picked up the mother by her soft cloth waist. Her wooden peg-doll head lolled awkwardly as he carried her up to his face.

"These you mean? Play materials. You make her act it out with these?"

"I won't *make* Molly do anything, Mr Vincent. But yes, the doll's house is one of the play materials commonly used in working with children who have experienced the kind of trauma that your daughter has had."

Ben stared at the doll with dark hair. Her head drooped mawkishly over his thumb. He *looked* like Gulliver now, the doll tiny and vulnerable between his thick fingers. I could sense his thoughts. *Not dark hair – Rachel had red hair. Lots of hair. A mass of red curls down to her back. Like those women in Renaissance art.* He flung the mother back into the living room in disgust. She landed on the father and then rolled off again. She lay on the simulation carpet like one who was dead.

"I think what my daughter needs now, after what she's been through, is help to forget, not help to remember."

Mr Searle smiled. He didn't mean the smile to look insincere but it did.

"Just because the memories are buried doesn't mean they go away, Mr Vincent. I can assure you that therapy now will pay dividends later. Your daughter will heal more quickly from this terrible trauma . . ."

"Will she get better and the nightmares stop? Will I have my daughter back the way she used to be? Can you can promise me that?"

Mr Searle gave a short dry laugh. "There's no guarantees in this, I'm afraid. All I can promise you is the possibility that if your daughter is encouraged to remember, and supported in that process, the chance that she will heal from this trauma is greater than if we do nothing."

*

Perhaps if it hadn't been for Mr Searle's smarmy smile, for the irritating habit with his foot. Perhaps if he hadn't been a man, or middle-aged. A nice young girl, not long out of training, with the light of conviction burning in her eyes. If he'd been, instead, like that. Perhaps if he had been less honest. If he had tried to convince Ben that he was a God, a magician, a miracle worker.

But even that would not have been enough. Because what it boiled down to in the end, as so many things in life do, was something so inconsequential, something that had nothing to do with the reason Ben was there. Nothing to do with my death, or Molly, or Mr Searle's powers to heal. It was to do with Mr Searle's shoes. He wore black patent-leather slip-on shoes. Like the Maths teacher Ben had at school when he was twelve. The one he had hated. He had told me about him in those early days when we were first seeing each other, when we wanted to tell each other everything, fearing that things not said would perhaps be a barrier between us. He had told me about Mr Gregory, with his little goatee beard and small cold eyes, who would send him to the principal's office for so much as smiling.

"I need time to consider this, I need a few days," Ben told Mr Searle.

*

When he got back from the hospital, Molly was sitting on my mother's lap, sucking her thumb like a baby. She stared at the television, a numb, glazed-over look in her eyes.

Mr Tumble was wearing his clown's costume, bright red nose on his face, dancing a jig and singing a song about an elephant.

"Well, how did it go, then?" Sylvia, my mother, asked. She sounded anxious. She was always anxious. She was missing my father dreadfully, and was worried about him being left on his own; he had been so withdrawn since my murder. He'd had a pacemaker fitted for an irregular heartbeat six months ago and my mother was living on a knife edge, watching him constantly for signs of a cardiac arrest. But if she had stayed in Wales and had left Ben on his own to cope with Molly she would have been worrying herself sick about *them*. Even more so. That was what my mother did. That was how she coped with her own grief, how she stopped it overwhelming her. Worrying about other people.

Ben walked over to Molly and kissed her on the top of her dark curls. She didn't look up. Mr Tumble was tumbling around in her world, filling it up.

"That psychologist chap, Mr Searle, he said Molly needs to be helped to remember. He said it would be better for her in the long run if she could get her feelings out. But there's something about him that I'm not sure about. I didn't really like him."

"But if it'll help Molly, Ben, help the police get some clues as who did this terrible thing to Rachel…"

My mother couldn't bring herself to say the word 'murdered'. Ben shook his head and said nothing, and she knew he was digging his heels in now and wouldn't be shifted. She didn't know about Mr Gregory, of course, who had sent him out into the cold corridor for smiling. Who ripped the page of sums out of his exercise book and tore it up in front of him, with the barbed words – *And what do you call this rubbish, then?* She didn't know about the black patent-leather shoes.

*

Detective Inspector Gardiner, who was handling the case, had phoned Ben up several days later to complain about his decision not to go ahead with Molly's therapy. It had been quite early in the morning. A little after nine. I'd been with Ben in the kitchen when he'd taken the call. He was still in his dressing gown. Sylvia was sitting with Molly at the breakfast table trying to entice her to eat her breakfast cereal.

"Come on, darling. Just another mouthful. Just another mouthful to please Granny."

He had his back to them, but he could hear Molly start to whimper and turned to see her push the spoon away and the porridge fall in a messy clump on to the open pages of her drawing book.

For God's sake, Molly…

The frustration was still in his voice when he spoke to the Inspector.

"Look, I'm not doing this to be awkward, you know. I have my daughter's welfare at heart. It's not in her interests to see this Searle chap."

Molly was crying now, quite loudly. I slipped my cool arm around her shoulders. But she didn't notice, she didn't know I was there. Ben put his hand over the mouthpiece and turned towards my mother. "Sylvia, leave it. If she doesn't want to eat, just leave it."

"She wants to watch television, Ben. She can't just do what she wants." My mother was feeling vexed and under-appreciated. She was trying to do her best for Ben and her granddaughter. She was missing my father. Nothing was working at the moment. And all the time she was fighting to keep those feelings at bay, the ones that threatened to engulf her. Her daughter was dead. Her only daughter was dead.

"Let her, let her do what she wants."

Ben was tired of the battles. Tired out with his daughter's pain. And his own.

He turned back to the phone, slid his hand away from the mouthpiece. "Sorry, Inspector. A minor problem with my daughter."

Gardiner must have protested about his decision, might have stressed that it was in their interests to pursue the play therapy if it gave leads to the killer.

"Inspector Gardiner, it's in all our interests, of course, to find Rachel's killer. Next to my daughter's welfare, that's the one thing that I want the most…"

I didn't know what she said next. Perhaps she accused him of a failure to co-operate. I felt him stiffen. I felt the anger steal into his blood.

"By exposing my little girl to more harm and trauma? I hardly think I'd be doing my job as a parent if I allow you to make use of her just because you're not able to do your job properly."

*

Ben went back upstairs now to his study. He had work to get on with, important emails to send to prospective clients, architectural plans to draw up. But how was he to make a start on anything, to find the powers to concentrate, with this tumult of thoughts on his mind? Had he made a mistake back then, he was wondering.

Should he have let Mr Searle work with Molly? Would she have been released from the trauma had he done so? Had his refusal to do so damaged her for good? He sat back down at his desk and looked out of the window again at the hills dotted with sheep. The scene wasn't as bright as it had looked earlier. The sun had been swallowed by dark clouds building on the horizon. He got an address book out of the top drawer of his desk and flicked through it until he found what he was looking for. He picked up the phone, slowly and deliberately dialled a number. I glanced over his shoulder. It was Gardiner's number.

Gardiner must have answered the phone. I heard Ben tell her that he was fine. That his life in Wales was working out. That it was the best thing he'd done, getting out of London. The best thing for Molly, too.

"… And Molly is fine, although she is mainly the reason for the phone call."

He paused – I could see the uncertainty on his face – *Should I tell her this? Will she think I'm crazy, after all this time?*

"It's just that Molly had a dream last night. About her mother. A nightmare, I suppose. She hasn't had them for a long while and then last night she had another one."

He paused again, as if attempting to summon up the courage to continue.

"She said something to me this morning. Something that made me think she is starting to remember. She said she dreamt that her mother was lying on the black and white tiles in the kitchen in the old house. She said there was blood – like a pool of it – under her head. She could even describe the summer dress her mother had been wearing, the one with little roses on it..."

He dried to a standstill. *She'll think I'm going crazy, losing the plot...*

In the blink of an eye I had left him. I was in an office. Magnolia walls, beige cord carpet, tidy grey filing cabinets. Shelves stacked with boxes. A large whiteboard on one wall with clippings from newspapers Blu-tacked to it. Beyond large windows I could make out another office space, much larger. A number of people with heads down over computers. I was standing next to a large polished desk where a woman sat talking on the phone.

4

Inspector Gardiner still wore her hair shoulder length, bleached blonde with dark roots showing. She still power dressed in dark suits, although it was a little dated now to do so. But I noticed the slight lines around her mouth that hadn't been there before, the weary shadows under her eyes.

Time had stopped for her. She was back there in that kitchen on the day that I died. The memories in her head slipped through me like water…

*

The forensic men in their white suits are slipping stray hairs inside tiny sterile polythene bags, taking samples of blood, taking cuttings of my hair and finger nails. A balding middle-aged man is snapping away with a camera.

Gardiner, staring down at the body. She has seen dead bodies before, lots of times. But they never fail to move her. She is noticing how the skirt on my light cotton dress is hitched up around my thighs. She is wishing that she could rearrange it, make me look more decent...

*

I felt her heart beat a little faster now. Perhaps she was feeling a little guilty. She hadn't spoken to Ben for months because there has been nothing to report. No new leads. Nothing.

The man who called to read the gas meter just before my estimated time of death had been taken in for questioning. He was young, attractive in his 'Jack the lad' way. He had read the meter. I had offered him a cup of coffee. It was raining. He tossed his dark hair out of his eyes and grinned at me. I noticed his small even teeth when he smiled, his green Irish eyes. He held the glazed red mug to his lips and drank the coffee, his eyes looking at me over the rim.

He was a married man with two kids. The gas board gave him a good character reference. He had no record of any kind, apart from a conviction for drunk driving back in his late teens. They had nothing to pin on him. Gardiner had to let him go. She was right to do so. I can't remember much about that day, but I know that when he left I was still standing there alive, on the black and white tiles in the kitchen.

*

There was a more serious enquiry that had to be followed up and eventually dispatched. It concerned Peter Bates who lived down the road. For a while Gardiner had seriously suspected that he must have killed me. His shoe size matched the prints found in the mud in the garden and slight traces of his DNA were found on the latch of the back garden gate. He wasn't without form either. He'd had a conviction some years ago for flashing at two teenage girls, who'd stood pert and giggling at the bus stop one evening. Nothing more harmful than that, but everyone in the area had got to hear of it and his crime had grown monstrously in the fertile fields inside their heads. He'd given me crooked shy smiles now and then when I'd walked by with Molly in her pushchair, and I'd smiled and said 'hello' because I'd nothing against the poor creature really. Anyone could see he was short of two shillings and no wonder, living with that awful mother of his, with her shrill voice and battle-axe face. I remember Ben hated him; all men hated him. Although maybe it was the things they feared in themselves that they hated the most.

"He's simple, Ben," I used to say, when he would go on about how dreadful it is that we lived so near 'one of those'. "In the olden days he'd be called a village idiot, if he'd lived in a village," I told him. "Nothing more than that."

"He may have a low IQ Rachel but don't you underestimate him."

"I'm not saying that children should be trusted with him. But just that he should be tolerated; he's to be pitied rather than hated."

Ben said I didn't know what I was talking about. That annoyed me when he said that. That patronising tone he'd had in his voice. Some awful story hit the papers later about a child who had disappeared, presumed dead. Local men, fuelled by drink and high passions, daubed red paint all over his front door. *PAEDO ROT IN HELL*. I went by the next day with Molly in her pushchair and Peter Bates was standing in the little front garden, his face strangely childlike, red and inflamed as if he'd been crying.

Anyway, the shoe size, the DNA traces, the previous conviction, a witness statement from a neighbour who lived a few houses to the left of mine, saying that she had seen him walking his dog along Gale Lane about twelve noon, just before the time it was thought I had been murdered, all that weighed against him for a while. However, all the evidence was circumstantial. Except perhaps for the DNA, but even that he could account for. He admitted under police caution that he'd stolen a pair of my knickers from the washing line about two weeks before my murder. Red satin ones, to be precise. He could even produce the knickers, in a drawer in his bedroom, along with a dozen other ones stolen from other women's washing lines.

"That's all I do, honest," he pleaded, his face red and screwed up with distress. "I've never touched anyone. I never touched that Rachel woman. I liked her, she was a nice woman. All I did was pinch her knickers." He had started to weep then, like a small boy instead of a man of past fifty, and his solicitor reminded the police that he was being interviewed in connection with a murder offence and not the far lesser crime of stealing knickers. In the end Gardiner could not charge him and he was released. There was no evidence that would hold up in a prosecution. He had admitted to taking his dog for a walk, turning right into the road from his council house and walking about a hundred yards down the road to the turning into Gale Lane. Then taking the right turn where the lane divided into two and following it along the edge of the cornfield, past the back gardens of the row of Edwardian houses that included my own, coming out further down the main road to the left of his house. This was a walk he did every lunchtime, he'd said, and there were neighbours around to confirm it. Yes, he had a knicker fetish, but that didn't imply at all that he would be capable of murder.

*

Peter Bates was upset for weeks after he'd been questioned by the police. So was his mother. She would stand at the garden gate, that fist of hers clenched against the world, daring anyone who walked by to utter one word of abuse or accusation at her son.

After I died I would sometimes find myself standing on the street outside their garden gate at night-time. Peter Bates would have the light on behind the drawn curtain of his room and I knew that he was lying in bed, sobbing in fear that they would come to take him away again. I sometimes went into his room and watched him. He would lie on his bed and moan as if he was in pain. I could see the memories that tormented his mind. Images, that flowed through me like water. That time in the prison when he had feared leaving his cell because of the way the other men looked at him, the covert threats they made under their breath. He had feared most of all going to the washroom or having a shower. That time when three heavies had pinned him up against the tiled wall and beat his face to a pulp. *Perv. Paedo. Scumbag.* In the end the guards had rescued him but they seemed to have taken their time in coming. He was only in prison for months, but still had nightmares about it. He would toss and turn on his bed. He would press the heels of his hands into his eye sockets to try to drive out the memories, but nothing worked. I would watch him, and almost feel sorry for him, almost wish that I could reach into his head and take the memories away.

Afterwards, I would pace backwards and forwards outside the gate into the small hours of the morning.

I don't know why I did that. Something compelled me. Perhaps I was waiting for those men to come again in the darkness with their red paint and their hate?

*

So anyway, all the leads came to nothing. Forensics had turned up nothing conclusive. They knew I had been bludgeoned with a blunt instrument on the back of the head, which had caused a serious compression in my skull. They knew that the injury corresponded to a blow from a club hammer; Ben had remembered that he had left one about that time on top of the rabbit's hutch in the back garden. He had been replacing some broken fence panels the previous weekend and had left the hammer out.

The hammer had now disappeared. No doubt my murderer had taken it. The police enquiry had concluded that I had been surprised by an intruder who had entered the garden through the gate from the back lane whilst I had gone out to take in the washing. The approximate time of the attack, around a quarter past twelve, was roughly the time that it had started to rain heavily. There was nothing in the washing basket except a pair of knickers – mine, and so the police surmised that I had been surprised by the attacker just as I was beginning to take down the washing. They knew that I had been walking quickly, or possibly running, away from the assailant, because of the positioning of the blow. They knew that I'd made it back into the kitchen through the back door and had collapsed on the tiled floor, and the severely compressed section of my skull, caused by the blow of this blunt instrument, had rapidly brought about unconsciousness, followed closely by my death.

Within minutes of my dying it was raining hard. A deluge of water. The washing left on the line was soaked through when Gardiner, along with Sergeant Williams and the crime investigation team, had inspected the garden. The garden lawn was soggy with water and the path that led across the newly dug vegetable garden to the back gate was mostly washed clean of footprints, except for a few vague traces that forensics picked up. A man's shoe, Clarks, size ten. Thousands of men wear the same size shoe.

Even the gas man.

Even Peter Bates.

Even you, Ben.

But none of them seemed to possess the shoes that identically matched the prints that had been found. And the murder weapon, the club hammer, was nowhere to be found.

*

"I know how you felt the last time this was suggested, Mr Vincent, but maybe you could consider the option of letting Molly work with a psychologist who could support her with these re-emerging memories?" Gardiner was saying to Ben on the phone.

She was remembering the phone call Ben had made to tell her his decision not to let Molly attend therapy sessions with Mr Searle. She had tried to persuade him to change his mind, but he'd dug his heels in and refused to budge. *I hardly think I'd be doing my job as a parent if I allow you to make use of Molly just because you're not doing your job properly.* His life had been swept away and he was grief-stricken; she had understood that. But still, she hadn't forgotten his words. They were coming back to her now, and she waited for him to protest again, to tell her such a thing was out of the question. Her reply made me assume he did not protest this time.

"I'm afraid though, the police wouldn't be able to set it up again… not after this amount of time has passed since the crime… It would probably have to be initiated by you and paid for privately… Whatever might be revealed… possible new leads… I might not be able to make use of them directly, certainly not in court as evidence… but I'd always be interested…"

After the phone call ended and Gardiner had hung up, I stayed with her awhile. I stood over by the filing cabinet at the back of the office and I watched her. She picked up a black biro and started to doodle on the pad in front of her. She drew circles, two interlacing circles, like Venn diagrams. Then she filled in the interlaced section of the circles. And then above the shape she wrote the name of her daughter – *Abigail* – in a looping and elaborate hand that was not exactly her own, but perhaps because such handwriting best suited the name, perhaps because of her love for the one who owned it. She was thinking of mothers, of the grief that dead mothers leave behind in the hearts of their children. She drew a heart around the name and then in anger, frustration, disappointment, because she hadn't been able to solve my murder, stabbed the point of the biro down heavily into the centre of the heart, and it fell into the 'g' in Abigail. She winced as if it had hurt her.

She turned very briefly and looked over to the filing cabinet and then, just for an instant, I felt her blue eyes raking through the space where I stood. The thought entered me like a shockwave – *She can't see me, but she knows I am there.* Then the door of her office opened and Sergeant Williams came in with transcripts of interview tapes to show her. Her attention went immediately to him and to work again and I felt myself shrink back and disappear into the grey metal of the filing cabinet, into the office's magnolia-painted wall.

*

Later that day I went with Ben to pick Molly up from school. We parked in the school car park and I followed him across the asphalt playground where children stood idly whilst mothers gossiped. A couple of the younger children stared at me with those wide-open eyes and I knew that they also had the gift, like the girl this morning with the blonde pigtails. We went into Molly's classroom. Miss Austin, who was not so prim now, whose composure was unsettled, who had high spots of red on her smooth plump cheeks, asked if she could have a little word with

Ben in private. Jill, the classroom assistant, entertained Molly whilst Miss Austin ushered Ben into the room next door and dangled a painting up in front of him. The name 'Molly' was roughly painted in large black capitals in the top right-hand corner.

"I'm a little concerned, Mr Vincent. Molly said it was a painting of her mother when she died."

Miss Austin's tone was hushed, shocked, reverential. She knew about my murder; all the staff at the school knew. Ben had given brief details when he'd registered Molly, and several of the staff had read about it in the tabloids two years previously, when our family had made it to the ranks of minor celebrity: Traumatised toddler witnesses her mother's brutal murder.

Ben stood and stared wordlessly at the two black figures: the one in the triangular dress, white with tiny pink dots that were supposed to be rosebuds, horizontal on the roughly painted black and white floor, and the one standing behind, a larger figure, and darker, and somehow clearly a male, in wide blotched trousers. But it was the redness that captivated him the most. That thickly daubed trumpet of colour smeared on to the black and white tiles and the dotted rosebuds. He couldn't tear his eyes away from the blood.

5

I know who it is now. The someone who is sometimes with me. And now that I know I realise that I have always known. It wouldn't mean anything to Ben – I have never spoken of this person to him – why should I have done when there was no need to? But when I was small, four or five, much the same age as Molly is now, my parents had a neighbour called Mr Jackson. We lived in a cottage in a quaint Sussex village in the Downs, not far from where the Long Man of Wilmington straddles Windover Hill bearing his staves. We weren't there long, maybe three or four years, but looking back, it seems it was an idyllic place to be a child in, a place belonging to picture story books, to English teas with scones and cucumber sandwiches and cricket on the green on Sundays.

We had a long rambling garden where I would get lost in the summer amongst the hollyhocks and foxgloves and rambling roses. I was waiting to start school in September and my mother was waiting for my baby brother to enter the world. She was heavy and huge and always tired and the garden belonged to me and my imagination. I remember I had lost a ball amongst the shrubs – what were they? Some sort of climbing rose, I think, with their sweet scent and soft yellow flowers and merciless thorns that snagged my cotton dress and ripped long bloodied weals on my arms. I started to cry and then a face peered down at me from over the fence. It was a soft red face, puckered like an old apple, with a feathery white beard and blue eyes that almost seemed to be laughing at my tears but had no cruelty in them at all. I don't know what was said to me, or what I said back, but my tears were halted in surprise and I stepped backwards, away from the clutches of the thorny branches. A long brown arm, taut with muscles that wove their way down the limb like ropes, reached over the fence and held out towards me a crumpled paper bag of Liquorice Allsorts.

"Go on, help yourself, my lovely, that'll stop the tears."

I took one. And then another. And then the arm retracted the bag.

"Don't worry, little miss. The fairies, they'll find your ball."

"There's no such thing as fairies," I said churlishly.

"You don't believe in fairies?" The crumpled face looking down at me put on a mock expression of shock and whether I would have re-thought the grounds of my non-belief and retracted my words, I don't know, because my mother suddenly came crashing into my world, her belly swinging heavily through the foliage of plants and flowers.

"There you are, Rachel. Are you bothering Mr Jackson?"

"Not at all, not at all," Mr Jackson answered. "Little lady got tangled up in the rose bush. Got a bit scratched up there, I think."

My mother held me out at arm's length and examined me. She noticed the red weals on my arms.

"We'll go inside and put something on that. Say goodbye to Mr Jackson, Rachel."

"Goodbye, Mr Jackson," I said meekly. He winked at me. I really wanted to stay and talk to him about the fairies and whether they were real or not, but I couldn't because my mother was tugging me gently away and into the house and it was another world I was entering now. All the promise of the garden and the bees and the pollen, the rich heavy scents of the summer day and the man who laughed at me kindly over the fence were dissolving, giving way to my mother's stinging cotton balls soaked with Dettol and exhortations that I had been out in the sun too long and it was time for my afternoon nap.

*

That was my first encounter with Mr Jackson. The following day, sitting on the path just in front of the pink climbing roses, was my multi-coloured ball. Whether the fairies retrieved it and placed it there for me to find, I do not know, but Mr Jackson from that time on took on an aura for me of things promised and fulfilled. I often sought out his crumpled face and equally crumpled bag of Allsorts on my forays into the summer garden.

"Don't you go bothering that Mr Jackson," my mother would say, but she was too caught up with the slow energy of her waiting, her growing, descending belly, to pay much attention to my world. Mr Jackson would offer me other things apart from the Liquorice Allsorts. A clockwork dog;

a tiny beaded pillbox; a Russian doll that revealed ever-decreasing miniature replicas within her belly; a wooden snake whose jointed body allowed it to zigzag alarmingly through the air when held by its tail.

Arrangements had been made for me to stay with Aunt Susan when the baby came; this was in the less enlightened days when there was no paternity leave. My father worked long hours as an accountant and couldn't take time off. But when the pains came sudden and fast and two weeks ahead of schedule and I found my mother clutching the edge of the table, white-faced and breathing with short, sharp intakes of air that filled me with fear, I fled down the garden shouting for Mr Jackson. He came round and sat my mother down. He held her hand and counted with her between the pains and we waited for the ambulance. I stood there watching in horror, wondering if my mother would die and that would be the end to the world. Aunt Susan was forgotten for the time being and Mr Jackson took me back to his house until my father came home.

Mr Jackson's house was full of interesting things to look at and touch. There was in particular a little fat pig on his mantelpiece. It was crude and roughly modelled out of clay and was covered with a pinky-white opaque glaze that had pooled thickly into crevices, into its eyes and ears and the deeply etched toes on its heavy feet, but was too thin in other places, letting the bisque terracotta show through. I kept picking it up and looking at it. Mr Jackson would tell me to put it down, at first pleasantly and patiently enough, but then as I picked it up again and again, he grew less patient and there was an edge to his voice. One final time, when he was out in the kitchen getting me lemonade and cake, I had it in my hand again when his little wire-haired terrier suddenly decided to rouse himself from his sleep on the rug before the hearth. He knocked against my legs and I stumbled and dropped the pottery pig. It fell on to the tiled hearth and broke into pieces. When Mr Jackson came back into the room, bearing a glass of lemonade in one hand and a small plate with a slice of Madeira cake in the other, he took in at one glance what had happened. He quietly set down the glass and plate on the coffee table. He picked up the broken pieces of the pottery pig and stood there silently staring at them as they lay in the calloused palm of his hand.

"I told you not to touch it," he said, his voice crisp and cold. "Why did you touch it? You're a naughty girl, doing that."

I wouldn't answer. Some hot disturbed feeling of either guilt or defiance, or a mixture of both, was shutting off my throat. He went out of the room taking the broken pieces with him. I sat on his stiffly backed armchair. *Play School* was on the television. The window was square today and through it was a rainbow and a boat riding a wave, but I couldn't enter its world. Mr Jackson came in a few minutes later with his cheerful face on again, trying to cajole me to drink my lemonade and eat the slice of cake that was sitting untouched on the coffee table. But I wouldn't. I stayed inside my hard, defiant little body and would not speak to him. I knew that I had done a terrible thing. That something more than a crude pottery pig had been broken. And it wouldn't be mended. I wouldn't ever let it be mended again.

*

When my father came home later and fetched me I walked out of Mr Jackson's house and wouldn't look back at him.

"Thank Mr Jackson for having you, Rachel."

I was studying the comic my father had bought me. I mumbled something half-heartedly.

"That's all right, any time," Mr Jackson said.

But I knew he was still seeing the broken shards of pottery sitting pitiably in his hand.

"Any news from the hospital?" he asked my father.

My father told him about the new baby son that had entered the world, red-faced and solid and weighing in at eight pounds. The following day I was taken to Aunt Susan's, where I had to compete with her two spoilt daughters. When I came home the summer was drawing to an end. My mother was smiling and conciliatory towards me, trying to make up for her betrayal, for bringing this noisy greedy usurper into my world. I was taken to Littlewoods where I tried on white blouses and grey pinafores for school. The garden and Mr Jackson were already a thing of the past for me, and although he came to the fence and talked to me occasionally I never let him into my world again.

I never forgave him.

*

That's why he's here.

*

My baby brother, John, was two months old before my mother questioned why I never spoke to Mr Jackson over the fence anymore. She had been out in the garden hanging out washing on the line. She came in, the washing basket tucked under her arm. Little John was on the floor on his special mat, under a frame that held all sorts of springing things and mirrors and rattles that he could stretch up and whack with his jerky little movements. It was a Saturday and I wasn't at school. I was colouring in a princess in my colouring book. Everything was pink. The crown on her head and her ballroom dress and the little dancing shoes on her feet.

"Mr Jackson asked about you, Rachel."

"Oh?"

"He said he hasn't seen you in the garden for ages. He wanted to know how you are getting on at school."

I was colouring in the princess's cheeks, her lips, her fingernails. They were pink too. Only her eyes were blue.

"Is everything all right, Rachel?"

"What?"

I looked up. My mother was standing in the kitchen doorway. The suffused September light framed her, creating an aura around her body, and I knew the summer was over and wouldn't come again.

"Did Mr Jackson take care of you, Rachel, when Mummy was taken to hospital in the ambulance?"

I said nothing. I was busy concentrating.

"How long were you around his house, darling?"

I stuck my tongue out, concentrating. The princess had five fingernails on each hand, including her thumb. They were long polished-pink fingernails.

My mother moved away from the doorway and the aura of light fell from her. She pulled out a chair and sat at the table opposite me.

"Rachel, did anything happen there?"

I didn't answer. At five and a bit I already knew the power of silence.

"At Mr Jackson's house, darling. When Mummy was taken in the ambulance. Did anything happen that day that you didn't like?"

I looked up slowly. I saw my mother's face fixed on me, alarmed and concerned and fearful of my answer. I wanted to hold on to this moment a little longer. I wanted to put it in a box and keep it there.

"No," I said, but not as if I meant it. I didn't really understand what could have happened at Mr Jackson's that would have alarmed my mother so greatly. But I knew it was more than a broken pottery pig. I knew it was more than an old man's displeasure that something he valued had been broken.

"Are you sure, darling? Are you sure Mr Jackson didn't do anything that you didn't like?"

I could hear, fleetingly, the frost in his voice again, see the lemonade losing its bubbles on the table, the uneaten cake. But I knew none of this came close to this secret meaning in my mother's words. I shook my head and I looked away, down at the pink princess again.

"But you don't like Mr Jackson anymore, do you darling? You don't like to talk to him anymore. Why is that?"

"I just don't," I said, in the way that children do, believing that feelings have no need for logic, no need to be subjected to scrutiny and reason.

My mother sat there quietly and looked at me. Then John made some noises from the other room – short punctured attacks of crying – and she got up to attend to him. Nothing more was said about me and Mr Jackson, except when my father some time afterwards – only months afterwards, not years, because I was in the same class at school – announced the firm were promoting him and transferring him to Brighton, and perhaps we could now consider buying a bigger house over there. I overheard my mother say, "That's a good idea, Ted. Then I won't have to worry about Rachel and that creepy man next door anymore."

"I don't know, Sylvia," my father said back. "I really don't think anything untoward could have happened that day. He seems such a pleasant man."

"Don't they always?" my mother said. There was something dry and unbelieving in her voice. There was something that wouldn't be shifted.

*

"You need to let go," he tells me now.
"I was never very good at that."
"But you need to learn how to. You need to forgive."

6

After I died I would be with Ben quite often. In the same room. Particularly in those first few months when he still lived in the house in Reigate.

He slept badly in those first few months. It wasn't just Molly that woke him. He had nightmares of his own to disturb his sleep, images seeping unbidden into his dreams. He would get up from bed sometimes, quite often in those early days, and go downstairs. He would sit in the dark, always in the dark, the curtains open at the window so that the moon would cast its cold light, making the room itself look as if it belonged to some other in-between world. I would be there, sitting in the chair next to him. There we were, the two of us together, not quite the living or the dead. Ben feeling as if he were almost dead, and I, so unwilling to give up the world of the living. He would lower his head down and rest his forehead on the heel of his hand and moan sometimes, even say my name, and I would answer.

I'm here, Ben.

I would take his hand, the one that dangled down from

his lap, and hold it in mine. It always felt so warm to me, so warm it almost burnt me. We would sit there together for ten minutes or more sometimes, Ben's hand lying still in mine, burning mine. And then suddenly he would pull his hand back and look at it, hold it to his mouth and suck it, as if it had become cold, too cold, and he was trying to restore it to life.

On one night like this, in those stark, tormenting early-morning hours, not long after my murder, Ben got up and went into the kitchen. He stared down at the black and white tiled floor. His eyes looked vacant, as if he was in a trance. Perhaps he was sleep-walking. There was no stain on the tiles that would have been apparent ordinarily, but I knew that he was seeing it. A pale blush of red on the tiles that were white. The stain of my blood. He went out of the back door, down the long lawn that was our back garden, past the rotary washing-line, the recently dug vegetable plot where nothing yet was growing except the weeds, down to the shed. He kept an axe there for chopping wood for the wood-burning stove that we'd had installed. He picked it up now and carried it like a man possessed, back up the garden and into the kitchen. He planted his feet firmly and lifted the axe high and brought it down upon the tiles where my head would have lain in its bath of blood. He swung the axe again and again until long dark cracks appeared on the tiles, fragmenting the bloodstain he could see in his head.

"Ben, Ben, what is it... what on earth are you doing...?"

Sylvia was there in the doorway, her limbs mottled and pudgy beyond the confines of her thin cotton nightie.

He lifted the axe up high again, poised for another strike,

but she was there at his side, her hand on his shoulder. I was there at his other side, my cold hands pulling down his arm, and although I doubt that he could feel me there, the resistance in his arm seemed to drain away.

"Got to get rid of these tiles. Got to get rid of the bloodstain…" He shook his head, as if trying to shake away the image of the stain. Light came back into his eyes. If he had been sleep-walking, he was waking up now.

My mother's warm hands and my cold ones covered Ben's hands; he lowered the axe to the floor and his clenched hands released. The axe clattered on to the broken tiles. Ben looked around, realised where he was, what he had been doing. He buried his face in my mother's hot flushed neck and sobbed, gulping noisy and painful breaths, as if something was being torn out of him.

"It's all right, Ben, it's going to be all right," Sylvia said. She awkwardly patted the back of his head, not quite knowing what to do with this moment. Men's grief, and her own, always a prickly area for my mother to navigate. If she gave in to her own grief then she feared she'd be overwhelmed. She couldn't allow that to happen, not whilst there were others who needed her.

*

I have no eyes, but yet I see things. I see things that are real, and are not real yet. I see my daughter in a future without me in it. I see you, Ben, with another woman.

Mr Jackson is here again. He moves forward, out of the shadows. I can almost see his face. Words form out of his cool breath.

"It is time now for Molly to remember. Time for you to remember."

"But if I remember, does that mean I will have to let Molly go? Let Ben go, too?"

He shakes his head, or what passes for a head in this place where we have no shape that is real in the way it used to be.

"You know what you have to do."

"But not yet. I can't bear it."

He has gone now and in his wake, a cold wind that makes me shudder.

7

Katie Clements. Aged twenty-six. Living and working in Cardiff. Pretty. Dark straight hair that falls past her shoulders. A pale, slightly angular face. A serious and studious manner that is suddenly offset by the warmth of her smile.

She sat back on her sofa. She was thinking about the phone call she had just received from Ben's sister, Susie. I watched her from a distance. She gave no indication that she knew I was there, but intuitions and sensitivities were passing through her all the time, unchecked, like water flows with no obstacle in its path. Perhaps she had lived with spirits all her life and thought nothing of it. She leant back on the sofa and closed her eyes. She was thinking, exploring her options. She always gave herself time to examine her various options and their implications. It was her nature. *Sun in Virgo, moon in Taurus.* How could she do otherwise? Although I would later feel that her interest in astrology ran contradictory to the outward persona she presented to the world, as having a cool head on her shoulders, rooted in the science of psychology and with a predilection for rational thought.

She closed her eyes and sat back on the sofa, her right hand continuing to stroke the black and white cat on her lap. I dipped into her memories. She had met Susie at university in Bristol. Susie had been studying English Literature and she, herself, psychology. Susie was headstrong and passionate, and made impulsive and spontaneous decisions based solely on visceral responses – *sun in Scorpio, moon in Aries* – and despite the contradictory nature of their personalities, and their seemingly astrological incompatibility, too, they got on remarkably well from the outset. Perhaps they each compensated to some extent for the lack found in the other. Katie would urge Susie to slow down and consider her options more carefully before jumping in with both feet, whereas Susie would cause Katie to realise that weighing up options on every possible decision did rather deaden an experience on the occasions when spontaneity was the order of the day. And so they had, surprisingly, clicked. They had formed such an easy and workable friendship that they shared a flat together in their third year and neither had lived to regret it. This was now six years ago, and each had gone different ways in life; Susie to live in York, marry Paul, a solicitor, and settle down with two children. Her career at present was restricted to occasional days filling in as a supply teacher at her local comprehensive. Katie had remained single. Although Toby, who she had parted from last year, had come close to getting her up the aisle, until – with that ever rational head of hers – she had finally decided to call a day on that relationship. Once again he had confessed to a minor transgression with another woman and she realised that, try as she might, he was never going to be the one who would make her happy.

However, a relationship break-up after five years of so-called 'togetherness' was not something to ever be taken lightly and it had heralded in its wake a desire to make significant changes in her life. So when she saw the advert in *Psychology Weekly* for someone to work with traumatised children in Cardiff she had tentatively applied. She had taken it as a sign that her life was meant to change in this way when she got the job – wasn't Jupiter sweeping through her sun sign now, with a new moon in Virgo, too?

She thought back now to the facts of the case. Susie had rung her the day afterwards, and in a very upset and agitated manner had rambled on about the murder of her brother's wife. The following day it made it to the front page of three of the tabloids. *Traumatised toddler witnesses mother's brutal murder.* She had told Susie to phone her at any time, whenever she needed to talk, but hadn't heard from her until several weeks later, when the worse was over and a funeral had been allowed to happen. Susie had filled her in on more of the details, this time in a calmer and more logical manner. Ben had been at work that day and had come home at around six o'clock to find his daughter, Molly – who was about three and half at the time – sitting traumatised by the body of her mother. Molly stopped speaking for several weeks, and when she did start talking again she spoke for some time in shortened truncated sentences, like a toddler. She wasn't able to tell the police what had happened. Susie phoned quite regularly for a while after that, and Katie had been able to piece together other parts of the developing story. She heard from Susie that the police had wanted Ben to take her to a child psychologist at The Royal Free to see if he could enable her to reveal memories of the trauma but Ben had refused. He'd thought it would do Molly more harm than good.

Katie thought back now to Susie's words on the telephone earlier that evening, spoken intensely and with passion:

Ben said Molly is starting to remember. Things are coming back to her in her dreams, in a painting she did at school. Details of that day. The black and white tiles on the kitchen floor. The kind of dress her mother was wearing. She remembers blood on the floor under Rachel's head. We want you to work with her, Katie. Ben's living in Wales now, only an hour's drive from Cardiff. We want you to take her on as a private patient. I know you're the right person to help Molly. I know you can do this.

Katie had felt a frisson of excitement. I'd felt it too. I knew that Katie Clements, this one I have chosen, was not an attention seeker, had no wish for celebrity status, but felt that to be involved in a case like this – one that had made it to the front page of the major tabloids – was a challenge she could not walk away from. It was the children she cared about most, but still, she was human… a little flash of ambition was now stirring her thoughts.

She would do it, she decided. She would phone Susie tonight and tell her. She would obtain Ben's phone number from Susie and then she'd ring him and make the first appointment.

I watched as she made the phone calls. I noticed when she talked to Ben that she tossed her head slightly, so that her straight dark hair moved and rearranged itself. She gave quick smiles, even though the man she was speaking to was many miles away and at the other end of a phone line. She would like the way his voice sounded on the phone. He always had an appealing voice. She would conjure up an image in her mind of him being attractive, which of course he was. He was giving her information on the phone, no doubt refreshing her memory about the details of the murder. By the time she'd finished the conversation and put down the receiver, they had fixed a time and date for Molly's first consultation.

Already I could feel the chill of losing Ben. Losing him to someone else.

8

Endings usually evoke beginnings, don't they, Ben? Is that why I am here, standing outside the house where I lived when you and I first met? It's dark. The curtains are drawn. There is light shining through them, life behind them. Life that I can't touch, can't belong to. I wonder if it's a young couple living there, with their lives ahead of them, as we had once. All that hope and promise...

I shiver; the cold rakes through me. I would never have known, when I was living, that the dead can feel as cold as this. Or so alone...

*

I had been living in Brighton then and working as an assistant forensic psychologist for the Sussex probation service. I had just bought this house. It was nothing special – a Victorian two-up, two-down terraced cottage, in a part of the town which was mainly given over to student lets and rented accommodation. There was litter on the streets back then, rusted old cars, youths walking around with beer cans in their hands and apathy on pale faces. The cottage had wet rot in the roof timbers and was in need of a damp course. The bathroom had a ghastly avocado suite and hideous brown tiles on the wall and the kitchen wasn't big enough to swing a cat in. But I loved it. It was the first real home of my own.

I got a local man in to sort out the wet rot and to put in a damp course. I bought pots of so-called revolutionary new paint, shades of white and cream, that were supposed to reflect the natural light, and when I took them home I stood in my house, in the tiny front room and cramped back dining room and the minuscule kitchen, and I knew that before the painting could begin I needed to open the rooms out, to find a way a way of bringing in more light and space.

Ben came around to help me draw up the plans to be submitted for planning permission. He was working as an assistant for a firm of architects that I had found on the internet. Gallagher and Dolton. He said he was used to jobs like this: people wanting to build extensions, garages, attic conversions. I took him into the little kitchen and the space between the work surfaces on either side was so narrow that we stood almost touching each other. He leaned back against the edge of the work-surface, his hands resting down on the edge, and I noticed the square surety of his palms, his long and capable fingers, the absence of a wedding ring.

"This one's a load bearer," he said placing one hand on the wall separating the little kitchen from the back dining room. "We can bring it down but we'll need to put a lintel here to take up the weight."

I asked if that would be expensive, and he said, "No, not really. Depends on who you get to do it. A small local builder would probably take it on at a reasonable cost, but not the big guys." Then he paced the length of my little kitchen, brushing past me as he did so, and opened the back door from the kitchen to step out to the paved patio area.

"May I…?"

"Please…"

He went outside and I watched through the kitchen window as he paced the length of the paved patio area, walked up the scruffy lawned garden. It was raining, a fine drizzle, but he didn't seem to care. Then he came back in. There was a fine film of rain on his cheeks.

"Do you know what I would do if it was my property? Of course, it depends on costs, how much you feel you can afford. I'd build out into the back garden here. An extension. A flat roof, with large skylights. These terraces are fine but light is nearly always a problem. You could build out to the full length of this adjacent paved area, and still have plenty of room in the rest of the garden. Maybe move the patio area to the far end of the garden away from the house. You could keep the back room as a separate dining room, or if you like bring down that adjoining wall as well and have a lovely open-plan space… The costs would be more but we're talking about added value here…"

He sounded almost excited, as if it was his property he was talking about. He was seeing in his mind's eye the space and the light, building sculptures with them in his mind.

*

I had him draw up the plans and they were submitted and approved, and then in the end he did the work for me himself. He said he could always use the extra money, that working as an architect's assistant doesn't pay that much, but I like to think that he took the job mainly because he wanted to be around me, to get to know me better. He had a couple of friends who were intermittently helping him to develop his own house, and he got them on board and they came and worked on mine on Saturdays, and occasionally, when work had reached a critical stage, the whole weekend. I hovered in the background, offering to help load bags of rubble, clear up the dust, make cups of coffee and quick impromptu cheese sandwiches. It took several months of Saturdays to finish. I had him bring down the dividing wall between the kitchen and the dining room in the end, as well as build the extension. I was captivated by the idea of the space. Eventually, we arrived at the stage where all the major structural changes had been done and it was only the finer finishing-off tasks.

By that time we had made our mutual interest in each other quite obvious. At the end of the day, his mates would leave at five to go home. Ben would stay and take a bath in my bathroom with its avocado suite, and we would go out later for a meal.

"Don't worry, we'll sort the bathroom out next," he said. He meant, of course, the hideous tiling, the avocado suite, the black mould growing on the peeling silicone edging. He seemed oblivious of how it sounded, the implied assumption in his words that he would be around in my future. That my little house would somehow be tied up with his vision of his own future. I pretended I hadn't realised the assumption but my heart gave a small jump of excitement, and as I moved around in my half-finished kitchen downstairs, tidying and sweeping up dust, I thought of his body stretched out in my avocado-coloured bath. I imagined the scum of water lapping at his ribs; his long legs stretching out, his feet perhaps jostling against the old chrome taps; the sharp shelf of his shoulder blades as he reached forward, groping perhaps for the plastic jug to rinse the soap suds out of his hair, water streaming down the long bridge of his nose and off his chin.

I stood in the middle of my unfinished kitchen and glanced up at the ceiling, which had a thick sheet of polythene fixed into place to keep out the rain whilst we were waiting for the skylights to arrive. A mist of bubbles from the rain clouded the polythene and I couldn't yet see the sky, but there was light on my face. I closed my eyes. I stretched out my arms on either side and began to spin round and round.

*

That is how we started. How can we predict at the start of things how they will finish? It began with Ben in my kitchen, standing so close in that shuttered space that I could have easily reached and touched him, could have lain my hand on his chest and felt his heartbeat. It ended with me lying dead on the tiled floor of another kitchen.

In between there were eight years. Ben went back to university and completed his MA in Architecture. He finished developing his property and then we sold his house, and then mine, and then rented a semi in Brighton, which was cold and too modern. But that was all right because we knew we wouldn't stay.

On the night he graduated we drank pink champagne and listened to an old Barry White CD and made love all over the house. After the third time Ben got down on one knee and asked me to marry him and I said yes.

Then we moved to Reigate. Ben set up in partnership with Timothy Banks. Vincent and Banks, Architectural Designers. It was the *Spend Spend Spend* days of New Labour. Tony Blair was sending our troops to Iraq and the banks were loaning out money to everyone who wanted it. House prices were spiralling. Property was being developed, big old draughty houses turned into multiple units. Old garages, warehouses: anything standing, bought at auctions and turned into housing. The work was pouring in from every quarter. I transferred from my job working for Sussex probation service in Brighton to a post at Wandsworth prison, which would involve a more specialised role in rehabilitation projects, work I was passionate about at the time.

We rented a flat for six months, then looked for a house that would take us into the future. We had this vision of light and space. *More* light and space. High ceilings, large rooms, big draughty sash windows. A rambling garden full of corners and secrets. We found it in Reigate. Virginia creeper had overtaken the brickwork at the front of the house. There were wrought iron gates, a brick paved driveway, a little winged cherub sculpture half hidden by ferns in the shrubs at the side of the house. Inside were the light and the space. There was original stained glass in the porch windows, in the large panelled window on the landing. The doors were original. Stripped panelled pine. There was an enamel bath with high clawed feet in the bathroom, an original Minton-tiled hallway.

We got married six months later. The ceremony took place at All Saints Church in Hove, followed by a lavish reception at a country estate about fifteen miles away from Brighton, hired out for weddings for a price that should have taken our breath away. But Ben's parents and mine chimed in to help pay for it, and we still had some money set aside after buying the house. This would only happen once in our lifetime, we thought, so blow the expense. My mother wore an oyster-pink satin outfit and matching hat, my father, a morning suit and waistcoat. Ben's parents had flown over from Marbella, where they now lived. His mother looked stunning in a tight-fitting ivory suit and his father broke with convention and was jovial in linen. Their tans made us all look grey and unhealthy. They shivered all through the service in the cold, draughty church. It was in the middle of winter, but a crisp bright day with frost on the ground. We stood outside in the grounds of the country estate and our footsteps melted soft prints on the frosted grass. When we looked at the CD of photographs sent to us later there was one where Ben was smiling like a clown into the camera. I was looking at him with this hard-to-read expression on my face. Perhaps I'd had too much champagne, perhaps the sharp January sun was in my eyes. There was a crooked grimace on my face and I looked more as if I was in pain than smiling.

"We don't want this one," I said to Ben later, when we sat down to choose what photographs we would buy.

"I like it," he said.

"But I look awful in it."

"No, you look just the way you are."

"How am I?"

"Ambiguous. Full of paradoxes."

"But I don't even look happy. You're grinning like a Cheshire cat and I look…"

"How do you look?"

"Weird."

"That's why I love you."

*

Eight years. We moved three times. We made love countless times. We got married once. Ben designed God knows how many new houses, how many multiple unit conversions. We thought of getting a puppy and went to look at one and then, feeling guilty about all the dogs wanting homes, trotted around Battersea Dogs Home twice and nearly brought home a heart-defective blue roan cocker spaniel called Bert. But then I found out I was pregnant and we didn't.

We only had one daughter. On the night she was born Ben told me that after he got home from the hospital, he ran for five miles around the dark streets of Reigate. He ran because so much light and space coursed through his veins and filled his heart. He ran for five miles through the dark winter streets just so that his veins would shrink and his blood would slow and he might, possibly, be able to sleep at last.

9

Katie Clements' grey suit jacket was cut low enough to reveal a cream chemise-style blouse, which was low enough itself to reveal the beginnings of a slight cleavage. Against her pale, slightly freckled skin lay a small gold crucifix on a thin chain. When she held out her hand for Ben to shake I noticed his eyes slide appreciatively down from her face to her breasts and then back up again, so quickly it hardly registered. Except with me.

"Mr Vincent?"

"Miss Clements."

Ben shook her hand. His handshake was firm.

"And this must be Molly?"

"Yes, Molly say hello to Miss Clements."

"Hello, Miss Clements."

"Do please sit down, Mr Vincent. And Molly."

Ben sat on the black leather sling-back chair. Molly, on the small wicker chair that Katie used for the children. Katie sat on a professional-looking cream upholstered chair. She looked calm and assured. She had done her homework.

She'd read the report sent over by Gardiner, the one that detailed the scene of the crime and all that was known to have happened that day. She'd read the post-mortem report and the notes made by Mr Searle. I had watched her whilst she had read them.

Now, she was taking her time surveying this man and his child. Her gaze was not penetrating; it was soft and non-direct. I knew she was recognising something of her friend, Susie, in Ben's face: in the firmness of his chin, in his slightly jutting brows. How would she describe him? Tall and rangy, perhaps, with his long wiry limbs and broad shoulders apparent under his light brown canvas jacket. His hair was dark; he wore it quite long so that it curled over the top of his shirt collar and hung in a loose casual fringe over his forehead. He had a habit of pushing it back with his hand when it got in his eyes. He was doing it now. She watched him, this girl. This one I have chosen. He crossed and uncrossed his legs, then opened them wide in what she knew was a classic 'crotch display' to belie his insecurity, and then leant forward. He rested his elbows on his knees and twisted and turned the gold band up against the bony knuckle of his ring finger. He had never removed his wedding ring. Why was that? Her gaze dipped down to his hands and now up again, back to his face, as if she hadn't noticed the ring, but of course she had. She turned her attention to Molly.

"That's a pretty top you're wearing today, Molly."

It was Molly's pink one with the yellow butterfly, its wings spread out across her chest. The wings were speckled with tiny sequins that caught the light as she twisted self-consciously in her chair. I'd been there when my mother had chosen it for her.

"Molly, I have to spend a little time going through a form with Daddy. I have to ask him some questions."

"Okay."

"Would you like to look at a book whilst I'm doing this? There are some over there in that box."

Molly shrugged.

"Go on, Molls, that's all right," Ben said. She got up and sauntered over to the book box and brought back a picture book about Sleeping Beauty.

Katie Clements picked up a clipboard with a form attached to it from her desk and settled it down on her lap. Ben answered her questions in a low and even voice. *Molly's first name. Molly's date of birth. Address. Phone number.* As the pen she held moved over the page, the gold charm bracelet she wore jangled softly on her thin wrist.

Molly was beginning to fidget. She closed up the Sleeping Beauty book. It didn't really interest her; she had the same one at home. She was growing out of princesses now. She folded up her right leg, tucked the foot under her bottom and fiddled with the clasp of her shoe.

"Would you like to find something else to do, Molly?" Katie indicated with a slight movement of her head a long draped curtain on her right. "There's some toy boxes over there on the shelves behind that curtain."

Molly glanced towards her father for confirmation again.

"You go see, Molls."

She slid off the chair and walked over to the curtain. She pulled it aside to reveal shelves stacked with games and toys. Below them on the floor were several wooden toy boxes on wheels. Molly peered into them one at a time.

She returned to the first one and took something out of it.

Katie had continued with the form.

"The name and address of Molly's GP?"

Molly was sitting on the brown carpet-tiled floor, cradling a doll in her arms. The doll looked like Miss Moffat. The same rope plaited hair, only brown not yellow; the same crumpled cloth face, the same crooked stitched smile. Only this doll was missing an arm, and was wearing an orange and green gingham pinafore, not a pink and yellow one like Miss Moffat at home.

Something had come over Molly. She was rocking herself gently on the floor.

Katie put down the clipboard.

"You like that doll, do you, Molly?"

"It reminds her of Miss Moffat, a doll she has at home," Ben said. But Katie wasn't listening to him. She was watching Molly intently.

"What do you like best about that doll, Molly?" she asked.

Molly pushed the doll's brown, plaited rope-like hair against her cheek. She had begun to hum a tuneless song under her breath, something she was making up as she went.

"Don't do that, Molly," Ben said. "Answer Miss Clements."

"No, it's all right, Mr Vincent. Leave her."

"Miss Moffat was the doll that Molly was found with the day when her mum was... you know..."

But Katie wasn't really listening to him; she was still watching Molly carefully. Molly removed her thumb from her mouth and put the doll down, placing it roughly on its face. She went back to sit in the chair and was suddenly back to herself again.

"She looks like my doll. She looks like Miss Moffat. 'Cept Miss Moffat has a different colour dress. She has a pink one. Not orange," she said, turning to look shyly at Katie.

"Which colour dress do you like best?"

"Pink. Pink is my favourite colour."

"She is seriously into pink," Ben added, laughingly. "Everything in her bedroom has to be pink. Pink curtain, pink bedspread, pink rug on the floor. Isn't it, Molls?"

"Yes. Pink is a nice colour," Katie said. She could sense Molly relaxing, sensed that my little girl felt comfortable talking to her.

"Molly, has Daddy told you why you're here?" Katie's tone was suddenly a little lower, a little more serious.

Molly twisted in her chair. She glanced towards her father, who smiled ruefully back at her, and then down at the Miss Moffat look-a-like on the floor. Then back over to Katie.

"You want me to talk about Mummy?"

"Well, that's nearly right, Molly. We think perhaps it's time that you did talk a little about Mummy. Do you remember your mummy?"

Molly shook her head.

"Not always. Daddy shows me pictures sometimes, then I think I remember."

"What do you think you remember most of all?"

"I don't know. Nothing really." She paused. "A song. She used to sing a song to me sometimes."

"How does the song go, Molly? Do you remember?"

She screwed up her face. She started to hum the first phrase of 'Frère Jacques' and then the tune died like a light petering out. Standing behind her, I began to hum the song softly into her ear. But I knew she couldn't hear me, I knew that the shutters had come down between us now, not like when she dreams. But it was almost as if Katie had heard me instead. She started to sing the song, her pretty Welsh voice lilting easily up and down the notes. She sang it right through to the end.

"Was that the song, Molly?"

"Yes," Molly said, in a small voice.

"Do you remember any other songs your mother used to sing to you?"

Molly shook her head. "Not really. I don't really remember her. Not the mummy before she died."

"What mummy do you remember, Molly?"

I sensed Ben holding his breath. If I had breath to hold, I would have held it too.

"The mummy that was dead. The one lying on the kitchen floor with lots of blood under her head. I dreamt about that mummy the other night. That's why I'm here, isn't it, Daddy?"

"Well, we think perhaps you need help to talk about it, sweetheart. What happened that day Mummy…"

Say it, Ben!

"… that day Mummy died."

"And you're worried about the painting too, aren't you, Daddy? The painting I did at school."

Our little girl. Always so pretty and so bright…

"I guess I was, darling. Yeah, I was a bit upset."

"Have you brought the painting? Would you mind if I

looked at it?" Katie said, directing the question at Ben. He shuffled around in the large canvas bag he had put down by his feet. He brought out the folded sheet of sugar paper with the painting on it.

"You don't mind, do you Molls?"

"No, I don't mind, Daddy."

He laid the sheet of paper over his lap and unfolded it. Molly looked dispassionately at it.

"Would you mind laying it down on the floor, Mr Vincent? So I can see it more clearly."

Ben leant forward and laid the painting down on the brown carpet tiles.

"Would you mind telling me about the painting, Molly?" Katie Clements asked her softly.

Molly looked vexed for a moment. *Can't you see it for yourself? Can't you?* She walked over to the painting.

"That's Mummy lying on the floor. Mummy's dead. That's the black and white floor. That's her dress with little flowers on it. That's blood where her head is hurt." Her voice was flat and mechanical.

"And who's that, Molly?" Katie indicated the darker figure.

Molly stared at it. She shook her head.

"You don't know who it is, Molly?"

"It's a man."

"Do you know what the man is doing?"

"No, not really."

"Where are you, Molly? You're not in the picture, are you?"

Without answering, Molly stood up, bent down, picked up the painting and then slowly started to rip it up. The painting hung in ragged strips. The mummy bit fell to the ground.

"What are you doing Molly? Stop that!"

"No, it's all right. Let her do it."

Molly left the painting in long ragged strips on the floor and came back and sat on her chair. She looked up at Katie, almost defiantly, the shyness gone now.

"I don't know," she said. "I don't know where I am. And I don't know who the man is. He hasn't got a face."

*

When Ben and Molly arrived home Sylvia was waiting to see them. She had driven over from her home near Talgarth, eager to hear how Molly's first consultation with Katie had gone. She had stopped off at the bakery in Brecon and bought a cake. Molly's favourite. Victoria sponge. The jam and buttercream were layered very thickly between the moist soft halves. They knew how to make it correctly, this bakery. The three of them sat together in the kitchen. Ben's cat, a smoky grey tom, jumped up on the table and he shooed him down again. It had surprised me, Ben's acquisition of the cat, as he had always been a dog man. But when he and Molly had moved in to the cottage the cat was there constantly, mewing to be fed, like a dispossessed soul, perhaps abandoned by the previous occupants, and so as Molly had loved the cat with a passion, Ben had taken him over. Molly had named him Jasper, after a cat in a storybook that Ben had read to her once. Jasper settled now in the corner of the room and watched me out of his aqua-green eyes. He knew. Cats always do.

Sylvia was telling Ben about the new shopping centre that had opened up near Hereford. She and Ted had taken a trip out to it yesterday. A shopping village, it was called. She showed him her new Calvin Klein bag, which she'd bought at a knockdown price. I sensed Ben thought sixty-five pounds is hardly a 'knockdown' price for a bag she didn't really need, but he didn't tell her so. I knew that he thought the bag was too young for her, too trendy, too green, but he didn't tell her that either. My mother didn't really have extravagant tastes but occasionally she went impulse shopping, maybe for the same reasons other women might binge on chocolate. To make herself feel better. She had been feeling anxious about these sessions Molly was starting with Katie. Anxious about what they might reveal. I could sense that she didn't want to ask Ben about how the session had gone, didn't dare to. Ben didn't dare to tell her either, didn't want to open old wounds for her. But Molly dared.

"Did you like that lady at the clinic, Daddy?"

"What, sweetheart?"

"The lady that spoke to me about Mummy."

"Yes, sweetie. I did. I thought she was nice. Did you like her?"

"She was all right, Daddy."

"That's good, darling."

"Do I have to see her again?"

"I'd like you to, poppet. I'd like you to see her a few times, if that's okay with you. It's just that we think it's helping you to talk about Mummy. Don't you think it's helping you?"

"I suppose so."

She looked at Ben and then at my mother. Sylvia was

thinking back, thinking back to that day. The memory was painful. Molly frowned, almost imperceptibly, and returned her attention to licking the buttercream filling from the side of her cake.

"Ted seems a little better these days," Sylvia said, needing to change the subject. "I think the depression is lifting. He spent some time in the garden yesterday. Tidied up the vegetable plot."

And because she had mentioned him, named him, my father was with us then in the kitchen. I saw him clearly, in the way the dead see, the way that doesn't belong to the living and their perception of time and space. He was wearing the shabby old corduroys he often wore when he was gardening. His face looked brighter than it had been for ages, since the day that I died. I was happy for a while, here with the people that I love. Although how possible it is to be happy when one is between the world of the living and the dead, I do not truly know.

*

Later, when Molly had finished her cake and was upstairs playing for a while, as it was too late now to go back to school, Ben told Sylvia about the painting. He told her how Molly had ripped it up, what she'd said about the man with no face. Sylvia's eyes widened with alarm. I knew that she was worried about my father knowing this, afraid that it would set him back again, if he knew. She was afraid of that heart of his beating out of time again. Of it stopping and never beating again.

"Are you sure it's the right thing to do? Making her to

talk about it, getting her to try and remember? I'm not sure, Ben. She's still just a baby…"

"Nobody is trying to force her to talk about it, Sylvia. It's a bit more subtle than that."

"Well, I suppose so…"

"That dream she had the other night, and the painting at school. It wants to come out whether we like it or not. She needs to be able to talk about it."

My mother grimaced. "I hope you're right, Ben. I suppose this woman, this Katie Clements, she must know what she's doing."

"Anyway, she might come up with something to help the police. God knows they need it."

"It feels like they've forgotten about it, Ben, like they've given up."

"Too right they have," Ben said, bitterly. Then he remembered Molly, playing upstairs on her own. "I'd better go and see what Molly's doing."

He went upstairs. Molly was quiet. The door to her bedroom was closed. He pushed it open slowly, expecting to see that she had fallen asleep, tired out by the session she'd had with Katie Clements, by the effort of remembering. She hadn't. She was sitting cross-legged on her leopard-print rug on the floor. Miss Moffat was lying next to her, spilling entrails of webbing and foam.

Ben crouched down beside Molly and clasped the disembowelled Miss Moffat.

"Christ! Molly, what's happened? What's happened to Miss Moffat?"

The scissors were lying open by her knee, their blades forming a cross on the leopard-print rug. They were the scissors that I had used for dressmaking. Ben still kept them in my old wicker sewing-box in a chest of drawers in the bedroom.

Molly lifted her head and looked at him strangely.

"I don't like Miss Moffat anymore, Daddy. I had to punish her for being bad."

"What had she done that was bad, Molly?"

"She didn't help Mummy when Mummy was hurt."

10

We're all of us guilty, Ben. And none of us are.

A paradox. I'm fond of those now, aren't I?

They're the only thing that makes sense. There is no sense.

Perhaps guilty is the wrong word. Complicit, then. We're all complicit in everything that happens. We may even have created the fact of it happening.

He is here again. That someone who used to be Mr Jackson, who was significant and yet insignificant in my life.

It is time soon for him to go, he tells me.

"Where will you go?"

He smiles. He says that he had a daughter once, and she is waiting for him. I think of that room full of light and warmth, the children playing. I think how good it must be to be in the only place where you want to be and for there to be no separation between you and the ones you love.

When I think of this I hurt inside. Only in this place where I am, which is no place at all, everything is inside. Everything in the world flows through me like water…

*

I knew he had a daughter. I heard my father telling my mother about her. It was just before we moved from the cottage in the Sussex Downs to the house in Brighton:

"He had a daughter, apparently. Mrs Fletcher at the post office told me. Years ago, when he was with his wife, they had a little girl. He doted on her and then she suddenly took ill with meningitis and died. She was only five when it happened. She had only just started school a few months earlier."

My mother said, "Well, I'm sorry to hear about that but it doesn't make any difference. I still don't think I can trust him."

She was still hanging on to those dark thoughts that had been festering for a year in her mind. *What happened, Rachel? Did something bad happen?* I could have stopped them taking root and growing, I could have stopped it if I'd wanted to, but I didn't. I was complicit in my silence; I was guilty. In that instant of overhearing my father speak I understood the meaning of the pottery pig and the sorrow Mr Jackson felt when I broke it. She had made it; his little girl had made it. She had modelled it roughly out of the clay. It had been fired in a kiln, and then she'd painted on the pinky-white glaze that had pooled thickly in the crevices in the eyes and ears, in the cleft feet, and then it was fired again. She'd probably made it at school, in those first few months of school just before she died. He had put it on the mantelpiece. He'd sat there at night-time and looked at it. Especially in the winter, when the fire was burning brightly in the grate and throwing up rich tones, so that the thickly glazed areas, opaquely white-pink, deepened almost to red, and every time he had looked at it he'd think of her, his little girl, and a flame of love would leap in his heart and warm him. It had probably stood there for years, in pride of place on his mantelpiece, and for years he had looked at it and been warmed by it, even long after his wife had passed on. And then I had broken it. Another little girl, about the same age as the girl who had made it.

"Mrs Fletcher said she looked like our Rachel. The image of her," my father said.

"How can she remember? It must've been years ago," my mother retorted.

"Well, that's what she said."

*

"You brought her back to me."

I see in that way that is outside time and space, a small child in a garden. The garden is Mr Jackson's garden, when he lived next door to us. There is a slide in the garden, a wooden dog on wheels that has an upright handle for pushing. The little girl looks like me, could almost be me, with her long hair in bushy pigtails, but it's blonde instead of red like mine, although it has reddish tints in the sun. She is wearing a gingham pinafore dress, with a bow tied at the back. She is clutching a rag doll that looks a bit like Miss Moffat.

"What was her name?"

"Melanie."

"That's nice."

"Yes."

"I'm sorry about the pig. I'm so sorry."

"I'm sorry too. I shouldn't have been cross with you. You were just a little girl."

"I didn't mean to break it. The dog startled me…"

"It was time to let it go. We can't hold on to things forever. Or to people."

"I was angry with you because I felt guilty."

"None of that matters. We need to see beneath the surface."

"How do we do that?"

"We need to accept. We need to release the things we hold on to."

"I don't want you to go. I don't want you to leave me for good."

"I will only be an instant away."

"So I will see you again?"

He doesn't answer. I am surprised by a temporary warmth, as if he has stepped towards me and hugged me. And then it is cold again.

*

That night I tiptoed into Molly's room. She was sleeping. Her dad had placed Rufus, the black and tan toy dog, next to her head on the pillow. He lay forlornly, one amber glass eye staring abjectly up at me. Molly was not clutching him to her chest the way she used to clutch Miss Moffat.

Where is Miss Moffat? Stray wisps of webbing and foam were curling like flotsam on the carpet.

I took Molly's hand in mind. It was warm and living.

I love you.

She stirred, but didn't wake. Her eyes flickered softly

under the warm fold of their lids and I knew that she was dreaming.

Something was coming back to me. An image, a memory. Almost like a haunting, as if I was seeing ghosts myself. I leant over my daughter and dropped the returning memory into her dreams.

*

She is playing upstairs and the doorbell chimes. She wants a pee and comes out on to the landing. She can hear me answer the door. She can hear voices, mine, and a strange man's voice. Not her father's. There is surprise and shock in my voice, then exasperation, anger, even pleading. She doesn't hear feelings move through the man's voice; she doesn't know his voice well enough to hear that.

She goes into the toilet and has a pee, all by herself. She wants to call out for me to come and wipe her, but there's this man's voice at the door, and there is something about the voice that makes her unsure, so she doesn't. She tries the wiping bit all by herself and is pleased with herself. She pulls the chain like she knows she should do and then she pulls up her panties. Out on the landing she can still hear the voices. The man's voice is loud, almost shouting. It's ugly with words she doesn't like. She knows they are bad words, although she hasn't heard them before. Her daddy never used words like that. She comes halfway down the stairs and then waits for me to turn and see her there.

"Mummy..."

"Molly... sweetheart... Look, my daughter is here. You must go, you must go right now."

A foot in a yellow boot plants itself inside the doorway, on the doormat. A hand comes around the door, then an arm. The arm is bare and has a picture of a butterfly that looks like a tiger on the thick rounded forearm. A face peers up at her. It is a face she has never seen before. It isn't an ugly face, and yet it frightens her.

"Hello little girl," *the mouth in the face seems to be saying. She says nothing back.*

"Please. You must go. Please."

There is something she hasn't heard before in her mummy's voice. It makes her feel a strange fluttering inside her tummy.

"You can't pretend it didn't happen, Rachel. You can't just fob me off like that."

"Please go… my little girl…"

"Say you'll meet me, then I'll go. Say you'll meet me somewhere."

Her mother's voice lowers and there are murmurings, things she knows she is not meant to hear. The foot in the yellow boot moves back beyond her sight. The arm with the butterfly-tiger, and then the face, disappear.

*

Molly moaned softly in her sleep and turned, one arm flinging out over Rufus' staring glass eye, and then she was sinking deeper, beyond her dreams, beyond any place where I might reach her. I left her, and in a blink of an eye I was in Ben's room. I watched him sleep for a while. I didn't want to touch him tonight. I knew he was dreaming of her. Katie Clements. His body twitched and jerked as he dreamt, and I knew that in the morning he would remember and be a little embarrassed by the dream. He would sit in the room opposite Katie Clements and try not to stare at the neat turn of her knees in her dark tan stockings showing beneath her black pencil skirt. Try not to notice the slim ankles, the narrow feet encased in red stiletto heels. He would try to think only of Molly, focus only on Molly, but all the time he would be feeling a new sense of being alive, more alive than he has been perhaps since the time we first met.

*

I didn't stay. I couldn't bear to.

11

The man with the tiger-butterfly tattoo walked over to the bedroom window, padding on the carpet in his bare feet. The window of the room overlooked a bungalow opposite. Some lights were on in nearby houses but the bungalow opposite was in darkness. He picked up the binoculars that were sitting on the seat of a wicker chair and trained them on the dark house. He was wearing a short-sleeved tee-shirt and the tattoo on his forearm crinkled slightly as his arm bent. He made a noise of exasperation and put the binoculars down again. He walked across the room again, back to the bed. He stripped off his jeans and his tee-shirt and left them on the floor. He was wearing blue and white striped boxer shorts. He walked over to the light-switch by the door and flicked it off and walked back to the bed in the darkness, holding his arms out slightly in front of him like one who is blind. The pale crescent moon brought a thin light into the room through the window. He left the curtains open. He got back on to the bed. He pulled the blankets half over his body. He closed his eyes.

I stayed with him in that room all night. I heard his breath deepen, slow down, and knew that he had fallen asleep. The crescent moon disappeared behind a cloud and the room darkened. He was dreaming now, but I didn't want to know his dreams, didn't want to touch them. In the small hours of the night there was the sound of a car slowing and stopping in the street outside. The man stirred on the bed but didn't wake. I stood by the window and watched a woman in her late twenties, early thirties get out of the car. The moon had slid out from behind the cloud and I could see in the vague light that the young woman had long light-coloured hair and wore it tumbling loose around her face and down past her shoulders. She leant forward, as if she was saying something to the driver. Then she turned and went up the path to the front door of the bungalow. A moment later the lights went on in a window at the front of the bungalow. The shadow of her body moved behind the lit window. It must've been a bedroom window. I saw her take off her silk beige shirt. Then she stood close to the window, in full view of anyone who might have been outside in the street, and revealed the smooth curves of her body under the tightly fitting chemise, her breasts lifting slightly as her arms stretched upwards to draw the curtains closed.

The man slept on. I stood by his bed and stared down at him. In this place where I am now, I am not supposed to feel hatred anymore. But I did. I could almost taste its bitterness in my mouth, if I still had a mouth to taste things.

12

Ben sat in the kitchen, sipping his coffee, and remembering his dream about Katie Clements. I knew he was wondering if she would know that he'd dreamt about her, if she could read his thoughts. I could. He was thinking that it wouldn't surprise him if she could; she seemed to know things other people didn't.

He wondered what she would say when he told her about Miss Moffat.

Miss Moffat was lying squashed under the cushion on the sofa. Ben had collected as much of the webbing as he could find and stuffed it back into the gaping vent on her belly. He had saved the cut-off pigtails and put them in the drawer in the hall cabinet. He would take Miss Moffat to my mother's and ask her to repair the doll. Sylvia was handy with a needle and thread. She could carefully sew up the gaping wound with neat little stitches that would hardly show, stitch the yellow pigtails neatly back on to Miss Moffat's head. The doll would look almost as good as new, but not quite. He would know, and Molly would know, that Miss Moffat was wounded, that there would always be a weakness there.

Upstairs, Molly woke up more slowly than she normally did. She didn't go straight downstairs, as she usually did, to where her father was in the kitchen getting the pancake batter ready; they always had pancakes on Sunday mornings. Still in her nightie, she searched the shelves for her sketch book and the tin that held her drawing pencils.

Molly loved drawing as most children do at her age, and although I know I am biased, I could see that she was clearly a natural artist. She drew everything, everything that was important in her world. She drew her father, giving him a large head and two long arms that protruded from halfway down his torso and ended in bunches of bananas for fingers. The face, though, was detailed. As well as eyes and a nose and mouth, it had eyebrows, sometimes lashes on the top of the eyes, ears that stuck out from the side of the head. Sometimes the face was smiling, and at other times, particularly in the earlier pictures drawn before the move to Wales, the mouth was down-turned into sadness. She drew trees and flowers, and little houses in a terraced row with large windows and brightly coloured front doors, like the row of terraced cottages where she lived with her father. She drew my parents' house, set haphazardly amidst a greenery of trees and grass, with a blue stream curving through the greenery, and a blue pond with big orange fish in another green area of garden.

She drew my parents. My mother was always smiling and wore large, triangular-shaped pink skirts; my father in wide brown trousers always looked sad. She drew Goldie, their Labrador, an oblong body supported by stick legs and coloured in yellow. She drew her teacher, Miss Austin, with a thin face drowning in round glasses. She drew some of her friends from school: Chloe, with her thick brown plaits and Charlie Craddock, who had ginger sticking-up hair and a smile that split his face from one side to another.

This morning she took the sketch book to the little desk that was set up in the corner of the bedroom. She turned the pages of drawings over and over, paying no attention to them, until she arrived at a fresh clean page. The dream was fresh in her mind. The man who had frightened her, with his loud unfamiliar voice. The strange tattoo on his arm. She started to draw a butterfly. I was helping her to draw it, almost guiding her hand. But she didn't know it was me that was helping. Making the movements of the felt pens over the page so fluent and easy, dropping names of colours into her head.

Well done, Molly.

It was quite impressive. The wings weren't quite symmetrical, but as close as she could get them to be. In the larger wings at the top, two large, slanted, lime-green eyes. The shape of a tiger's nose, drawn with a red crayon, formed the bottom of the butterfly's body. She had coloured the butterfly in orange, with black smudgy stripes; at the edges of the wings the orange lightened to yellow and then faded out to white.

She took a small pair of children's safety scissors from the tin of pencils, and cut close to where the paper joined the stapled spine so that the drawing was free of the sketch book. She put the scissors and the pencils back in the tin and placed it back on the shelf along with the sketch book. She picked up the drawing and started to go downstairs. But then she heard the sound of the doorbell chime and because the memory I had given her in her dream was still clear in her mind, she froze. She sat down on a step near the top of the stairs and stared down the stairwell towards the glazed front door at the muted shape of a figure standing outside on the doorstep. Ben was at the bottom of the stairs about to open the front door. He turned and saw her there.

"Molly, what's wrong? What is it sweetie?"
"Don't open the door, Daddy. Don't."
"Darling, don't be silly…"
"Please Daddy…"
"Don't be silly."

His hand was on the door latch. He turned it. Molly got up and ran upstairs back to her room. She had dropped the drawing, and the sheet of paper lay, trembling slightly, precariously balanced on the edge of a tread. Ben shook his head – *silly girl* – and opened the door. A woman, a neighbour who lived several houses down the road on the opposite side, stood there in the slanting October sunlight smiling at him. She had a sponsor form in her hand. She asked if he would be interested in sponsoring her for a charity marathon she was taking part in to raise funds for a local hospice. This woman, he knew, had recently lost her partner to cancer, and how could he refuse? Of course he would sponsor her, he said. He took the form from her and leant up again the wall of the hall. With a bitten-down stump of a pencil he found in a drawer of the hall cabinet, alongside Miss Moffat's severed plaits, he committed to twenty pounds if she finished the whole run.

"You'll be out training every night now, just to make

sure you get my money off me," Ben joked, handing back the sponsor form. The woman smiled and thanked him warmly. She turned to go and he shut the door and called up the stairs, "Molly, are you coming down for breakfast? I'm making pancakes."

Pancakes were her favourite. She always liked them on Sunday mornings. She liked to help him make them, to let him cup her small hands with his large strong hands over the handle of the frying pan and help her to toss them. She liked them drizzled with lemon and sugar and rolled up into a sausage shape.

No answer. Ben put a foot on the bottom rung of the stairs. The sheet of paper had drifted in the draft from the open door down a few more steps. Ben climbed up the stairs towards it, stooped and picked it up. The tiger's lime-green slanted eyes stared out at him from the pattern on its wings. He looked at the drawing, faintly impressed. Something she'd copied out of a book? He was used to his daughter's skill in art, but the detail in this was beyond her usual work. He called upstairs again, and this time Molly's voice answered. Yes, pancakes, she wanted pancakes.

She came slowly back downstairs and into the kitchen. The drawing now was forgotten, the memory of the dream fading at the thought of pancakes for breakfast. She sat at the kitchen table and watched as her father poured batter into the large frying pan on the hob. The hot fat sent up a white curl of smoke, then a sizzle as the batter went in.

"Want to help me toss it?"

She got up and held the handle of the pan with him and together they awkwardly tossed the pancake. It shifted into the air and landed back in the pan half-folded.

"Not bad, not bad. You straighten the folded half out with a spatula."

"Let's do it again, Daddy."

"Okay, but I need you higher." He lifted her up and sat her on the work-surface and they tossed again. The pancake went up and this time fell neatly on the other side. They did it again. She giggled with pleasure.

"Okay. That's done." Ben slid her down and she sat at the table again. He slipped the pancake, which was a little too thick and doughy and burnt faintly at the edges, on to her plate.

"Now, how about that? Have you had a better pancake than that, ever?"

She was busy squeezing the lemon, ladling on sugar that melted into crunchy crystals on the hot pancake. The drawing of the tiger-butterfly still lay there on the table, the eyes staring up at him. I stood by his shoulder, leant forward, whispered softly into his ear.

Ask her about the drawing, Ben. Ask her.

He picked it up. "This is lovely, Molly. A tiger-moth?"

Her mouth was full of spongy pancake. She mumbled indistinctly, "Butterfly, Daddy."

"What, sweetheart?"

She swallowed the mouthful. "Tiger-*butterfly*, Daddy."

"I've never heard of a tiger-butterfly, honey. A tiger-moth, yes. But I don't think it looks quite like this."

"It doesn't matter, Daddy. It doesn't have to be real. I made it up. It's a butterfly, that's all." She was a little angry with her father now because she had to explain her drawing to him. Why did grown-ups always need things to be real?

"Yes, well, it's beautiful anyway, darling."

Ask her.

"Where did you get the idea from? Was it something you saw in a book?"

She dug the side of the fork into the pancake roll for another mouthful.

"No. I saw it last night."

"Last night?"

"In my dream. I had a funny dream. I dreamt that a man came to the door and he had a tiger-butterfly on his arm."

"A man? What man, darling?"

"The man in my dream. Only not just in my dream."

"What do you mean, sweetie?"

"I think it happened. When I was little. Before Mummy went to heaven."

I could feel Ben's heart start to race.

"Was he the bad man, Molly? Was he the man who hurt Mummy?"

Ben said this tentatively. He was thinking perhaps he shouldn't be saying this. Perhaps this was something for Katie Clements to be saying.

"I don't know. He came to the door in my dream. He was cross, that's all."

She shoved another mouthful into her mouth and munched it slowly.

"Is that why you were scared, sweetie, when someone knocked on the door just now?"

She glared at him and mumbled sideways through the mouthful of pancake. "I *wasn't* scared."

She swallowed the mouthful and jammed another in straightaway. She didn't want to talk about it anymore.

*

In the afternoon Ben drove the twenty minutes car journey to my parents'. They lived in a cottage that bordered a stream near Talgarth. Molly loved their garden; it was tiered and full of little hidden areas that she liked to explore. There was a pool on the tiered lawn set furthest away from the house; it looked like a natural pond although it wasn't really. My father had dug it out himself, with some help from a neighbour, in the months soon after they'd moved there from Brighton, before stress and the grief of losing me had sent his blood pressure soaring and his heart into fits of irregular beating.

The pond was bordered by reeds and bull-rushes, marsh marigolds and water forget-me-nots. Molly wasn't supposed to visit the pond without supervision, but sometimes Goldie would chase off towards it and Molly would run after her. For a few minutes she would be out of sight whilst my parents and Ben sat in the kitchen, which didn't have views over to the pond area. Molly would kneel down in the wet grass and look at the water-boatmen skimming the pond's surface and her hand would reach into the dark, cool water and stir the algae, hoping to catch sight of the goldfish.

I would stand just behind her, holding my cold breath in case she fell in.

Ben sat in the kitchen with Sylvia, telling her about how Molly was getting on at school. Molly stayed in the living room with my father. She sat on the footstool close to my father's armchair. He was pretending to watch the football on the television, but I knew that he was aware of her; he was always aware of her. She was colouring in pink princesses, just as I used to do. Then she stopped her colouring and swivelled around to face him. She stroked his trousered knee with her small hand. My father glanced down at her and gave a smile that was more like a grimace. Her upturned face and the roses in her cheek had brought a sudden memory back to his heart.

"You all right, darling?" he said. His voice was gruff with concealed emotion. He squeezed her hand.

"What's wrong, Granddad?"

"Wrong? Nothing's wrong, darling. Why should anything be wrong?"

"Because you look sad."

"Don't be silly, 'cos I'm not. I'm happy to see you. Always am."

*

Later, Ben and Molly put on jackets and let Goldie out of the kitchen door. They went over the lawn, past the vegetable patch, past the fruit trees and down to the pond on the tiered area below. I stood back at some distance and watched. But I didn't have to hold my breath this time because her father was there with her, leaning over her, one firm hand on her shoulder.

"Look, Molly. See the fish!"

There in the dark water, they could see the gold flash of the fish, its scales mirroring the light, and for the time being Molly forgot my father and his sadness.

Until later, on the way home.

"Why is Granddad sad, Daddy? Is it because Mummy died?"

Ben's heart threatened to race like my father's used to do.

"I expect so, darling. I guess you remind him of Mummy sometimes, when she was a little girl. But that's not a bad thing."

Molly winced. She glanced out of the window. She wanted to think of the pond and the golden fish, but she couldn't now.

"I can't remember Mummy really. Not the mummy before she died. Only sometimes in my dreams I do."

And now I felt sad, because she was forgetting me. And I had to let it happen.

*

Later that evening after supper, when Molly was engrossed in watching a DVD of *Shrek* on the television, Ben went upstairs and into her room. I followed him. He was looking for it. Looking for the tiger-butterfly. It was nowhere to be seen. It was as if its wings had lifted themselves from the paper and flown away. He searched through her things. Through the books in her little bookcase and stacked on her desk. He rifled through the chest of drawers, lifting aside the pink knickers and vests, the little tee-shirts and ruffle skirts and little black leggings, to look for it.

Under the bed. Look under the bed.

He knelt on the carpet and peered under the bed. There was another world under there, dark and hidden. A world of missing Lego pieces, chewed pencils and broken pens, scraps of sweet papers, half-eaten biscuits and fluff. He could see glittering in the dark the plastic ring with the red glass 'ruby' that she'd once lost and cried over. And the drawing.

He pulled it out. All over the butterfly's strangely patterned wings, thick black marker pen lines. A furious, deliberate scribble.

13

He is back with me now. Mr Jackson. With him comes the smell of the earth after a rainfall. A flurry of autumn leaves.

"You haven't gone yet then?"

"No."

"When will you go?"

"Very soon."

"Where will you go?"

"To be with them."

"Your wife and child?"

"Yes."

"Will I ever be able to leave this place?" This place that is no place yet every place as well.

"When you are ready."

His words make me sad. There is the chill of winter in them. Because I'm not ready, not yet. I'm not sure I'll ever be.

"I'll miss you."

He doesn't answer. And then he gives me a kaleidoscope of images. I see the little girl with strawberry blonde hair *wearing a gingham pinafore, playing in the garden. Then I see a small figure in a white hospital bed. I see Mr Jackson, a younger Mr Jackson, with dark hair and without a white feathery beard. He is sitting by the hospital bed. Then he is sitting in his small front room holding his head in his hands. I see a wreath of pink and white flowers, the small crudely made pottery pig sitting on the mantelpiece. Then the broken pieces in Mr Jackson's broad palm.*

"Nothing stays the same; everything changes," he tells me.

"Is anything real?"

"Love is real."

"How can I know that?"

But he has gone again. If I had a face to feel it, I would feel wetness on my cheek. It must be the memory of rain that he has brought back to me…

There is a harsh wind building, a biting chill of snow. He is gone now, but I know he will be back.

14

Molly perched on the edge of her seat. She was on her own in Katie's consultation room. Ben was waiting outside, under the kindly eye of Katie's receptionist, a young woman with a mess of hair dyed in multi colours who went by the rather exotic name of Saffron. (She had told him on the previous visit, when he had commented on the unusual name, that her parents had done the hippy trail to India back in the seventies and had conceived her in a trailer in Goa under an auspicious eclipse of the moon.)

Katie had asked to see Molly on her own when Ben had phoned to tell her about the drawing and Miss Moffat.

"I think she may perhaps open up to me more, when you're not there," Katie had said.

Molly now gazed self-consciously around the room. I stood over at the other side of the room and watched her. She was curious. She was curious about the drawers and cupboards that seemed full of secrets. About the hessian sacks with their drawstring cords at their necks that she could see on the floor behind the nice lady's chair.

"Would you like to choose a toy to play with, Molly? There are lots of toys in the little sacks over there. You could open some up and take a peep, see if you can find something you'd like to play with."

Molly slid gingerly off the chair and walked over to one. She pulled loose the red drawstring cord and looked in. What she saw didn't seem to please. This was the bag of heroes. Batman and Catwoman and Spiderman and Superman. The Incredible Hulk with his slime-green muscles. Heroes dressed as cowboys and soldiers and swash-buckling pirates, all of them brandishing weapons of all different kinds.

Molly drew the drawstring tight, closing the heroes down into the darkness.

The second bag she chose was full of villains. A crocodile with a leering red mouth; Captain Hook; a monstrous alien with a cyclops head; a Dalek from *Doctor Who*; a witch with a luminous green face. Molly took her out for a moment and considered her, then shoved her back into the little sack, pointy witch hat first, and pulled the drawstring tight.

Out of the third bag tumbled soft fluffy animals with battered vulnerable faces. A one-eyed teddy bear, a dog with a missing ear, a little grey mouse patched and mended on its back, a rabbit with big black stitches across his belly. The Miss Moffat look-a-like with the missing arm was in the bag, too. Molly clutched the one-armed rag-doll to her chest.

"Didn't you say you have a doll that looks like that, Molly?"

She nodded.

"You didn't want to bring her with you, this week, then? You could've done, you know."

Molly shook her head. "I left her at home. She's poorly."

"Oh that's a shame. She's like that doll, then. She's poorly, too. She's lost an arm."

"Yes."

"What's wrong with your doll?"

Molly didn't answer. She clutched the one-armed Miss Moffat impostor to her chest, then let it go and pushed its face down on to the floor.

"If I told you you wouldn't like me."

"Why do you think that, Molly?"

"You wouldn't like me if I did something bad."

"I'll always like you, Molly."

"Even if I was bad?"

"I wouldn't think you were bad, Molly. No matter what you did."

"Promise."

"I promise."

"I cut her up. I took the scissors from Daddy's room. They are funny scissors. They have teeth on them, like crocodile teeth. I stuck them in Miss Moffat's tummy and cut a zig-zaggy hole in her."

"Were you angry with Miss Moffat?"

"Yes."

"Would you like to tell me why you were angry, Molly?"

"She let someone hurt Mummy. She was there and she didn't help her."

Katie Clements sat as still as a rock, her slender hands folded in her lap.

"Were you there, too, Molly?"

Molly hung her head. Her dark hair fell forward across her face.

"No."

"But Miss Moffat was?"

She nodded.

Katie Clements gently opened the folder on the small table by the side of her chair, revealing Molly's drawing of the butterfly patterned like a tiger.

"Was the man there?" she asked Molly, softly.

"What man?"

"The man with the butterfly tattoo on his arm. A butterfly with the face of a tiger."

"I don't know."

"Would you like to play with anything else, Molly?"

Molly picked up the Miss Moffat look-a-like from her undignified position face down on the floor and tucked the doll under her arm. She got up and walked slowly around the room, the doll's legs poking out from under her armpit. She stopped at a cupboard. She turned the handle on the cupboard door but it was locked.

"What's in here?" she asked, her voice small and barely audible.

"There's more toys in there, Molly. Puzzles. Art materials. Would you like me to open it for you?"

Molly nodded, silently.

Katie Clements walked over to a cabinet and took out a key from the top drawer. She walked over to the cupboard and unlocked the door.

"There," she said. "It's open now."

Molly didn't move. She stared at the door.

"Do you want to have a look inside?"

She nodded again.

Katie Clements gently opened the cupboard door. Molly stood still and stared into the dim interior. She could make out a wooden cart of bricks, a pull-along dog, a red plastic car for toddlers to sit in. More dolls, large ones. Katie Clements walked back to her seat. She knew what was going to happen now. She knew because of her intuition, that sense of knowing without knowing why. That's why I chose her. Molly moved forward slowly towards the open door. She went into the cupboard; she hunched up, crouched down, pulled the cupboard door shut behind her. The door creaked as it closed.

And in the blink of an eye I was in the cupboard, too. Sitting next to Molly in the darkness.

A few minutes later – only a few, she wouldn't think it was safe to leave her too long – Katie Clements opened the cupboard door again. A long shaft of light fell in upon us. But Katie saw only a little girl, sitting next to the plastic car, amongst the large dolls, the Miss Moffat look-a-like clutched hard to her chest.

"It wasn't her fault, Molly," Katie Clements said softly. "It wasn't Miss Moffat's fault. She was frightened, Molly, like you were. She needed to hide, she needed to feel safe."

15

Six o'clock. The hour of dusk. The man with the tiger-butterfly tattoo walked up and down the road outside his block of flats. I followed behind him like a stalker. Sometimes he slowed, as if he almost sensed me, his head turning slightly as if he was about to look behind. But then he'd change his mind and walk on.

He walked past the bungalow where the woman with the blonde hair lived. He stopped for a minute outside and glanced over to the dim windows that had no sign of life behind them, no light. He walked on, his head turning now to the right, as if he was scanning the cars that were parked. I suddenly realised that he was looking for *her* car; he wanted to know if she was already home.

He carried on, a hundred or so yards down the road, to a small playground set back from the road behind a fence. It was almost empty. It wasn't the time now for children to play. They would be at home now. Their mothers would be making the tea, their dads coming home and swinging them up in their arms, spoiling them before they go to bed.

Like Ben used to with Molly.

A mother was pushing a toddler in a swing. She was very young, this mother, little more than a child. She wore her black hair cut short in a spiky style. Her skinny body, in jeans and a fake fur jacket, darted forwards and backwards in quick, sudden movements as she pushed the swing, as if she was always vigilant, always on edge. The man paused outside the gate to the playground and the young mother's head swung around to look at him, her hands moving up instinctively to the chains of the swing to slow its momentum. The man turned and walked back in the direction he had come from; he wasn't interested in the young skinny mum. She wasn't his type. He had someone else on his mind.

He passed the house again where the blonde woman lived. He slowed down, glanced at his watch. He crossed the road as if he had decided now to walk back to his flat. Then his head jerked up and he stared down the road. A car was coming. A red car. Her car? He walked to the side of the block of flats, stood concealed around the corner and waited. What was he waiting for? For the sound of the engine switching off, the car door opening.

She got out of the red Honda Civic. She was wearing her office suit. A skirt and jacket, with a faint thin charcoal stripe against a slightly paler grey. She walked to the rear kerbside door and opened it and the top half of her body disappeared, then re-emerged with a little boy in her arms. The child was sleeping. She propped him over her shoulder and supported his body with one arm, whilst the other arm opened up the boot. She lifted out a pushchair – one of those light easily collapsible types – and shook it open. She carefully lowered the sleeping child into it and fastened him in.

The man crossed the road again, back to the side where the car was parked. She hadn't noticed him yet; she was too busy lifting plastic carrier bags out of the boot, hanging them clumsily on the handles of the pushchair. The little boy's legs kicked forward, as if he was about to wake, and then he relaxed again into sleep. The woman turned towards the gate and opened it, struggling to get through with the laden pushchair. When the man walked past he muttered something that sounded like *Good evening*, but she was too busy concentrating on how to manoeuvre the pushchair to hear him. One of the bags caught on the gatepost. It tore open, contents spilling on to the ground. A bag of sugar, rice, a plastic tub of margarine, a jar of coffee, a tin of baked beans. Apples spilt out of a paper bag and rolled down the camber of the pavement into the gutter. A bottle of wine fell on to the tarmac and smashed, red wine spooling over the pavement, trickling down to stain the apples in the gutter.

"Oh bugger!" she said.

He was there in a moment. "Let me help you." He stooped down and began to pick up the fallen items, avoiding the broken glass, the wine that was the colour of blood.

"That's very kind of you," she said. "I've an empty bag in the boot. Just a minute – I'll fetch it." She walked to the back of the car, opened the boot up, returned with the bag. She took the items out of his folded arms and put them into the bag.

"You live here, don't you?" he said, jerking his head towards the bungalow.

She nodded yes.

"I live in those flats over there. I've seen you go in and out."

He faltered a bit then. Maybe he thought it sounded creepy. She was looking at him strangely, as if she didn't quite know how to respond to this.

"Look, why don't you take your little boy inside and fetch me a dustpan and brush. I'll tidy up this broken glass. Can't leave it here for some kid to cut himself on…"

"If you're sure you don't mind…"

He smiled. "'Course not."

She struggled up the path with the laden pushchair and fiddled with her key at the lock in the front door for a moment, before disappearing into the bungalow. Moments later she reappeared with the dustpan and brush and some newspaper and passed them to the man.

"We can wrap the glass up in the newspaper. The apples, too. Don't fancy eating them now."

He took the newspaper from her and opened out a sheet. Then stooped down and picked up the apples, one by one, that were lying in the gutter. The red wine stained his finger ends.

"You're very kind… thank you," she said. They could hear the sound of a child's wail through the open front door of the house.

"I'd better go… I've left my little boy in the pushchair in the hall…"

"I'll knock on the door to return the dustpan and brush when I finish," he said.

She could have said, would he mind leaving it on the doorstep? It was only a dustpan and brush.

But she didn't.

He knocked on the door only moments afterwards and she opened it, and before she had time to doubt the wisdom of letting him into the house he was following her into the kitchen, carrying the dustpan and brush and the newspaper parcel of broken glass and apples, a red smudge of blood leaking on to the paper from a cut on his thumb. I followed after him.

"Oh dear! You've cut yourself! Let me look at that."

She held his hand up close to her face and peered at the weal of blood.

"It's quite deep," she said.

"It'll be all right."

"I'll stick a plaster on that for you, but you'll need to hold it under the tap and make sure it's nice and clean."

He stood at her sink, holding his thumb under the tap. Blood thinned and streamed pink in the running water. I stood at the back of the kitchen watching them. The child, who was still fastened into his pushchair, was wide awake now. His saucer blue eyes stared over to where I stood, and I knew that he could see me. I lay my cold finger against my lips.

"This should do the job."

The woman tore off a piece of kitchen roll, then took a plaster out of its wrapping. He stretched out his hand towards her, palm upwards. She steadied his hand in hers and peered closely at the wound again, dabbing it dry with the kitchen roll paper, then snapped the plaster cleanly over the cut and smoothened it down to seal it.

"Are you a nurse, or summat?"

She smiled at him. But I noticed the wariness in her

eyes now. She wanted him to go. She had been at work all day and now she had the child to attend to, his meal to prepare. She released the man's hand and turned away towards the child.

"Anyway, thank you again. You've been very helpful…"

"That's all right. Always willing to help a damsel in distress."

She was stooping to undo the straps on the pushchair that held the child secure. The child reached up his arms to her and she lifted him out and stood up straight with the little boy perched on her hip. She planted kisses on his flushed cheek. His tousled head rotated so that he could still see me.

"Suppose I'd better go then," the man said. There was something about the woman and the child that made him feel uneasy now. He started towards the door that led back into the hall.

"I'll show you out." She moved quickly out in front of him and down the hallway, still holding the child, whose head was swivelling around trying to see me. She opened the front door.

"Well, thanks again for your help," she said, a little awkwardly.

"Oh well, if you need any help for anything. I'm quite a handy man, and I'm only across the road…"

"That's very kind, but I don't think that'll be necessary," she said. There was a curtness in her reply that she hadn't really intended. The man's shoulders stiffened slightly at the words. He was feeling knocked back by her. She closed the front door quickly on him and the night. She hugged the child tightly in her arms, relishing his warmth.

"Come on then, Leon. Time for supper. What do you fancy, darling? Fish fingers and chips, maybe?"

"Lady. Where the lady going?" the child muttered, as he watched me glide through the closed door and disappear. I heard his mother laugh.

"What lady, silly? You got an imaginary friend now?"

She could not see what he could see.

16

"I'm leaving."

"Are you going to join them now? Your wife and child."

"Yes."

"Will I see you again?"

He is silent. I sense already the thick glass pressed up against my face. The bright lights of the other room, the laughter. I sense a fire burning in a grate in the room, and there, on the mantel above it, the pottery pig sitting as if it had never been broken, its pink glaze burnished to shades of red in the firelight.

"If I joined you, I would have no one there waiting for me, as you have. The people I love the best are here."

"There is love everywhere. You don't belong here anymore."

And then he is gone. Gone for good. The loneliness is more than I can bear. And because I need comfort, because I need to feel loved, in the blink of an eye I am with my father. He sits in his chair reading the paper. Goldie is by his side, her heavy head resting on the arm of the chair. My father's hand drifts down from the paper, strokes the top of the dog's head. She stirs in delight at the touch. My father can hear Sylvia talking on the phone out in the hall to John, my brother. John is working as an engineer out in the Arab Emirates. My mother misses him; he has always been her favourite, although she was always fair, and had never made it too obvious. She is laughing at something John is saying. My father rarely feels like laughing, and when he does it still feels uncomfortable to him, a betrayal of my memory.

He folds up the paper and lays it down on the carpet by the side of the chair. He closes his eyes, lets his hand drift down again, rests it on the dog's back. Behind his closed eyelids he is seeing pictures. He is seeing pictures of me when I was four or five. I am bringing him back the pictures. Bringing them back to comfort him, to comfort myself...

I am crouched by the coffee table colouring pink princesses, like Molly did the other day...

I am sitting up on his shoulders, coming back one summer evening from the fair in Wilmington. His hands are holding my lower legs firmly, to steady me. The hedgerows are scented with wild flowers and midges nudge into my hair...

I am six or seven. There is thick snow on the ground in the garden of our house in Brighton. I am wearing a red duffel coat and a scarf that muffles my face. My father is building a snowman. He builds it quickly, expertly. It looks like one of the Wild Things from the book I love so much. When it is finished, he takes a photo of me standing next to it. It is easily twice as tall as me, perhaps even more. I am grinning from ear to ear...

Flash forward. I am twelve, and winning a trophy for

swimming. My body is taut and slim and there are small budding breasts under my swimsuit...

I am fourteen and playing Titania in the school play of Midsummer Night's Dream. I am wearing a long cotton dress and a garland of flowers in my hair. I hold hands with Oberon and take my final curtsey to a flashing of cameras from the local press...

I am sixteen and out with my first boyfriend. He is thin and has spots on his chin and mumbles my name nervously when my father opens the door. I wobble out of the door in heels and a tight mini skirt and my father worries...

I am off to Swansea University to study psychology. My father is driving me there. My new life is packed up in a big suitcase and my mother cries as she hugs me goodbye. My father has tears in his eyes, too, when he says goodbye to me in the halls of residence, but brushes off his feelings with a joke. "Now, you watch out for these young men. They're only out for what they can get. I should know; I used to be one..."

Then, before I can bring back any more images, my father brings in one of his own.

I am lying in the morgue. The compression on the back of my head is hidden. They have cleaned up the blood, brushed my hair. My face looks unreal, like a wax effigy...

And now, because the image is causing him a stab of pain, my father jerks his hand away from Goldie's back and places it on his chest, so that he can feel the pulse of his heartbeat, to make sure it is not racing again.

My father wonders sometimes why his heart continues to beat at all.

"It's all right, Daddy."

He doesn't hear me. He sighs, as if the breath might

release this tight constriction in his chest. Goldie gets up and stretches out her back legs; she is stiff, feeling her age these days. She saunters away into the hallway to see if she can get some attention from my mother, who is saying goodbye to John now and hanging up the phone.

"I'm sorry. I'm sorry I had to leave."

My father grimaces, slightly shakes his head. He feels the tightness in his chest relax. He picks up his paper, begins to read it again.

*

I want everyone to forgive me, it seems.
   Especially you, Ben.

17

I have to go back. It seems important that I have to go back. I don't want to, but I have to.

I have to go back now to when Molly was about two and a half.

Ben and I were both working hard then. We had to. We had put down a large deposit from the sales of our previous two homes by the time we bought the house in Reigate, but nevertheless our mortgage was substantial and we needed two decent salaries to support our lifestyle. Four years later, when Ben sold the house and moved down to Wales, there was less equity in it than at the time we had bought it. The bubble had burst.

But you can't know in advance how things will turn out. You imagine later that you can know, that you should have known, you should have seen things coming, but you can't.

I only worked three days a week back then; it was important to both Ben and myself that Molly got some quality time at home with me rather than attend the private nursery in Reigate full-time. But it never felt as if I was only working part-time. Rather, that I was cramming five days work into three.

So Ben and I were both working hard and spending less time together. Perhaps we had drifted a little apart. But not seriously though, not then. Just the pressures that life brings as you get older. Earning a living and raising a child.

I enjoyed my work, though. I had just started a new position at Wandsworth prison and was responsible for setting up a rehabilitation project for sex offenders. We wanted something that could be statistically seen as being successful, where the re-offending risk was lower, so that there would be a greater chance of securing future funding. So we were careful with our selection. We chose men who had not committed offences against minors. And younger men, men who had committed fewer offences, and those whose sexual offences had not involved serious acts of violence. The milder edge of the spectrum – if rape could ever be described as mild.

I had been on a course in sex offenders' rehabilitation, and was fired up with enthusiasm for the project. It was my baby. There were others involved, of course. Several of the prison social workers, the occasional attendance from a locum psychiatrist. But the actual business of making it work was my job.

I remember the first meeting we had with the men on the project. Ten had been selected and they all turned up, probably because there were privileges for those who kept up good attendance. Everyone was on their best behaviour. Watched their Ps and Qs. Didn't act out by losing it in torrents of swearing or by walking out in a temper.

Nicholas Hedges impressed me from the beginning.

For a start, he was very good-looking. Tall, with a solid physique. A man who kept himself fit, who worked out, who prided himself on the importance of a six-pack and well defined pecs. He turned up that first time in well-fitted and spotless jeans. Prisoners weren't permitted to dress too scruffily – jeans with the crotch right down near their knees, sort of thing – but Nicholas seemed particularly well turned out. He wore a black tee-shirt. No slogan or image emblazoned tackily across the front. Just a plain black tee-shirt, a good quality one, and short-sleeved because it was the height of the summer and the weather was hot, and the room where we held the therapy group was close and airless with small high windows that naturally were barred.

I noticed the tattoo on his right forearm straightaway. Its colours were bright and rich. He must've had it done not too long before the time of his conviction. He would keep his hands, which were strong – broad in the palms, and with long supple fingers and impeccable nails – placed lightly upon his thighs, his legs wide open in that bold and thrusting way that young men do. The tattoo lay on the smooth, slightly tanned skin of his forearm like a giant butterfly, patterned at its centre into the face of a tiger, that had settled upon his arm and was held there against his skin as if it were under some kind of a spell.

Was I just a little spellbound, too?

There was an attraction, yes. Probably from the start. But for a long time it was like that feeling you have when you are on a diet, and something forbidden, something unashamedly loaded with calories that you have denied yourself, is put within reach and for a long time you go on as if you haven't noticed it there. You do not react to it, but at the same time can't quite forget that it's there.

And then something happens. After that, even if you don't reach for it, cram the forbidden treat to your mouth and relish it, you can't pretend that it isn't there again.

*

Something happened in the group, something subtle yet definitive, that made it impossible for me to pretend to myself afterwards that I wasn't rooting for him, wasn't clearly on his side. More so than with the other men, although of course I tried not to show favouritism in the group.

Even before the 'something that happened', he was always polite and attentive to me. Not just polite in that way that the other men of the group were. A certain ingratiating politeness that had a trace of insincerity about it, based more on a desire to retain the privileges that attending the group afforded them. But with Nicholas, there was in his manner a degree of attentiveness to everything that I said, and a desire to please me. It seemed to me then, perhaps in my vanity, to spring from an admiration of who I was and what I was doing.

*

The 'something that happened' was on the third meeting of the group.

Nicholas had been talking about his mother. She'd been a model, although what sort of model she'd been he was never quite certain. Or he didn't like to clearly spell out.

Probably on the glamour end of modelling, even touching on porno stuff I should've thought.

He was describing a single incident. It didn't seem particularly significant or tragic; I'd heard so much worse in my time. But there was something poignant in the story and the way that he told it.

It involved an outing he'd made with his mother to Southend. He wasn't sure how old he was at the time; he thought maybe six or seven years old. He remembered sitting next to her on the train and feeling happy. He said it was strange, this feeling of happiness. It was like something he wasn't used to, that didn't come very often. He said he sat still and behaved and did all the right things, so that to the outside world he would have presented as a nice, well-mannered child. But inside he had this bubbling of anxiety, a sense that if he wasn't careful, if he didn't stay completely vigilant, the happiness would suddenly dissolve, as if it was based on nothing more than froth without substance.

He remembered his mother was in a good mood, and perhaps he remembered that because her good mood was a rare thing, also. She was paying him attention, pointing things out to him through the window, playing I-Spy with him. She had bought him one of those Kinder Egg things, and together they had broken the thin white chocolate body and found the tiny plastic bits inside that his mother had painstakingly put together into the shape of Pluto the dog. He had wrapped this dog up in a piece of tissue paper that his mother had found in her handbag, and kept it tucked down in the pocket of his trousers, where it stayed all day.

When they got out at Southend they had found their

way down to the seafront. It was a hot day, an August day, and the beach was thronged with bodies and the bright colours of swimming costumes, towels and beach balls, plastic buckets and spades. Out there on the ruffled teal-blue water he could see a sail boat, the white sail tugging this way and that in small flurries of movement in the wind. He'd gazed at this sail boat for a long time, willing it not to disappear, not to capsize, and his anxiety, too, was like that white sail being pulled this way and that by the uncertainties of his love for his mother.

Then this man had come walking down the strand towards them both. His mother had shrieked with a silly excitement and ran off into the man's arms and he'd stood waiting, feeling stiff and awkward and unreal, as if he himself had slipped like a white sail beneath a wave and had disappeared…

*

I am using my own words, of course; I know that. And although the words that he used were not the same they evoked the same feelings. I remember how he had held the room captive with his low and careful manner of diction, with the precise and evocative memory he described of that small boy on an outing with his mother, and the feeling of desolation that had overcome him at that moment when the strange man appeared.

He went on to describe the rest of the day, and it was all downhill from there. There was a meal in a pub, where he was forced to sit on his own with his burger and chips in some desolate 'children's room', while his mother, seen dimly through a window, sat with the man at a table near the bar. He could see from the way her head moved, and her shoulders, the thrust of her chest and the arch of her back, that she was happy in this man's company – talking, laughing, enjoying herself. He remembered what happened afterwards only in fragments. There was a room somewhere where he was left on his own with a man who kept staring at him, and smoking and slurping beer from a can. He was given some bitten-down pencils and some paper, and expected to pass the time drawing. The man kept on staring, and hardly spoke to him. He wasn't sure where his mum was. Perhaps she was in the house, too. He didn't know. Upstairs, perhaps, with the man she had met at the seafront. She reappeared at some stage, then went away again, and then someone gave him a sandwich, with bread that had a stale, unwanted odour and greasy cheese, and then he was back on the train going home to London with his mum. It was dark, he was very tired; there were some loud drunken youths on the train and he thought he remembered someone throwing up. His mother was closed into herself now and hardly seemed to notice he was there. The happiness had gone completely. It was hard to imagine it had ever been there.

When he got to the bit in the story when he described how he felt when the strange man came walking down the strand towards them, and his mother had sprang from his side and into the arms of this stranger, and the white sail of himself slipped under the wave and disappeared, there were tears shining in his eyes as he spoke. I think there were tears in mine, too, as I listened.

He noticed. He looked over to me and he noticed. After

that it was hard to deny the attraction that flowed between us. Although I did my best not to let it show.

*

After that session, I went back to my office and pulled out Nicholas Hedges' file and read it again. What was I expecting or hoping for? That the facts around his conviction would have somehow changed? Softened, altered themselves, so that I could feel righteous in this tender feeling of compassion that his story had aroused in me? That I could continue to shore up a sense of denial – i.e. he wasn't there because he had done an unspeakably bad thing but was simply a victim of an unhappy childhood?

But the facts were there in black and white, staring me in the face. He had formed an obsession with a woman who lived in his street. She had gone out with him a couple of times and sexual intercourse by consent had taken place, but then she had wanted to end the relationship. He couldn't accept it. He'd sent her numerous texts: she changed her mobile number. He put letters through her letterbox: she never answered them. He came around night after night, banging on the door of her flat, demanding to see her, letting rip with a string of insults when she didn't answer the door. She would sit there, night after night, even when he didn't come round, frozen into a pitiable heap, the television, her iPod off, so that he would think she was out. But she never went out, didn't dare to, except in the daytime to go to work. And even then she would have to steel herself to open the door and let the world enter in, although her car was never far away, was only parked in the allotted space outside the small block of flats.

Finally she grew tired of her own fear. That was what she had said herself, apparently, in court. *I grew tired of my own fear.* Nicholas came again, banging on the door at night and demanding she opened it. But this time she went to the door, forcing her face into a mask of cold rage.

Look, fuck off! Fuck off and leave me alone. I don't want to see you again. I don't like you, in fact, I bloody hate you!

There wasn't much violence involved. He was strong; there didn't have to be. Her testimony in court said he dragged her on to the sofa and lay on top of her. He was heavy; she couldn't struggle. He said he would hurt her if she started to scream. He wedged his arm up under her throat while he did it, and she could hardly breathe. She thought she was dying. She didn't mind if she was dying; she thought that dying was preferable to what he was doing.

Dying doesn't hurt. Although what precedes it might.

*

How easily we can pretend, we can cling to a distorted idea of the truth. I told myself that a man who can cry when he tells a story about himself as a small boy disappointed in the loss of his mother's love, couldn't be capable of that. He was changing; he *had* changed. The man who had become obsessed with that woman was an aberration. Maybe the account of the crime in his file was not the truth, the whole truth. He had said in court that she had willingly let him in and acted as if she was willing to have sex with him and then had changed her mind. She was playing games with him, he said. He wasn't sure what she wanted. Still wrong what he did, but somehow more defensible.

Paul Brentwood, the senior psychologist at Wandsworth, thought I was in danger of losing my perspective.

"But Rachel, haven't you read the report of the trial? Men like that don't change. Psychopathic personality types. They rarely change. But they're clever, cunning. They'll go on a charm offensive, they'll suck you in."

"What are you saying, Paul? That I'm gullible?"

"I'm saying that he's a psychopath, that's all."

"I'm not sure. I think he can change. I think he's responding really well to the therapy group."

Paul didn't agree. He thought that if Nicholas Hedges was granted parole and an early release he could well revert to type when out again in the community. But I thought he had hope. I thought the therapy group was working. He'd cried again, openly, when he'd been asked to give an account of his crime in the group. He'd spoken about the girl and how much he'd thought that he loved her, and how he realised he'd been wrong, very wrong, to have done what he did.

"You can't make people love you back. I know that now. You can't force them to feel the same as you feel, no matter how much you care," he'd said, wiping away the tears in his eyes with the back of his hand, like a small boy might do if he was upset. And I thought of that little boy in Southend and his mother's betrayal. I was sure his remorse was genuine, and that surely meant that he couldn't be psychopathic, because psychopaths are never truly capable of feeling remorse. I was convinced that he was changing, and that my work with him had been a main agent in bringing about that change. When I had to prepare my report for his parole board I said I was sure Nicholas Hedges was capable of showing genuine remorse for what he'd done and that the risks of his re-offending were negligible. Because I had been the one who had worked more closely with him than anyone else on the programme, my opinion counted for a lot. Parole was granted.

*

He came to see me the day before his release. I was writing a report for another prisoner when Nicholas knocked on the door of my office.

"Just want to thank you for all you've done for me, Mrs Vincent." He held out his hand and I shook it. His grip was firm and strong.

"That's all right, Nicholas. You just repay me by leading the good life. Don't want to see you back in here ever again."

"Not likely. No, you can be sure I've seen the light. I'll never disrespect a woman again."

I thought the word 'disrespect' was a mild word for describing the offence he'd been prosecuted for, but I didn't say anything. We chatted for a few minutes longer. He told me he would be moving in with his uncle who lived in Redhill, in Surrey. His uncle was a builder and would be able to give him some work until he sorted out what he would do next. He had qualifications in joinery and maybe would later consider working for himself. He was considering doing a plumbing course at some time in the future, as well. A trade like that would set him up for life, his uncle had told him.

I remember thinking that it was strange that he was moving to a town so close to where I lived. I could bump into him somewhere. In a shop in either Redhill or Reigate. In a cafe, or a pub. At the train station – I often went to Redhill to catch the train into London. What would I do if I did bump into him? Acknowledge him, or pretend I didn't know him?

He didn't, of course, have any idea that I lived so close and I wasn't going to tell him.

He shook my hand again before leaving. He looked directly into my eyes. I had to look away. I couldn't hide the way I felt. This lingering attraction between us.

"You're a lovely lady," he said. "Your husband is a very lucky bloke. Hope he knows that."

I felt my cheeks warm into a blush. Perhaps he held on to my hand for a little too long before releasing it. Perhaps I held on to his.

"Good luck," I said, before he left.

I remember staring at the door after he'd left and feeling a little sad that he had gone.

18

Ben was sitting in his office staring at the phone. I sensed he was restless, ill at ease. He stroked the receiver as it lay in its cradle. He picked it up and then placed it back down again. He had two phone calls in his head and wasn't sure which one he should make first, if any at all.

He had just got back from visiting a woman who wanted him to design an eco-friendly house. I'd gone there with him. It was a big job and there was a lot of money in it, if he was up to the task. Eco-friendly houses were a little outside his field of experience; they hadn't been much in demand in leafy suburban Surrey. The woman was in her fifties and an artist. She came to the front door of her cottage wearing paint-splattered jeans and a baggy man's shirt. She had a mane of unruly faded reddish hair that was streaked with grey. She made him think of how I might have looked if I had reached that age.

She had inherited a considerable sum of money from her parents and this house that she wanted him to design for her was her dream. She had already purchased a plot of land, on a hillside overlooking the sea in Pembrokeshire. He told her that his experience at designing eco-friendly houses was limited, other than installing solar roof-panels and using timber frames, but she said it didn't matter, she trusted him. She had heard of the wonderful wooden-framed house he had designed for the Grahams, fellow artists and friends of hers, and anyway she had a good feeling about him and she always trusted her instincts; her instincts rarely let her down. He got out his laptop in front of her and opened up a website that showed some ideas for green designs: organic rounded-shaped houses, hobbit-like partially concealed ones in the side of hills, houses made mainly of wood with straw-bales used for insulation.

She said she wasn't sure she could live in the side of a hill – she'd feel like a rabbit, she said, too claustrophobic. But the straw-bale insulated ones were interesting. They brainstormed some ideas together and he made notes and quick sketch ideas to entice her. He said he'd get back to her as soon as he could with some detailed preliminary designs.

He was supposed to be working on the designs now. But he wasn't.

He was thinking of Katie Clements. He was thinking of her neat breasts under the roll-neck jumper she had worn the last time he'd seen her. He was thinking of the curve of her instep when the loafer had slipped off her foot as she'd crossed her right leg over her left. The way she tilted her head slightly upwards when she smiled, showing the smoothness of her throat.

He was thinking of Molly too, and what Katie had said

the other day on the phone. *Did you have a cupboard under the stairs in the house where your wife died?*

He thought back to the house. He hated having to think of the house at all these days. It was like a dark stain in his mind; it filled him with a sense of unbearable loss and yes, if he was honest, guilt as well. His thoughts ran through me like film clips. He was remembering the heavy wooden front door painted in Buckingham green. The porch inside the door where we'd hung our coats. The glazed door that opened to a wide arched hallway. At the far end of the hallway, the door to the kitchen, and just before that, a door on the left that led to the spacious cupboard under the stairs where we'd kept the hoover, mops and brooms, boxes of tools and other odds and ends.

He told her yes, there had been a cupboard under the stairs.

"Was there room in the cupboard? Room for a child to hide?"

"Yes, it was a large cupboard. It had a lot of things in it, but yes, in the front area just inside the door there would have been quite a lot of room…"

"Enough for a child to hide in?"

"Yes. Plenty. Enough for two people to hide in even."

"Mr Vincent, I think that may have been where Molly was hiding when your wife died. She may have witnessed the murder… I'm not sure. But she would have been terrified, of course, and powerless to do anything, whether she saw it or not. I think she opened the cupboard door and hid inside to protect herself…"

"Thank God! Thank God she did."

"I think she had Miss Moffat with her. It is likely that

she felt guilty that she could not help her mother. Later, she would have repressed that guilt. Now the memories are surfacing and Molly is projecting that guilt and anger on to Miss Moffat."

Ben thought of Miss Moffat, the entrails of webbing spilling from the jagged slash in her belly. He shuddered inwardly.

*

After picking Molly up from school that day he'd taken her to McDonalds at Merthyr Tydfil, as he had to see a client who lived near there. He'd let Molly choose whatever she'd wanted. She had a double cheeseburger, fries and Coke, and mini doughnuts to dunk in chocolate sauce.

All of it rubbish of course, and normally he would avoid taking her there despite her pleas but today, today she could've demanded anything she wanted from him and if it was in his power to give it to her he would've done. He'd have given her a toyshop, if he could've, if she'd wanted one. Anything to erase that memory from her mind of the dark cupboard under the stairs.

He wished he had the power to erase it from his own mind as well.

"Mr Vincent, I don't think I'll see Molly for a few weeks. I think we'll let it settle, and see if she's remembered enough now to find her own way of processing the trauma. Of course, if she continues to have distressing nightmares, or if she acts in any way that concerns you, then please let me know…" Katie Clements had told him.

What had he felt when she'd said those words? Relief

of course, that Molly might be okay now. But even more than that if he was honest, consternation. An edge of panic even, tightening his diaphragm. If he didn't bring Molly for these consultations, maybe not ever again, then how was he to see Katie Clements?

He picked up a brochure from the desk in front of him. I looked at it over his shoulder. It was a programme of events that were showing at a theatre in Cardiff. Beginning this coming Friday, there was a new production of *Equus* that would be running for the next few weeks. Surely a psychologist would be interested in a production of *Equus*, even if the play was rather dated these days?

He had it all worked out in his mind. He would phone Katie and mention that he was in Cardiff on Saturday visiting a client and thought he'd take in a trip to the theatre whilst he was there. He had already booked the tickets (a small white lie), and was supposed to be going with his mother-in-law (another lie) but she had cried off. He didn't want to waste the ticket; perhaps Katie might go with him instead? He would suggest a meal perhaps, in a restaurant before the production, or afterwards… Molly would stay with my parents for the weekend – they love having her to stay. What did Katie think about Turkish food, or Thai, or even Iranian? There was an Iranian restaurant he knew that was very good…

He picked up the phone again. He sighed. He put the brochure down casually on the desk and dialled a number. But it wasn't Katie Clements' number that he dialled first.

*

Gardiner sat at her desk. Before her on the desk was a photo of a missing child. A blonde child in a blue school uniform, smiling sweetly. Another child that she felt responsible for and hadn't yet been able to find. Another child that reminded her of her own daughter. I could sense her harassment, her irritation, when the ringing phone disturbed her from her thoughts. I filled in the gaps from her conversation with Ben:

Molly's had another dream. She dreamt about a man with a tiger-butterfly tattoo who came to the house. He could possibly be Rachel's killer...

"Molly said that the man who killed her mother had this kind of tattoo?"

Not exactly. Molly dreamt that he came to the house. There was some sort of row, he was cross about something...

"Cross?"

The word sounded small and insignificant to her.

That's Molly's word...

"Mr Vincent, that's hardly evidence that this man killed your wife."

My daughter was frightened. Maybe he was more than cross... verbally abusive...

"You said Molly saw this man in a dream?"

The dream brought back the memory. I just feel that this man might be connected with what happened to Rachel...

"Feelings have got nothing to do with police work, Mr Vincent... nothing to do with evidence."

I'm just passing it on to you. It might mean something. You said to let you know if Molly remembered anything significant.

Gardiner sighed. She picked up her biro from her desk

and started drawing doodles again on her open pad. A heart this time. She shaded one half of it in.

"Yes, of course, Mr Vincent. There might be a connection. You yourself have no memory at all about who this man might be? No association with anyone who came to the house prior to your wife's murder?"

No. None at all.

"Well, let me know if Molly remembers anything else that is significant."

Gardiner hung up the phone. I leant towards her and whispered – *You didn't ask what you wanted to ask – Did your wife have any lovers, Mr Vincent? Do you think she was ever unfaithful?*

She put up her hand and brushed the side of her cheek, as if she had for a moment felt the hoar of my breath upon it.

*

Back in a blink with Ben in his office, I could feel his irritation. *She told me to tell her if Molly dreamt of anything significant… This was, and yet she makes me feel like a fool…* He got up and went into Molly's room and pulled out a book from her bookcase… *A World of Dinosaurs.* He had placed the picture Molly had drawn of the tiger-butterfly between the pages of the book to keep it safe. The book fell open in his hands to reveal the drawing. The bright orange and yellow picture that was criss-crossed with black scribble. He looked at it hard. *Katie Clements… she takes it seriously. She takes everything my little girl says and does seriously…*

He slipped the picture in between the pages of the book again and slid the book back into the bookcase. He strode purposely back into the office again and picked up the phone and dialled another number. When he heard the voice on the other end of the phone he rearranged himself in the chair, leant forward, fiddled with the brochure again, and tried to make his voice sound more even and confident than he felt.

"Hello. This is Ben Vincent here… Molly's fine, no problems… Actually, it isn't about her that I'm phoning… it's just that I'm in Cardiff this weekend visiting a client and I thought I'd stay the evening and take in a play. It's a new production of *Equus*. Very good reviews. I was going with my mother-in-law but now she's told me it's not quite her cup of tea. She wouldn't think too much of watching teenagers gouging horses' eyes out. It would be a shame to waste the tickets – I've already booked them. I hope you don't think I'm being presumptuous but I'm wondering, that is, if you're free on Saturday, whether you would like to see it with me…?"

When he replaced the receiver he leant back languidly in the chair, interlacing his fingers behind his head. He smiled broadly. The irritation he'd felt earlier had vanished. I stood and watched him, and would have felt the bleak winds of loss blow around my heart, if I still had a heart to feel them.

19

We are all of us guilty, Ben.
We are none of us to blame.
Another paradox.

*

Was your wife ever unfaithful, Mr Vincent?
Gardiner *did* ask Ben that question. On one occasion, she did.

*

That evening, when he came home and found Molly sitting by my dead body, he'd called the police, his voice shaking and barely coherent. Gardiner and the sergeant had turned up, with a crime investigation team right on their tail. Ben phoned my best friend, Joanne – we'd met at Wandsworth prison where she had worked as a social worker – and she came over immediately. It was arranged that she would take Molly back to her house for the night whilst Ben accompanied the police back to the station to help with enquiries.

They took him into an interview room. Someone made him a cup of tea. They spoke gently to him, respectfully. They knew he was still in shock. He wasn't being treated as a suspect or anything like that. Although of course, Ben would have realised that they couldn't rule it out altogether.

Gardiner conducted the interview herself, in attendance with Sergeant Williams. He was a large man with a paunch that hung over his trousers and a florid complexion. It was warm and airless in the room, despite there being an electric fan, and Williams kept inserting his forefinger between his fleshy neck and his shirt collar and working his tie loose. Ben felt compelled to watch him do it; it distracted him a little. The question, when it came, returned him fully to the present.

Mr Vincent, do you know of any time in your marriage when your wife was unfaithful? Do you know if she ever took a lover?

He knew they had to ask such questions. And yet it startled him. His heart began to beat faster. But it wasn't the possibility of my infidelity that caused the flash of anxiety, but his memory of his own coming back to haunt him.

*

I have to go back again. Back to when that happened.

When was it? I need to reckon the passing of time by the age of our daughter, because since she was born all time has been measured by her. As if time began with her, or a different concept of time, anyway.

She was a little over three years old.

We had celebrated her third birthday in August. Joanne had come to Molly's party with her two girls, and Tina from the pilates class on Thursday evenings with her little boy, Jack, and my parents, because that was just before they had moved to Wales, when my father was still working in Brighton. And three more children and their mothers that Molly knew from the private nursery she attended.

I had made the birthday cake myself, staying up late the night before to get it done. It was in the shape of a ladybird. It had turned out well, except for the colour of the ladybird, which was more cerise pink than red. Although Molly didn't care, and probably the pinkness added to her joy in it.

It was a Saturday and Ben and I were both at home. We sat all the children around the dining table, propping up the little ones on cushions if they couldn't quite reach their plates. I brought out the ladybird cake from the kitchen, which was glowing with three lit candles. We sang 'Happy Birthday', painfully off-key as it nearly always is, and then Ben said, "Go on, Molly, blow the candles out," but had to help her because she didn't quite know what blowing meant, or how to do it. She'd suck in a deep breath then puff her cheeks and hold the breath in tightly instead of blowing it out. I remember we laughed at that.

Then Molly put her small hand on the handle of the knife and I covered it with mine, and together we cut into the cerise pink wings of the ladybird. Molly ate the sponge and the jam and buttercream filling, but left the thick pink slices of icing that made up the wings, as if she couldn't quite bring herself to eat them, as if they were too beautiful, too pink, to lose by eating. I had to wrap them up in tissue paper and keep them in the fridge for several weeks, so she could take them out and unwrap them and look at them again, the sight of them bringing the joy back to her face.

*

We encapsulate memories with objects, as if we are seeking to make them less transient.

But everything is transient. Why can't we accept that?

*

So that's how I remember when it was, when Ben betrayed me. It was the October after the August when Molly turned three. The ladybird wings were still wrapped up in the fridge, growing hard and brittle, and Molly had long stopped asking to look at them.

That's when I discovered Ben was having an affair.

I found out the usual way. So usual and so familiar it is almost cheesy. I found a message on his iPhone. He'd left it at home one morning, one of those mornings when I wasn't at work. I was upstairs, repainting the spare room, and I heard it ring. I recognised it to be his phone because of the guitar rift sound of its ring-tone; mine had Beethoven's 'Ode to Joy'. I put my paintbrush gingerly down on a stool and went downstairs. I found the phone lying on the sofa. It stopped ringing just a second or two before I picked it up. I checked *recents,* just in case it was something important

– Ben's father in Spain hadn't been too well lately – and I saw that the last call was from a Claire, with a Guildford number.

I thought nothing of it. Most likely it was one of Ben's clients, I remember thinking. But then I thought, a few minutes later perhaps, I'd better return the call; if it was a client I could take a message and tell them Ben would phone this evening. So I pressed the number at the top of the *recent* call list. A woman answered. A youngish woman, although it's sometimes hard to tell on the phone.

I told the woman who I was, and said that Ben had left his phone at home and could I take a message, and she said, "Oh no, it's not important, it's all right." Her voice was weak and strange, as if somehow I had caught her unawares. I had the beginnings then of an instinct that something was not right. That she wasn't a client, or 'not only' a client. I asked her in fact: "Are you one of my husband's clients?" I said. She said she was, but repeated that it wasn't important, she'd phone him another time, and then she hung up. Without saying goodbye or thank you, or anything; she just hung up.

I stared at the phone; there was a hollow feeling in my stomach. I pressed *contacts* to see if her number was listed. There was a Claire. No surname, just *Claire*, and a landline number. Then I noticed Ben's iPhone had a little red flag by the voicemail icon. So I pressed it. I listened to a woman's voice, this same woman's voice, but this time not small and strange, but breathy and provocative.

"I missed you last night," it said. "I *ached* for you."

*

Shock does strange things to the body. Where I am now, stuck here beyond the glass, beyond the land of the living, I feel no shock, no physical symptoms of shock, but I still have their memory. The way the stomach lurches and hollows, a feeling of wanting to throw up.

That's how I felt then. I sat down. I put down Ben's phone. I didn't want to hold it any more. I felt tainted just having it in my hands.

I missed you last night. I ached for you.

I remembered, very vividly then, what it felt like to ache for my husband. I had felt that in those early months, just after I'd met him. If I didn't see him, even for one evening, I would lie in bed and every part of me would ache for him to be there, holding me, touching me. Just for the nearness of his body, just that.

He had planned to see a client last night, but he had to cancel. He hadn't mentioned it until he came home. It was a potential new client, he'd said. She'd phoned him that morning. She wanted an extension done at the back of the house, a large one. Could be worth a lot, he said. He couldn't see her in the day because she worked full time, and was away that coming weekend, so he thought he'd see her in the evening. I said, Had he forgotten my pilates class? He looked a bit flustered, a bit irritated.

"You'll have to see her tomorrow night," I said. "Your turn to babysit."

Maybe I was a little curt with him, disappointed that he'd forgotten that Thursday was always my night out. It wasn't just the pilates class. I also went for a drink and a catch-up with Tina from the class afterwards. We would go to a little wine bar near the train station. It was my time to unwind, that hour in the wine bar with Tina. Sometimes Joanne would come to meet us there, too – Joanne and Tina hit it off very well together – and then it was girl-talk and giggles, just like in the old days when we both worked in the prison and would go out on a Friday after work.

Ben had looked at me strangely, as if he was put out by what I was saying. I guess I just thought he was reacting to the tone in my voice. He went upstairs to get changed. When he came back down he said that he'd phoned the client on his mobile and rearranged the meeting, so yes, of course I could go out.

I supposed I could have wondered why he didn't use the landline downstairs to make the phone call? But I didn't. Why would I? I had no reason then to be suspicious.

*

After listening to that voicemail message I didn't know what to do. I contemplated phoning this woman, this *Claire*, and asking her outright if she was having an affair with my husband. But what would be the use? She'd deny it, of course. Then I thought of phoning Ben and telling him that I had listened to the woman's voicemail, that I knew that he was having an affair, that there was no point in denying it. But then I thought if I did, and he admitted it, what would I do then? What good would tears and accusations and threats and ultimatums do over the phone?

Better face to face. Always better face to face.

And then, when the shock was settling down into something cold and hard and determined inside me, I got up and I began to clean the house.

I pulled on Marigold gloves and filled the sink with washing-up liquid and bleach. I wiped down all the work-surfaces, the cupboard doors, and then went over the kitchen floor with a squeeze mop. Then I went upstairs to the bathroom and sprayed everything with those antibacterial sprays. I cleaned the bath – working the cloth in hard on the silicone edging around the bath where mould always threatened to encroach. I cleaned the basin, the toilet.

Then I hoovered everywhere, and tidied up Molly's room, putting her toys away into her toy box, then tidied up the study where Ben had his plans strewn out on his desk. I was tempted to open the drawers on the pedestal desk and rifle through, to see if I could find any more evidence. But I resisted. I had the voicemail on his phone; that was enough. And perhaps I was scared of what I might find. Scared that the wave of nausea would overcome me again, the lurching in my stomach.

I went to pick Molly up from nursery. Even though it had been one of my days off, Molly attended nursery that day, so that I could make good headway with decorating the spare room. I'd promised Lucy's mother that Lucy could come home with Molly for tea. It was hard for me, having two little girls to have to entertain, making fairy cakes with them for tea, little salmon paste sandwiches with the crusts cut off, when all the time my mind was screaming at me that my husband was having an affair. When finally Lucy's mum came to pick her daughter up, I stood in the hallway making small talk with her, my face frozen into a pretence at cheerfulness.

Then it was six o'clock and time for Molly's bath. Ben came home just as I was sweeping her up out of the water into a fluffy towel. I got her into her pyjamas and she came downstairs to sit on her father's knee for a while and to act as a buffer between us until it was time. Time to tell him what I knew.

But how do you start a conversation like that?

Do you do it calmly? Or do you shout, throw things, behave like the scorned woman that even the fury of hell cannot match? And what did I want to happen? Did I want him to pack a suitcase and go to *her*? Did I want our marriage to be over?

In the end I did it quite calmly. I waited for hours. I took my time. He did ask me once or twice if I was all right. I just nodded and muttered, yes, why wouldn't I be? "You're quiet," he said. I said I was just tired. But inside me there was that cold knot of anger hardening and biding its time.

I waited until the ten o'clock news was over. Then I went and fetched Ben's iPhone from the kitchen and placed it on the coffee table in front of him.

"You left your phone at home today."

"Yes. I realised as soon as I got to work."

"Somebody phoned."

Was I waiting for a sign of guilt? Colour to rise in his face. A clearing of the throat. But he gave me no such sign.

"Did you take a message?"

"I didn't make it to the phone in time. The caller left a voicemail message. I listened to it just in case it was important."

"Was it?" His hand went up to touch his mouth. You're trained to notice these gestures when you work with criminals.

"Yes, I suppose so. A woman called Claire."

Was it something in my voice? A shard of ice penetrating the words I was speaking. I had my signs now. His gaze flicked towards my face, then quickly downwards. He licked his lips. One hand went momentarily up to pull at his left ear lobe. I could tell he wanted to reach forward and pick up the phone but he couldn't quite bring himself to do so.

"Why don't you listen to her message yourself?"

He sat unmoving, as if he had turned to ice himself.

"Rachel…"

"Listen to it, then. *Listen* to it."

He turned to me; there was a pleading in his face.

I picked up the phone and threw it on to his lap and it must have hit hard on his genitals because he winced, his hands cupping himself protectively.

Then I left the room and went upstairs. I raked through the airing cupboard on the landing, retrieving a duvet and a sheet and some spare pillows, and threw them all downstairs. They landed in a soft pile at the bottom of the stairs.

"You'll need these," I shouted.

I didn't sleep a wink that night. I turned restlessly over and over, as if I was lying on a bed of nails.

*

Jealousy, the green-eyed monster, has a creative side. It imagines things. It fills in details. When there is a void, an absence of facts, it supplies material in abundance. It easily relegates its owner to the role of second place. It loses whole histories and supplants them with this new usurper. It tears the one who possesses it to shreds and invalidates any evidence of love. I could easily have imagined, over the next few days when jealousy possessed me like a tormenter, that Ben didn't love me and never had loved me and never ever would again. And all those countless incidents of love that my mind would turn back to, in my little terraced house where we first met, in the house in Brighton that we rented later, and in this house in Reigate, where Molly spent the first years of her life, where I myself was to die, were written off as inconsequential, the tenderness of these memories deceptive.

*

Over the next few weeks, in between bouts of unrelenting silence, when just being together, in the same room, even in the same house, was painful beyond words, in between my outbursts of anger and accusations, and the tears that came after the silences, Ben told me everything I wanted and didn't want to know. Something in me yearned and ached for the truth. Demanded it. Needed desperately to know it. As if my very life depended on it. But feared it greatly, too.

*

Claire Bishop, I learnt, was thirty-five years old. She owned her own advertising agency. She was smart, intelligent, successful. She had just come through a divorce with a banker who worked in the City, and lived in a salubrious area of Reigate, in a large detached house facing over the park. She'd ended up with the house. She was pencil slim and childless. (I had put on a stone since having Molly. I walked around in baggy jumpers that hid my breasts, with orange juice stains down the front of them.)

Claire Bishop had started off as one of Ben's clients. He'd had two consultations with her, then came back with the designs for her extension – a large glass-ceilinged space at the back of her house; it would extend her kitchen and provide a substantial breakfast room that would let in the sky and show off the foliage of the elm and beech trees that bordered her large garden. He had submitted the plans to the council and then had to make amendments, which had entailed a third visit to Claire's.

That's when it first happened.

Ben hadn't told me the details of how she'd seduced him. (*She* had seduced him, he'd insisted, as if that really made any difference to the way I might feel.) He didn't tell me the details but I could imagine them. I played them out in my mind, over and over. When she opened the door to him she was dressed seductively. Perhaps in a short black skirt, a low-cut top that hinted at the black satin of her bra underneath. She poured him a glass of wine, and then another, and then she reached over the table to where he was sitting opposite her, and stroked the inside of his wrist with her long index finger. She was wearing red nail varnish, siren red; her nails were long and curved like a temptress.

She kissed him first. (That part of my fantasy was true; Ben had found it necessary to tell me that.) Initially he hadn't wanted to kiss her back, but then he did, and soon he was lying with her on her bed. I imagined such a woman would have cream damask sheets, a wide, super king-sized bed, a bedroom where everything was cream: cream curtains, cream carpets, cream furniture.

I did not imagine the finer details of their lovemaking; I could not bear to imagine them. I did not want him to tell me them either, although of course he didn't try to. But I did want to pin him down on times. *How many times?* It seemed vital that I knew. *Three times*, he told me. Perhaps it was true, or perhaps he had conveniently left out a few more. It meant nothing to him, he said. (How easily men can say that!) And how readily I made myself believe that those three times or more, that meant nothing to him, had overruled all the countless times of our lovemaking. Had turned them all to ash.

*

Of course he ended the affair. Of course he spent the next few weeks and even months, trying to make it up to me. And, of course, I hung on to my cold wrath, metered out forgiveness like a miser. I did not so much as bring it up and chuck it in his face whenever we had an argument – nothing as crude and blatant as that. But it was not easy to forget all the real or imagined details of Ben's betrayal. They gnawed at my insides like a cancer.

It was a long time before we made love again and when we did it was like I was watching myself perform the act whilst keeping the innermost part of me separate, my true sense of who I was in an inviolate and protected space.

I have heard that rape victims can feel like this during the act.

*

Enough of going back.

20

Nicholas Hedges was watching the bungalow again from the window of his second storey flat.

He had seen the black Saab arrive at eight that evening and park outside the bungalow. It was the new type of Saab, the number plate belonging to the previous year. He'd seen the driver get out and go and knock on the blonde woman's front door. The man was probably in his mid thirties, dressed casual-smart in clothes that were well cut and expensive. He looked like a man of means, Nicholas thought. Not necessarily loaded, but a man who could afford good clothing, a nearly new Saab. He saw the blonde woman open the door. She was wearing a red low-cut tunic top which revealed a few inches of the hemline of a satiny black skirt. She was smiling, laughing; her body was energised in that way that he recognised when a woman is pleased at seeing a man, shifting her weight readily from one leg to another, swinging her arms, moving a hand up as if to rearrange her hair. He watched the man step easily into the lit interior of her hallway. The door closed.

He sat for a few moments at the window doing nothing at all. I could feel the heaviness of his thoughts. Was he remembering that moment in Southend, when his mother had deserted him to run off and throw herself into a strange man's arms?

*

For days I have followed him as he has walked past the woman's bungalow at the time he knew she was due home from work. He would walk as far as the playground, where sometimes the skinny mother was pushing her child on the swing, or sometimes another mother, and often a group of youths swigging cheap cider out of cans, their bodies slack and restless with the wasting of time and the knowledge that they have all the time to waste. He would stop at the fence and look at them, the mothers with their children, or the youths, and I would feel his thoughts unravel backwards to his own teenaged years, when he would rarely be with a group as these youths were, but instead on his own. Alone in his room usually, listening to heavy metal music and obsessing about some girl at school that he wanted to ask out but could not summon up the courage to do so. Whilst his mother was out, in the arms perhaps of yet another strange man.

There were always strange men. Always. I have dipped into his memories, and I have seen them there. Sometimes late at night when he was a boy he'd wake up, disturbed from his sleep, and hear the muffled springs of the sofa downstairs creak in an urgent rhythm. He would bury his head under the pillow to muffle out the sound and loneliness would sweep over him like that wave drowning the white sail of his self again.

*

Several trips he would make, on these evenings, always at the same time. Walking past her house and down to the playground. Waiting, watching. Turning and walking back to her house. Waiting, turning, and walking back down to the playground. Waiting, watching, walking back to her house again. And me, drifting behind him, keeping my distance, as if I had become a stalker myself. As perhaps I had.

I have learned something too, about the psychological rumination of the stalker. I have felt his obsessions about the blonde woman, what he'd like to do to her if he had a chance, trickle through me like muddy water. Now it was as if I was morphing into him, or something like him. My thoughts turning obsessively around him. Just as his did about the blonde-haired woman.

But for different reasons. For very different reasons.

*

A few days ago, when he had been doing his usual walking to and fro at the time when she was due home from work, she had been particularly loaded with shopping again, and had accepted his offer to allow him to carry the bags to the front door. He watched her struggling to turn the key in the Yale, the little boy straddling her hip.

"Let me take the bags through to the kitchen for you. You've enough to manage with your little lad."

She nodded. Perhaps a little tersely, but he didn't heed it. He followed her into the hallway and through to the kitchen. He put the bags on the table. She swung the child down to the floor. The boy scrabbled up on to a chair and started to fumble with the bags.

"Want jammies, Mummy. And juice."

"Jammy Dodgers," the woman explained to him, smiling. "His favourite biscuits." She fumbled through one of the bags and found the packet of biscuits and a six-carton pack of apple juice. She broke into the biscuits and gave the child one. She prised apart one of the cartons of apple juice from the rest, detached the plastic straw from its side, stabbed it through the carton's foil-covered hole, and plonked it in front of him.

"That'll keep him quiet for a while," she said.

"By the way, don't think I told you my name," he said. "It's Nick. Nick Hedges." He held out his hand to her, rather formally. She hesitated for a short while – he noticed the hesitation – before slipping her cool hand into his and letting him shake it.

"Sharon," she said. He nodded and grinned at her. I felt the flash of his elation. By giving him her name he felt she had given him something important.

"That's a nice name," he said.

"Oh, I don't know," she said, with a slight, self-conscious laugh. "I've always hated it. You know, all those Sharon and Tracey jokes."

"I like it," he said. "I think it's very feminine." *Like you are*, he was thinking, but he daren't say that yet.

She had turned now to the bags on the table and was taking out packets of cereal. Special K and Weetabix.

"Here, let me help you unload those," he said. He opened up another one of the bags and started taking things out. *Her* things. The things that *she* had chosen; it pleased him, thinking that. He handled her groceries as if they were precious things. Olive oil spread. Pesto sauce. A packet of pasta. Shallots. A fillet of cod. Greek yoghurt. Kiwi fruit. He handed the items to her and she put them away. It felt intimate to him, what they were doing, as if they were married. A married couple unpacking their groceries together. He took out a can of deodorant shaped suggestively like a penis.

"I'll put that away in the bathroom later," she said, taking it from him. Her hand touched his for an instant. Did he see her blush, as the penis-shaped can passed from his hand to hers?

Afterwards she made him a cup of tea. The little boy had finished his biscuit and was demanding another one. His mouth was smeared red with raspberry jam. She gave him another.

"I'm a bad mother now," she said. "He won't eat his tea."

"What's his name?"

"Leon," she replied.

"That's French, isn't it?"

"Maybe I'm pretentious. French always sounds more interesting to me than English."

She gave a quick smile.

"I don't think you're a bad mother. I think you're a good one," he said.

"Ah well, you don't really know me." She was looking a little coy now, as if suddenly aware of what her words were suggesting. *Not yet. You don't know me yet.*

"My mum was a single mother. She brought me up on her own."

She looked at him quite intently now, as if suddenly seeing him in a new light.

"Did you know your father?"

He shook his head. "No, he was never around. I'm not even sure who he was. She was always very unwilling to talk about him and I guess I soon learnt not to ask."

"I'm sorry," she said. She looked at him as if she meant it.

"That's all right. You get used to things. What about Leon? Does he know his dad?"

"Oh yes. He stays with him every other weekend. He's a good dad, he thinks the world of Leon."

"Well, that's good, then. Good for the kid. Kids need their dads, especially boys."

He didn't really want to be talking about the kid's dad. To think about the kid's dad meant to be thinking about her with another man and he didn't want to think of her with any other man but himself.

"Yes, I'm sure you're right," she said. "I can't complain too much about his dad. It may not have worked out between us but he does right by Leon."

"Well, it can't be easy being a single mum, even if the boy still has his dad around sometimes. I think you're doing a great job."

She picked up a Jammy Dodger and bit into its edge. She smiled at him, a little self-consciously. Perhaps she thought he was being too personal; what did he know really about the job she was doing with her son? There was an awkward silence for a moment.

"A woman on her own needs a man around sometimes,

to help out with those jobs around the house. You know, fix things that need fixing. I'm quite handy at that sort of thing. You know you've only got to ask."

"That's very kind of you to offer, Nick. I usually manage though."

Her tone was friendly enough, but I sensed he was aware of having been knocked back by her.

"Or maybe you've a boyfriend or someone to help you out with that sort of thing." He was fishing, of course.

She gave a short mock deprecatory laugh. "I am seeing someone actually, but no, I wouldn't quite describe him as a handyman. Not in that way, anyway."

I sensed the hardening in his belly. He hadn't missed the sexual connotations of the words, even if they hadn't been what she had intended.

"Well, like I said. The offer still stands if you need any help…"

She looked thoughtful. "Actually, there is something. I'm thinking of putting some shelves up in my spare room so I can use it as an office. I was going to ring around for a quote. Is that the sort of thing you could do?"

"No problem at all. That's my main trade, joinery. Went to college for it. Proper credentials."

"But I wouldn't dream of letting you do it unless I paid you, of course," she said.

He knew she was setting boundaries, giving unspoken messages. *You'll never be my boyfriend and do things for me for free…* The words he had wanted to ask her would remain unsaid now: *How are you fixed for babysitters? I was wondering if you'd fancy going out with me one evening? For a drink or a meal, or summat…*

He nodded. He had made his face look neutral to hide a multitude of feelings.

"I could show you now, if you like?" she said. "Then you could drop me over an estimate when you're ready."

"Yeah, that's fine. Why not."

She stood up and picked up Leon from the chair, who was stuffing the last bit of biscuit into his mouth. She nestled him into a straddle position on her hips again.

"Crazy child! What you smiling at, sweetheart?" She kissed her son on the top of his blond curls. "You know, all the time we've been sitting here, he's been staring over towards that corner with an inane smile on his chops," she said, turning back to Nicholas.

"Yeah, I noticed that," he said.

"Lady," Leon muttered. "Funny lady."

"What lady, darling?"

The child, from his position still on his mother's hip, pointed at me and smiled. "Over there. Lady over there."

Sharon and Nicholas both turned and stared over towards me but I could tell by the vacancy in their eyes that neither of them could see me.

"I told you he's a crazy kid! His imaginary friend, I suppose." She kissed Leon on his sticky rosy cheek.

"I never had one of those. Never had too much imagination either," he said. I felt a shadow sweep through his mind; he was suddenly thinking of his own childhood. Those empty, hollow hours when he was left in the council flat alone. The thoughts that used to spool through his head. Wanting to hurt someone, perhaps. His mother, the man she was with, even himself.

He followed Sharon down the hallway. I followed after

them. He was noticing the round pertness of her arse in her snugly fitted jeans, resenting the child's leg stuck out across it, spoiling his view. They passed the half-open door of her bedroom. He would know it must be hers because he could glimpse the bed with its mocha and pink duvet covering. A pair of fluffy pink slippers sat on a sheepskin rug on the floor. In the small spare room that was little more than a box room but would take a modest-sized desk and some storage units quite easily, he stood so close to her that he could see the rise and fall of her chest under the shiny material of her blouse.

"That wall, I thought," she said. "Wall to wall shelving. Quite deep. Maybe a foot. And about eighteen inches between each shelf."

"What are you thinking of?" he asked her. "MDF, plywood, or solid wood?"

"Oh, plywood. Quite thick. The shelves will have to be strong enough for box files and text books."

He looked at her, impressed.

"This to do with your job, all these books and stuff?"

"I'm starting a degree course with the Open University. It'll boost my salary as a legal secretary," she said.

She's clever, he was thinking. It was a turn-on to him, clever women. He was thinking of her bedroom next door, the mocha and pink covering on the bed. He wondered if she slept naked under it at night. He felt a stirring in his groin. He was imagining how soft her naked body would feel if he was lying there with her under him right now. He resented the child for being there, nestled into his mother's hip.

"I'll come over tomorrow if that's okay and take

measurements. Then I'll get something priced up and drop it off to you in a day or two." His voice was gruff to hide his rising excitement.

"That's fine, there's no hurry," she said.

*

He turned from the window now. *That's him, then; that's the boyfriend. Maybe this is the weekend the kid sees his dad. That'll be handy for her. Give her a free rein, so that the black Saab could stay parked outside all night.* He imagined, now, seeing it still there in the morning. He imagined how he would feel if it was.

He walked over to the small table against the wall in his room. There was a sheet of paper lying on it, with his pencilled quote for the shelving work. He had stopped over at B&Q the day before to get pricing for the plywood. He thought for a moment about screwing it up and chucking it in the bin, but the thought of her bed with its mocha and pink covering, the thought of her naked body lying next to his in that bed, stopped him. No, he wouldn't give in that easily. She was his. She *would* be his. He would teach her to come on to him like that. He would show her he wasn't someone that could be just played with and then thrown away.

He lay on the narrow bed. He tried to shut out of his mind the thoughts of her with the other man. Tried to shut out the pictures in his mind about what they might be doing. *He isn't handy, at least not like that.* She was a tart. All women are tarts. Hadn't his own mother been one?

*

He turned on his side. I heard his breath quicken and I sensed what he was about to do. It disgusted me.

In the blink of an eye I was gone.

21

This strange compulsion that I feel sometimes, that draws me back to stand outside the house where Peter Bates lived with his mother...

*

It was the kind of house derelicts might live in, or squatters. A general feel of neglect about it. Rather tattered curtains hung against the grimy bay window and the paint on the window frames and front door was peeling and weathered.

I waited here for Peter Bates to come out of the house, as he regularly did at half-past eight in the evening, to walk his dog. He had a small black and tan terrier. If dogs are supposed to resemble their owners than this one certainly did. It walked with a certain diffident bow-legged gait, as did Peter Bates, and both of them, dog and its owner, kept their heads down, as if they were always perusing the pavement for something they had lost.

Peter Bates followed a different route these days on his

nocturnal walks. He used to turn left when he came out of his front garden, and walk the fifty yards or so down the main road to the turning that led to Gale Lane. Gale Lane led into a T-junction, where the lane ran almost parallel to the main road. If he turned right at the junction instead of left, he would pass by the back gardens of the row of Edwardian semis where Ben and I used to live. If he continued up past the houses, Gale Lane would eventually come out onto another road that would link up again with the main road where Peter Bates' house was. This was the circular route that he used to take.

I know this because I used to see him sometimes from my bedroom window passing by my garden gate. Especially in the summer when the evenings were light. And sometimes around lunchtimes on my days off work, as well. His head would be looking down at the ground, as it always was, and the dog would stop every so often and sniff at the hedgerow that bordered the lane on the left-hand side that separated it from the cornfield.

But now the route wasn't quite the same. He wouldn't turn right at the T-junction but instead would turn left, and follow the lane down to the end where it met a high fence that bordered a scrap yard. A stile led to a footpath that would take walkers over the cornfield. He would climb over the stile but instead of taking the well-worn footpath over the field, he'd walk along the edge of it, parallel to Gale Lane, until he came to the gap in the hedgerow that took him out again to the road.

Normally I left him at the stile, fearing for some reason to follow him in the dark along the rough and rutted ground at the edge of the cornfield. But tonight for some reason, I felt compelled to follow him. It was dark and I could hardly see him. Despite the rough and rutted ground he seemed to find his way with ease, as if this untidy pathway was so familiar to him he could find his way along it blindfolded. Then he stopped suddenly, so suddenly I nearly collided with him. The small terrier was cocking its leg up against a large tree. Peter Bates was fumbling in his pocket for something. Moments later the flare of a cigarette lighter revealed a scraggy roll-up held between his thin lips. His thin face was grimacing with a distracted and pent-up anxiety. He lit the cigarette and drew deeply on it. He crouched down and moved the flame of the lighter towards the ground. He stared at the ground in front of the tree. He stared at it hard, as if he had found the place where something was buried, this valuable thing that he had lost. I looked down at the ground. But I could see nothing there in the darkness.

I'm sorry, I'm so sorry.

His shoulders through his thin jacket were shaking. There were sobs in his voice, like a child struggling to hold back its grief. I wanted to touch him. To feel the shaking of his shoulders through his thin jacket, and to calm him. To let him know that I was there. But I couldn't. Something in me feared to touch him, as if I might hurt myself if I did so. Although in what way can the living hurt the dead?

He started up again as if something had suddenly alarmed him and the terrier, having relieved itself now, jerked once more into motion at his side. I followed him all along the edge of the field to where the gap in the hedgerow gave access to the road. He turned right into the road, then in fifty yards, right again, then walked the short distance down the main road to the house where he lived. He pushed open the rusted wrought-iron gate and went up the front path to the door. He opened it and went in. At first I hesitated to follow him in. But then I asked myself again, *How can the living hurt the dead?*

And I was curious. The curiosity of the dead is as compelling as that of the living. I wanted to see the inside of his house, to see how he lived. So I went in, gliding through the door just after he had closed it. What hit me first was the gloom of the hallway, and the clutter in it. Then the odour of greasy carpets and stale cigarette smoke, and the stained, unwashed doors that led into the other rooms in the house.

Peter Bates was opening the door at the far end. It opened into the kitchen where his mother sat, large and solid at the littered kitchen table, watching a portable television that was perched on a cupboard.

"You back?"

He grunted and released the dog. It went straight to its food bowl where remains of its supper clung messily from the sides.

"Where did you go with 'im?"

"Usual," he said. He sat down with her at the table and drew the tobacco tin out from the pocket of his jacket. He began rolling another cigarette.

"Along Gale Lane?"

"Yeah."

"Not back across the cornfield?"

"Naw. 'Course not. Too dark."

"You want to avoid that field," she said. She hadn't taken her eyes off the television.

"I do," he said.

"You watch you do. Don't want you getting upset again."

He lit the cigarette and drew on it sharply.

"Can't 'elp it."

"Yeah, you can. If you do what I tell you, you can."

They sat there for some moments in silence. Peter Bates drawing on his cigarette and his mother still fixed on the television. Some American courtroom drama was on. I leaned against the kitchen door and watched them and thought how ordinary their lives were, and yet so extraordinary. I thought of how his thin shoulders had shaken in the cornfield, the sobs that had racked him. I thought of the words he had muttered. *I'm sorry, I'm sorry.*

"Got cold in here suddenly," his mother said. "Shut that door, will you, Pete."

She indicated the door to the hallway that had been left ajar. But as her gaze swung around to look at it she seemed to stare right into my face. If I had a face to stare into.

It startled me so much that in the blink of an eye I had left.

22

Gardiner sat slumped at her dining-room table, staring at the photos she had brought home from work. The courtroom drama was still on but the sound was muted. She didn't want to watch it. Her daughter Abigail was tucked up in bed, feeling unwell.

I had been with her earlier that evening when Gardiner had phoned her father and said that Abigail had complained of a sore throat and headache and was possibly coming down with a touch of flu. If Abigail was still unwell on Sunday evening, could he come over and look after her on the Monday?

Gardiner hung up the phone and stared once more at the photos of the missing child. She picked up one and examined it closely, as if trying to discern some clue in the girl's wistful grey eyes, in the tendrils of hair that fanned across her cheeks. The child looked about nine years of age – the same age as Abigail. She was fair too, like Abigail, and pretty. What would she be feeling now if it were Abigail that had gone missing?

She turned the photos over and pushed them away from her. *Enough, enough…*

I dipped into her thoughts. The case depressed her completely. The child had been walking home from a friend's house. The friend lived only a hundred yards from the missing child's own house, and it was a short walk that she regularly did on her own, that her mother and stepfather trusted her to do. The streets were quiet and suburban, a leafy middle-class neighbourhood. Two people remembered seeing the child walking happily down the road in pink jeans and a grey hooded top. An elderly lady who was walking home from the bus stop after a shopping trip into town, and a man in his thirties, who was outside his home washing his car, had seen a girl of that description. She was just walking by quite happily, nothing amiss. They didn't know, and nobody knew, what had happened to her after that. It was as if she had suddenly, miraculously, vanished into the ether…

"She was a sensible girl, always sensible. You've got to give them some independence, haven't you? You can't wrap them in cotton wool," the mother said to Sergeant Williams, who responded to the call when the child had failed to come home.

Gardiner imagined the haunting, the heartbreak, that would have been on that mother's face, and now possibly would never leave her. Because after three days of being missing, what else could have happened to her beloved sweet sensible daughter but the unthinkable, the unimaginable?

No doubt the girl's body would turn up one day, and until it did her mother wouldn't sleep, would hardly eat.

Every unaccountable sound in the house would spring in her heart the hope that her daughter had returned to her. Until the day, that is, the body is found...

Gardiner put her head in her hands. She was tired. She should go to bed early herself, but something was troubling her. It wasn't just the case of the missing girl. It was something else.

Had she detected the slight drop in the room's temperature, my chill breath behind her as I stood by her shoulder and brought back to her the memory of the phone call she'd had earlier that day with Ben? *A man with a tiger-butterfly tattoo... he might be the one that killed Rachel...*

She shook her head, as if trying to shake away the thought. *A child's dream... what kind of evidence is that!* But now she was sitting up and pulling her laptop towards her. She typed in the code word for the website that would allow her to search for people with a criminal background on just a few selective physical descriptions. *Male ... Tiger-moth or butterfly tattoo... on what arm?... It doesn't matter...*

The profiles of dozens of men came up who all had a tiger-butterfly or tiger-moth tattoo on their arm. Some had it on their left arm, some on their right. Some had it on their forearm, some higher up near the shoulder. There were young men, older men. Men who were still serving jail sentences and men who weren't anymore but had done. Men with shaven heads and balding heads and men with thick heads of hair. Black men, white men, Asian men. She scrolled down through their profiles and one of them was Nicholas Hedges.

I leant forward to get a closer look, my breath now on her cheek. *That's him, that's the one.*

Perhaps it was coincidence, or perhaps Gardiner had sensed my thoughts. She paused and stroked the details briefly with her thumb. She read the details of the crime.

Prosecuted five years ago for rape of a former girlfriend. Found guilty and sentenced to five years at Wandsworth prison. Released on parole after three.

Something tugged at her memories now. *Wandsworth prison? Wasn't that connected with Rachel Vincent's murder?*

She went out of *Quest* and into the files of unsolved crimes that were stored in a special database. She found the information that stated that I had been a prison psychologist and had previously worked for eighteen months at Wandsworth prison.

This association with the prison had been followed up at the time of my murder. All the men that I had been in close association with in the course of my role there – and in particular, the men that had attended the sex offenders' group – had been interviewed. If their sentences had been served at the time of my murder and they were released, then their alibis had been followed up. No evidence was found to suggest that any one of them was guilty.

Nicholas Hedges? The name was ringing a bell. She searched the files that recorded the notes made of the informal interviews with the men from Wandsworth prison that I had worked with. Yes, here he was. *Nicholas Hedges.* The notes said that at the time of the murder he was living in a housing trust flat in Redhill, Surrey. He worked as a self-employed general handyman and was taking a course in plumbing at East Surrey College. On the day of the murder he had been repairing a shed roof for a lady who lived in Redhill and this alibi was followed up and confirmed. He had been at the woman's house from ten that morning until six. Then it was noted by the landlord at The White Swan that Hedges had been in there having a few pints until about eight that evening. The time of my death was recorded as being in the region of mid-day. So he couldn't have done it.

She sat upright and stretched. She was tired now; she should go to bed. I was standing behind her shoulder, leaning over her, my cool breath on her cheek. She reached up with her hand and touched her cheek and shivered. She glanced quickly back over her shoulder. She shook her head. She was imagining things, she thought. Just like she used to as a child sitting at the kitchen table doing her homework, when she would imagine her mother's soft hand on her shoulder. Even though her mother had died when she was nine, mowed down by a hit and run driver. When Gardiner had grown up she sometimes wondered whether she *had* imagined it; maybe she was psychic, or something like that? But when she joined the force she had dismissed this notion completely. No room for such whimsical beliefs in the police.

She closed the computer down and went upstairs to bed.

23

Katie Clements was trying to decide what she would wear. Four outfits had been flung on to the bed. A red satiny tunic top and black trousers. Perhaps a bit too formal. A skirt and blouse. The blouse was too large for her now she'd lost weight. A white tunic top and black leggings. The white tunic fell too straight from her shoulders and made her look shapeless, and hadn't black leggings gone out of fashion now? The ubiquitous little black dress.

She had tried it on and it fitted her like a glove still, and had a nice scalloped neckline that showed just the right amount of cleavage but not too much. It was sleeveless and the day had been cool and cloudy so she'd need a jacket, or perhaps a cardigan, but that was okay. It would disguise her arms, which she'd always felt were a bit too thin and waif-like. She could brighten it with some costume jewellery. She had laid out on the bed beside it a red choker made of flat glass beads and a string of plain imitation pearls. The pearls, yes. They would be better. Simple and not ostentatious. Ben Vincent was a man, she felt, who liked simple things in women – nothing too overdone or gaudy.

She was acting as if it was a date. *Was* it a date? Or had Ben invited her mainly to make use of the ticket? What had he said on the phone? *I've got a couple of theatre tickets for that new production of Equus. I was going to go with my mother-in-law but she's changed her mind. Doesn't want to see some crazy teenager gouging out horses' eyes. Can't find anyone else to go at this short notice and I wondered if you'd care to go with me...*

Of course, it was the sort of thing a man might say who was reticent about admitting he might fancy someone. Keep it casual. Make it seem like a date that wasn't a date. Wait until you get some inkling that she might be interested.

And of course, there was the professional etiquette of it all. He was, after all, the father of a child she was treating. Although it wasn't exactly him that was attending therapy, and anyway, hadn't they decided to take time out for a while to give Molly a little breathing space?

She picked up the little black dress. She'd wear this one. She would wear sheer black stockings with it, those red stilettos that she liked so much. She held the dress up against herself and smiled slightly at her reflection in the mirror. *All right. So it's a date. Yes, of course it is.* She turned and put the dress carefully over the back of a chair and hung the other outfits back in the fitted wardrobe. She shuffled through her drawers for a set of black lacy underwear. A short oyster-coloured satin petticoat. The sheer black stockings. The string of pearls.

When she was dressed and ready she stood and viewed herself in the full-length mirror. She knew she looked good, very good. A woman who could snatch a man's breath away. She put her hands behind her head and dragged up her long brown hair, so that the smooth nape of her neck, the neat small shells of her ears, were revealed to me as I stood behind her.

The doorbell was ringing downstairs. She grabbed her dressing gown from the hook on the back of the bedroom door and went down to answer it. When she opened the door to the man standing on the doorstep, I was standing behind her and just for an instant I thought it was Ben. He was about the same height, the same build, had dark hair that fell floppily across his forehead. He wore a dark green corduroy jacket over an open-necked checked shirt and jeans. Ben had a similar style of dress. But this man's eyes were a little closer together and there was a pudginess around his jaw-line that Ben didn't have. And when he smiled it was a quick tight smile that seemed to miss the eyes. Ben never smiled like that.

"Toby. Oh my God! What are you doing here?"

"That's a funny way to greet the love of your life."

His tone was jocular, but I picked up the bluffness in his manner, the feeling of unease that the humour was trying to mask.

"I didn't know you were. Or at least, I didn't know I was the love of yours."

"*Katie...*"

"Sorry... but you have taken me somewhat by surprise."

"A surprise? I'm hoping that's good."

"Well, maybe more of a shock..."

"You look as though you're ready for bed. I hope I'm not interrupting anything."

She blushed and grasped the neck of the dressing gown to close it over her chest.

"I was just trying on a dress for tonight."

"Ah, tonight. You're going on a date, I take it?"

"Toby, I don't really think that is any of your business." There was a slight sternness in her voice that he reacted to by pulling a mock scared face.

"I know, I know. I should have phoned, sent you an email. I shouldn't have just turned up like this. Invasion of your privacy. You can go out with whoever you want. I'm history, and all that."

"I seem to remember that was what you wanted at the time. To split up."

"Invite me in, Katie. It's cold on this doorstep."

"I can't. I'm going out soon. You really should have phoned…"

"I know, I know." The banter suddenly dropped from his voice. "Maybe I was afraid to. In case you hung up on me. I need to speak to you. Ask me in, Katie. A tea, a coffee, something stronger. I promise I'll go when you want me to."

She grimaced, but more for the sake of it, to make a point, then anything else. She stood aside and he came in.

"We'll talk in the kitchen, then."

He followed her through the hall and into the kitchen. He perched on a stool at the breakfast bar counter.

"It'll have to be tea or coffee. I'm not going to offer you anything stronger."

"Coffee, then."

She was filling the kettle, setting out mugs, spooning coffee into the cups.

"Nice in here. You've decorated?"

"Yes. The week after you told me about Elsa, I think."

"Ouch."

"Well, what about Elsa, Toby? Are you two an item or is she history too?"

"Elsa was a mistake, Katie. You know that."

"Well, maybe a mistake that I found out."

"No, a mistake. Pure and simple."

"And before that? What was her name? Another foreign sounding name."

"Natasha. Actually she wasn't. Born and bred in London. Polish parents, though. Yes, she was a mistake too…" He was still attempting a seriousness in his voice, although he knew he was on a losing wicket.

Katie poured hot water from the kettle into the mugs. "Milk? Sugar?"

"You've forgotten."

"Six months is a long time, Toby. People change."

"Black. One sugar."

She pushed the mug down the work-surface towards him.

"Anyway, I haven't. Changed how I feel about you, that is," he said, but it was hard now for him to sound convincing.

She sipped her coffee. She had high spots of colour in her cheeks. Her hands were shaking slightly in their clasp on the mug.

"Any port in a storm, eh, Toby?"

"No." He said it fiercely. "That's all changed, I promise. It's only you that I want. I've been a bloody idiot, Katie, I know that I have. Just give me another chance. I promise I won't let you down." He put his hand into his jacket pocket and brought out a dark blue presentation box, the sort that would hold a ring.

"I want you to wear this again, Katie. And this time never take it off."

She glanced up at him, disbelievingly. She looked down at the box. I could read her memories. She had worn it on her finger once for a whole three months before she had taken it off and given it back to him in the original dark blue presentation box it had come in. She hadn't given it back in anger; more with a kind of sad resignation. *This will not work; better to recognise it now and end it than to be hurt more in the future.* She didn't think she would see this box again, or its contents. She picked it up and opened it. The pale blue sapphire glinted in the autumn sunlight that slanted into the kitchen. It was that kind of light, low and mellow, that softened everything, gave things a new perspective, but could get into your eyes and blind you.

She put the ring back in the box, closed it, and slid it down the counter towards him.

"I can't, Toby. I can't go back now. I love you and in a way I always will. But I've moved on. I've met someone else."

"Someone special?"

"Well, it's early days, but yes, he could be. I think he really could be. Very special."

Toby looked dejected for a moment. He sat slumped in his chair. Then he brightened up. Or pretended to.

"Maybe I should have something stronger, Katie. To toast your good fortune. And his. Mainly his. He's a very lucky man!"

She means you, Ben. You're the one who could be special.
   The winds of loss would have blown around my heart at her words. Except that I haven't a heart anymore.

24

Sylvia was sewing up Miss Moffat. The doll lay across her knee, its torn and severed belly exposed. She had stuffed the webbing back inside the ragged vent. Her left hand clasped against the doll's slack neck, her right hand holding the big darning needle. The needle snagged the cloth on either side of the vent and pulled it closed.

My father was watching her.

"Maybe we should just buy her a new one. New doll, I mean."

"That's no good. She loves this one. Had it since she was a baby, remember?"

"Seems to me she doesn't love it very much to do that to it."

"She didn't mean to."

"I thought Ben said she fetched the dressmaking scissors from Rachel's own sewing basket?"

My father rarely used my name. It hurt him to do so, even now. I felt him wince inwardly, his tender heart shrinking a little.

"That sounds deliberate to me," he added.

Sylvia rested the hand holding the needle on Miss Moffat's nearly sewn-up belly.

"She's hurting, Bill. When we hurt we can damage those we love, can't we?"

She wasn't expecting him to answer. It wasn't a question that needed an answer. He shrugged and sighed.

"I sometimes wonder if it's a good thing, Molly seeing this woman in Cardiff. If it's making her do things like this…"

"Ben thinks it's going to do her good. In the long run, he says. Molly's having a break from the sessions at the moment, anyway."

Sylvia finished off the last stitch, drawing the thread repeatedly over the same place to make a little knot to hold it. She curled the thread tightly around her finger and snapped it close to the knot.

"There. Good as new. Almost, anyway."

My father looked at Miss Moffat and said nothing. I knew he was thinking that nothing is ever as good as new. That the scar was still there, and always would be. The sewing was neat enough, but done in a thick black thread that tracked over Miss Moffat's belly from one side to another, as if she'd been opened up like a woman having a caesarean. The stuffing was back, but it didn't look quite the same; it looked a little lumpy in places. He still wished that the doll had been put in the bin and thrown away. So he wouldn't have to see it now, scarred and imperfect. He thought of his own scarring, where they'd opened him up and fitted the pacemaker, and his hand went involuntarily up to his chest, to feel the scar there, a little lumpy and knitted under his shirt. He thought he felt a twinge in his chest, a vague arc of discomfort that rose and fell again, a tightness in his breathing.

"Do you think this will be serious, this woman and Ben?"

Sylvia looked across at him. He had voiced what had already been on her mind. Things were changing now, there was change afloat, and the change was affecting Ben's world and Molly's, and their own worlds, too. Since I'd died everything had been as in a deep-freeze. The memory of me, mummified, a corpse preserved in an airtight casket. Now with Molly's memories returning in her dreams, in her sessions with Katie, the casket has been opened, the bandages unwrapped. Nothing would be the same again.

"I don't know, Ted. It's just a trip to the theatre. He said he had a spare ticket – someone from work had dropped out – and this Katie woman might enjoy the play… Something about a psychiatrist… the sort of thing she would be interested in…"

"You believe that? I think he must have planned it."

"Well, even so, who can blame him? Can't be easy for him, can it? Being on his own with a young daughter. A man at that age."

"No, of course not. I'm not saying that. Time he got out more and went on dates…"

My father lapsed into silence. He was thinking of me. My white waxen face in the morgue that dreadful day. And now he, with his poor battered heart, just going on living…

He leaned back in his recliner and closed his eyes. I wanted to comfort him. I wanted to take away that awful memory and give him one that would cheer him.

*

It is June. Not the June when I died but six years before. My wedding day. You look elegant and suave in your grey morning coat. The weather is very unseasonal; it rains all day, except for an hour in the afternoon when we all rush out into the garden of the hotel and photos are taken in the watery sunshine. Ben and I stand smiling together by the side of a large rosebush. When the photos come out later they are so clear and sharp we can even see the raindrops glistening lightly on the pink petals of the flowers.

Earlier that day, beneath the high, imposing Gothic arches of All Saints Church you gave me away. I rested my hand lightly on your arm and we walked slowly together up the aisle. When we reached the altar you moved aside to leave me standing next to Ben. I glanced back at you; there were tears in your eyes, one stray tear threatening to roll down your cheek.

I mouthed, "I love you, Daddy," and you smiled.

My father smiled now, warmed by the memory. He thought of Molly and how much she sometimes reminded him of me. It didn't hurt him anymore that she did; he was glad that this was so.

*

That curiosity again. It brought me to this restaurant, almost against my will.

Ben sat with Katie at a table close to the window. I stood out on the damp street and looked in and felt like that child again, shut out from the party, her face pressed up against the glass. Behind the two of them the restaurant looked crowded; I could see the flickering lights from red lamps on other tables, the dimly lit bodies of other diners, waiters in white shirts passing swiftly amongst them.

The white linen jacket Katie had been wearing was draped now over the back of her chair. The red tones from the Persian-type lamp on the table warmed the skin of her slim pale arms, her throat, the curve of her breasts just showing in the dip of the scalloped neckline of the black dress. She leant on her elbows towards Ben, her fingers laced under her chin, so that her face was tilted up towards his. Ben was talking, entertaining her, making a joke; I knew this because she suddenly threw back her head, exposing the smooth curve of her throat to him. I could hear the peal of her laughter through the glass. Ben's hand was lying palm down on the tablecloth, very close to her elbow. He moved it closer; he touched her briefly.

Those winds of loss again. I placed my hand that wasn't a hand over my heart that wasn't a heart. Even though I could feel it aching all the same.

25

In the morning before Ben arrived, Sylvia presented the repaired Miss Moffat to Molly over breakfast. Molly took the doll and inspected her coolly.

"I can see the stitches in her tummy, Granny."

"Yes, darling, of course you can. We can't pretend that they're not there. But she's okay now, isn't she?"

Molly didn't answer. She put the doll down on the table, picked up her spoon and went on eating her Frosties.

"If you don't like her anymore, darling, you don't have to keep her," my mother said, a little anxiously.

"No, it's all right. She can go in my hospital when I get home. I have a dog with a torn ear and a hippo with a bad leg. She can go in there and the doctor can come and make her lumpy belly better."

Sylvia looked disappointed. She didn't think the doll looked that bad.

"Miss Clements has got a bag full of sick animals, too. There's a mouse and a dog and a rabbit. The rabbit has a bad tummy like Miss Moffat. Oh, and there's a doll who looks like Miss Moffat, too. But she's got only one arm."

"Do you play with these toys when you go and see Miss Clements?"

"I can if I want. I can do anything at Miss Clements' that I want to do. She even let me hide in the cupboard the last time."

"Hide in the cupboard?"

Sylvia looked alarmed. She didn't like the sound of this.

"Yes. I liked it in the cupboard. I felt safe in there. It was better than hiding in the cupboard the other time."

My parents are both staring at Molly now with a look of confusion and bafflement, and yes, fear too. They felt for a moment as if they were picking open a wound. As if they were unpicking the lumpy stitching across Miss Moffat's belly and the webbing was spilling out again. They heard Ben's car pull up outside on the gravel drive and were grateful for the distraction.

"Daddy's here!" Molly cried. She clambered down hurriedly from the table and ran towards the front door. Miss Moffat, jolted by the movement, fell down from her dangling position at the edge of the table and landed face down on the floor. Sylvia picked her up and placed her over the arm of her armchair. Both my parents followed Molly out to greet Ben, who came striding merrily over the gravel, a smile on his face and a swing in his step, and it was clear to them, and to me as well, that his date had been a success. My father felt that wind of change blowing again. His hand went up unselfconsciously to feel the lumpy scar under his shirt.

And because it hurt me too, in the place where my heart should have been, I left them.

26

And anyway, I had somewhere else I needed to be. Somewhere I felt compelled to be.

*

He was in his spare room. He was sawing sheets of plywood into the required size. The shelves on the walls were cluttered with his tools and equipment: boxes of nails and screws, hammers, chisels, power tools, planes and files. Against one wall, off-cuts of MDF, chipboard, more plywood, planks of wood.

He enjoyed the feel of the tools in his hands, particularly the manual ones, the planes, files and chisels whose smooth rounded handles worked rough calluses into his palms. He preferred working with manual tools rather than power ones. They were more flexible, more sensitive. They responded keenly to the pressure of his hands, to the movements of his body. He could work for hours, planing or sanding wood, watching the wood come off in fine, curled shavings or dry powdery dust. It was the closest he ever got to quietening the obsessive thoughts in his head, which had mostly to do with women and sex.

I know this because of something he said in the sex offenders' group once at Wandsworth. He'd been talking about this girl he'd sat next to on the bus when he'd been young, barely out of his teens. The girl had been wearing a short green skirt that had risen up her thighs, which were large and beefy, bare and blotched with bluish-red marks. She was wearing a fitted white shirt-type blouse, not unlike the ones schoolgirls wear. It was a warm spring day and her sleeves were rolled up, the top buttons of the blouse unbuttoned to reveal her ample cleavage swelling under a black lace bra. She was almost certainly a schoolgirl, because she looked young, no more than fifteen, but she must have gone to one of those more relaxed comprehensives where the teachers have given up trying to enforce strict uniform standards because she wore no tie around her neck, nor did she have any sign of a blazer. And she wore make-up. There was definitely mascara on her lashes, and on her lower lids, a smudgy eye-liner. Her cheeks were reddened – not just from the warm weather but from too much rouge that had been messily applied.

Nicholas had put his hand into his pocket to reach for his mobile. He had suddenly remembered he had arranged to meet a fellow apprentice for a pint after work and couldn't now make it; his uncle, who ran a building firm and had taken him on as an apprentice, had a rush of orders in and had asked him to work late. He fumbled in his trouser pocket for the phone, and as he brought it out, his hand briefly touched the girl's leg. She turned and leered at him. Not smiled; it was definitely a leer, and then in response to his flushed embarrassment she parted her thighs a little. Not much, just enough to send a message, to make the skirt ride up even higher and stretch against her blotched and generous flesh. The inevitable had happened then.

He'd got an erection. It pressed achingly against the fly of his jeans, and although he attempted to hide it with his hands cupped against his crotch, it was not adequate to hide his predicament. The girl giggled then. Her hand went up in a mock attempt to hide her giggles, and she leaned over to whisper to her mate who sat across the aisle on a parallel seat, another girl in a short green skirt and white school-type blouse, but a skinnier girl, much lesser endowed. The two of them giggled openly now, fat undisguised chortles designed to humiliate him.

In the face of such embarrassment the erection didn't last long, but he kept his hand there, cupped in his crotch, just in case, and stared gloomily out of the window. He didn't relax until the girls stood up and swung carelessly down the aisle to disembark at their bus stop, hanging on to the leather straps as the bus lurched round bends and changed down gears as it slowed, the bigger of the two girls stooping as she went to allow any seated male passenger the best opportunity of glimpsing her impressive cleavage.

When he got to work, he was immediately given the task of planing smooth six panelled doors to be fitted in a new house that was near the completion of construction. Although he was still churning with the remembered humiliation, in a short time all he was conscious of was the feeling of his body tilting forward and backward into the motion. He rested first one palm, and then the other one, over the wooden handle of the plane, and the curled, thin slivers of wood rose and fell away from the sharp lip of the tool. He became oblivious to the sound of the other men working away in various parts of the workshop, the high-pitched whine of drills and the ragged noise of saws, so lost was he in the rhythm of the movement. It was almost sexual, I'd thought, listening to him as he spoke about it, the pressing forward and the tilting back. But this time he was soothed by it and calmed by it; the churning humiliation had gone.

*

"A kind of meditation," I had said to him, quietly, when he finished his story.

"Dunno. I don't know what mediation is."

"It's like a concentrated focus on something. Anything really, but it brings you right into the present moment. Everything else, all the clutter in the mind, diminishes."

"Yeah, I guess it was then," he said. And he looked slightly baffled with himself then. That he, Nicholas Hedges, who went to the gym regularly and worked out, who prided himself on his muscular and masculine torso, could be capable of something as airy-fairy sounding as meditation.

*

He was finished now. He stacked the boards for the shelving up against the wall. He put the tools away tidily in a box on one of the shelves. He folded up the workbench and stacked it away in the corner of the room. He took a dustpan and brush from the shelves and knelt down and cleared up the shavings and sawdust from the laminate flooring. Then he fished his mobile out from the back pocket of his jeans and went into the living room. He sat down on a worn black vinyl sofa and pressed his *contacts* buttons. He scrolled down until he found the name 'Sharon' and rang the number.

"Hello. It's Nick. I've got the boards ready for the shelving. Maybe we could arrange a time for me to come and fix them?"

*

In the blink of an eye I was with Sharon and Leon in her kitchen. Leon was sitting at the table with a colouring book. Not princesses for him in pink, but ships and planes and trains, and the only colours he was using were navy and crimson. He still gripped the thick wax stumps in his fist, like a baby does.

Sharon was making a cake. She was following a recipe from a book. Lemon drizzle cake. She had been sifting the flour into a large bowl when she'd answered the mobile. There were cloudy white patches on her red plastic apron.

"That's great, Nick. What about Tuesday evening?"

He must've said that would suit him.

"Thanks for phoning. See you then."

She put down the phone and carried on sieving the flour for the cake. Leon had raised his head from his colouring and was staring at me, his blue saucer eyes wide open, not so much with fear but curiosity.

"Mummy," he said. "Funny lady back."

"Oh, not that again, Leon!" She pushed the bowl over towards him and placed his chubby hand on the handle of the sieve. "Go on, you have a go." He shook it too energetically and white flour clouded his face. He laughed, and I was forgotten for now.

I walked out of the kitchen and into Sharon's bedroom. Perhaps I wanted to see the scene of the crime before the crime was committed. The bed was tidily made. Its silky pink and mocha duvet cover was straightened and pulled up to hide the plump pillows. The pink slippers were tucked under the bed. On a wicker chair over in the corner of the room, a teddy bear sat staring out of one brown glass eye. In the place where the other one should have been was just a wisp of thread. He was very old, this teddy bear. I guessed he was a relic from her childhood, or perhaps even her mother's childhood, perhaps even her grandmother's. Like one of those antique Steiff bears that fetch a small fortune at auctions. He had matted brown fur and those jointed limbs that can swivel round 360 degrees. I looked back at the bed. I was having a vision of that silken duvet, disarrayed and out of place, revealing two bodies struggling on the bed.

And all the time that ancient teddy, that had seen so much of childhood, sitting placidly in his chair with his one glass eye staring.

27

Molly is dreaming about Oranges and Lemons. She plays it with the other children out on the asphalt playground at school. The children are passing in pairs through the arch made by the arms of the first two children. The pair that is caught out on the last word, 'dead', form another arch beside the first one, and so as the game progresses the arch becomes an ever-lengthening tunnel through which the children have to run faster and faster. Molly is paired with Charley Craddock. He is grasping Molly's hand firmly in his, dragging her energetically through the tunnel of children as if she's a dog on a lead. She loves being paired up with Charley. His desperate determination not to be caught gives her a surge of adrenalin that increases both the terror and the exhilaration. But she knows with Charlie she will not be caught. Not until the end, the very end.

When the terror is at its greatest pitch, she almost believes that 'dead' really means dead, although, of course, she has little idea what being dead means. Except that it is something *bad, associated with blood, because of what happened to me, and that it takes you to a place from which you never return. If she was to find herself with such a fate she wouldn't mind, she thinks, if she was with Charlie.*

I reach into her dream, disturbing it like water rippled on the surface. It is time now, to give her another memory. The one that has returned to me…

*

We had been up to London to the West End. It was several weeks before Christmas and I had wanted to take Molly to see the lights and the tree in Trafalgar Square. We had missed the official tree-lighting service, but most afternoons there was a Salvation Army band playing there. Portly men mainly, buttoned up in their thick military-style coats, their cheeks reddened with the cold, and extended as they blew into fat brass mouthpieces pressed hard against their flattened lips. We had stood for a while and listened to them play 'Away in a Manger', 'Jingle Bells' and 'Little Donkey', a menu chosen mainly to entertain the children, as there were many there standing with their parents. Then they played 'Silent Night' and this time they were joined by a trio of violins and a woman soprano. The men softened their lips against the mouthpieces and subdued the sound of the brass. It was so lovely it brought tears to my eyes.

I was still feeling fragile about Ben's affair; it was only about two months since I had found out. We were at that stage where we were being too formal with each other and too polite, and avoiding as much as we could talking about anything real and honest, like how much it had hurt me, torn my heart out, and how much Ben resented me for making him feel such a heel.

We had made love only once since I had found out. That time when I had felt I wasn't real, I wasn't really there. Then not again. Ben had tried, but I had turned my back on him, pushed him away. *I can't. I just can't.*

We both knew that it was only a matter of time. That, if we didn't sort this, didn't find a way back to each other, then we would be over. But at that time I didn't know how that would be possible. I wanted forgiveness to be some commodity you could buy in a shop and use. Like washing powder. I didn't know it would be so hard and so difficult.

Ben wasn't with me that weekend. His parents were over from Spain and staying with his sister in York, so he'd gone up there to see them. Perhaps Molly and I should have gone with him, but I didn't feel ready to play at being happy families yet with Ben in front of my in-laws, so Ben said he'd give some excuse. He'd tell them Molly had a party she was going to attend, one she couldn't bear to miss.

After the rendition of 'Silent Night', when the soprano's voice had risen on the high notes with such a crystal clarity on the cold winter air it had made me want to cry, we caught the Underground to Covent Garden, where we delighted in a display of Santa's Grotto and watched two men with painted clown faces doing incredible feats on giant-sized unicycles. I bought some Body Shop products in Christmas Cranberry – handmade soaps for my mother wrapped in brown waxed paper that looked like tempting tablets of something sweet and edible – and spicily scented aftershave, overpriced but stylishly packaged, for my father. I had hesitated over what to buy for Ben. I settled for a coffee-table book on Indian architecture, which had amazing richly coloured photographs of highly decorated temples, all manner of Hindu gods and demons lavishly layered up on the steeped roofs.

Then I took Molly into a cafe in the square. She had orange juice and strawberry ice-cream, while I warmed myself up with hot chocolate with gooey marshmallows on the top. Then we took the Underground to Victoria to catch the train home.

I was standing in the station, which was thick with Christmas shoppers, staring up at those large monitors that give the train times and platform numbers, when I felt a hand touch my shoulder and a voice behind me say, "Mrs Vincent – it is you, isn't it?"

If I said I recognised the voice I would be lying, because I didn't. When you have heard someone speak in one setting, and that setting was something as closed and set apart from the world in general as a prison, it isn't easy to transfer that voice to somewhere that belonged as much to the larger world as Victoria train station. I swung around, and I must admit there might have been annoyance on my face, as I do not like being touched by strangers, even if that touch is non-sexual in nature. But then my annoyance was offset almost at once by this rather handsome smiling face.

"It *is* you!"

I may have looked quizzical, bemused, as if I didn't recognise him.

"Nicholas. It's Nicholas Hedges."

When he said his name it all came back to me and I saw him – in that strange visual way that we often have of encapsulating memory – sitting in that airless room at the prison, dressed in neatly pressed blue jeans and a black tee-shirt, the flamboyant tiger-butterfly resplendent on his right arm.

"Nicholas. I don't believe it! How are you?"

"I thought it was you. I was over by that kiosk buying a paper, I saw you walk by and I could have sworn it was you."

He was grinning broadly, obviously pleased with himself.

"Oh, well, it's a small world. Fancy seeing you. How long has it been?"

"Well over six months. Since I got out of… oh well, you know where."

"I guess it must be! How's life treating you?"

"Great. It's great. I'm working for myself. General handyman work. Maybe not the greatest job but I do all right and I don't have to answer to anyone, which is good."

"I'm so glad to hear that, Nicholas."

"Yeah, and I'm doing a course in plumbing. Widen my skills, so to speak. There's plenty of money in plumbing these days."

"You're right there. I've just paid a fortune for a plumber to service our boiler."

"This your little girl, then?"

His gaze moved down and fixed on Molly.

"Yes, this is Molly. Molly say 'hello.'"

But Molly wasn't in the mood. She averted her eyes, stuck her thumb in her mouth and sucked it glumly.

"Sorry, she's a bit shy," I said.

"That's all right. If I was her I wouldn't talk to strange men either." He gave a short laugh.

The intercom was announcing the train to Redhill. I took Molly's hand and picked up our bags.

"You catching this one, too?" he said. "I live at Redhill."

"I live at Reigate actually, but I usually get a taxi home from Redhill."

He seemed about to say something and then changed his mind.

"If you don't mind, maybe we can sit together on the train. It would be good to have company."

"Yes, that would be nice," I said.

*

But I did mind really. I felt unnerved by the chance encounter. I couldn't quite forget how I knew him, the context in which we'd met. It made me suddenly aware how all the people that you see – in the street, in shops, in crowded places like train stations –have their own lives and their secrets, the bits of the past they might not want anyone to know. Here was Nicholas Hedges looking perfectly respectable. Nice, even. Normal. But I had met him for the first time in Wandsworth prison on a sex offenders' course I was running. I couldn't forget that.

The unease continued throughout the entire train journey.

We tried to make small talk for a while but then gave up. There was such a hub of voices and different conversations going on in the carriage – people talking loudly into mobiles telling relatives what time they wanted picking up and that sort of thing. He did ask me, though, if I still worked in the prison, keeping his voice low and discreet, although with the noise around us I doubt that anyone would have particularly overheard, or cared much if they had.

I didn't still work there. I was office-based now, working in Guildford for Surrey and Sussex probation services, but I was professional enough not to want to divulge too much. He was an ex-con, after all.

"Oh, yes, same old."

We got off the train at Redhill and when we had gone through the ticket barrier I turned to him and held out my hand for him to shake.

"It's been good to see you again, Nicholas. I hope everything continues to work out well for you."

"Hey, I've got my car parked here. Let me give you a lift home."

"No, no, it's fine. I'll get a taxi."

"Honestly. I don't mind at all. In fact, I'd love to."

*

There are some moments in life when you hesitate, and that hesitation can create a window through which you can jump to consequences you will always regret. This moment was one of them. It was bucketing down and I could see that there was a queue for the taxi. Okay, he was an ex-con who had served time for raping his ex-girlfriend, but hadn't I believed in him back then? Believed that he had worked hard in the group, had been willing to face up to his issues. Was rehabilitated. A different man. Older and wiser, and trying to get on in the world.

"I don't want to trouble you, Nicholas. You'll be going out of your way…"

He took my heavy shopping bags out of my hand and with his other hand gently steered my elbow, taking me with him, guiding me over towards the car park.

"After all you've done for me in the past, Mrs Vincent, least I could do."

He had a white Mondeo. The estate version. It was fairly old but he obviously took good care of it. The interior was very clean and tidy as if it had been quite recently valeted. There was a lemon-scented air freshener hanging from the mirror. I settled Molly on the back seat with the central lap belt around her. I sat next to Nicholas in the front. I must say he handled the driving well, although the traffic did turn out very congested, it being a Saturday and close to Christmas.

We chatted most of the time quite openly now, in the close confines of the car. Molly's head nodded down on her chest after a while and she was asleep. He told me he lived in a housing trust flat in quite a nice area of Redhill. I did think – *he's going right out of his way to take me home* – but didn't bring it up. There was no point. And to acknowledge this would have made us both aware of the possibility that something more than an act of kindness on his part was provoking him to take me home. I told him I'd just been up to London with Molly to show her the tree at Trafalgar Square and do some Christmas shopping.

"I don't have to worry about that," he said.

"What about your mother? Don't you buy her anything?"

He shrugged, gave a wry smile.

"She dropped out of my life when I was eighteen. I mentioned it once in the group, but I guess you wouldn't remember. Last thing I knew, she'd gone off to Ireland with some bloke."

"I'm sorry," I said.

"It's all right. She didn't do me much good as a mother. Maybe I'm better off without her."

"No other relatives?"

"Just that uncle that I stayed with when I first got out of prison. Before I got my flat. He used to live in Redhill but he's moved to Margate now. Semi-retired."

I was trying not to, but I did feel something close to that wave of compassion I had felt when he'd talked about that trip to Southend. *A lonely boy*, I thought, *and now a lonely man*. Or perhaps not.

"No girlfriends, Nicholas?"

"Been out with a couple of girls. Nothing serious, though." He paused, and then shot me a quick look before negotiating a right turn. "And don't worry, I don't go over the top with them anymore. If they want to let go, I let them go. Anyway, it's usually me that ends it. I don't feel I'm ready for commitment yet. Want to better myself. Have something to offer a woman."

Because he was talking like this, so sensibly, all my qualms about him had disappeared completely by the time we got to my house. He parked outside.

"Nice house," he said.

"Do you want to come in for a drink, Nicholas?" I asked him. "'I could offer you a Christmas drink, but you're driving so I'd better not. Tea or coffee, perhaps?" I felt it was the least thing I could do after he had gone out of his way to drive me home.

"Your husband won't mind?" he said. Maybe that should have alerted me, that question. But it didn't.

"Ben's away for the weekend," I said. I had the words

in my head – *but he wouldn't mind anyway. What's there to mind?* – but I didn't say them.

"Well, if you're sure. A cup of tea would be favourite."

I took him into the house. Molly had a glass of orange squash and a biscuit in the kitchen and then went upstairs to her room to see if Miss Moffat was better. She had been playing at 'hospitals' that morning and Miss Moffat had been complaining of a sore head. She'd received from Doctor Molly a large crepe bandage that had obliterated half of her squashy pink face. I guess she must have got involved in the game again because she didn't come down for ages, but answered me in nonchalant tones from her room – *Yes, I'm fine* – when I called up the stairs – *You all right up there, Molly?*

I sat in the kitchen and talked to Nicholas. I don't remember what I talked about – nothing in particular. The house and how much I had just been quoted to have a new kitchen installed; his handyman work and how some people quibble over the price of everything and others don't; Ben's work as an architect, something about the castle restoration project in Scotland he was hoping to soon begin work on. Whatever it was, at one point – that was the other window that opened that I jumped blindly through – Nicholas looked at me, this strange expression on his face and he said, "Rachel, you're not happy, are you?"

I'm not sure what I had said to him before to provoke this comment, but I felt a tweaking behind my eyes then, a catch in my throat, and before I could check myself I was crying and telling him about Ben's affair. He slid an arm around my shoulders and said to me, his voice low, his mouth dangerously close to my cheek – "If you were mine, I wouldn't let you out of my sight, let alone ever want someone else." Then, in spite of the fact that it was doing my dented ego so much good, I had warning bells in my head – *What are you doing, Rachel? You hardly know this man, except what you knew about him back then, in the prison…*

I dried up my tears with the back of my sleeve and stood up. I put the teacups in the sink. I said that I would prefer it if he went now; I had to get on and make my daughter's tea. To his credit he said, yes, of course, he'd go now. He thanked me for the tea. I showed him to the front door, but before I had a chance to open it for him he pulled a white business card out of his jacket pocket and gave it to me – "Just in case you need a friend," – he said. It had his name on, and the words – *General Handyman – kitchen fitting/decorating/tiling/joinery – no job too small.* Underneath, in small italics, his mobile phone number.

"Anytime you want to, call me, Rachel…" he said, and then he leaned down to kiss me. I thought he was just going to kiss me on the cheek, but he turned my face slightly towards him, his fingers lightly guiding my chin, and I caught the kiss on the lips instead, and in a moment I'm kissing him back. Then I remembered Molly and came to my senses.

"Go, you must go now…" I said, the palms of my hands up against his chest, fending him off. I opened the front door and he went out and when I closed it again, abruptly, sharply, wanting to forget what I had allowed to happen, I turned and saw Molly standing at the top of the stairs staring down at me. Her face was flushed and shocked. She turned and ran back to her room. I went up the stairs and into her bedroom. I sat down on her bed and put an arm around her stiffened body – "I'm sorry, Molly. Don't be angry. What you saw – it was nothing… it didn't mean anything…"

She picked up Miss Moffat, whose bandage had been replaced by a small sticky plaster on her forehead. "Mummies only kiss daddies like that," she said.

"Yes, darling, you're right. It was silly. I won't do it again."

She warmed up eventually and came downstairs. I made her fish fingers and chips for her tea, and let her stay up for a while to watch a DVD after her bath. Later, when she was in bed and I had finished reading her bedtime story, I leant over to kiss her goodnight, and said, "Molly, that silly thing you saw me doing with that man… kissing him… it's our secret, okay. There's no need to tell Daddy. No need to tell him anything."

She considered this. "He'll be cross if he knew."

"Yes, darling. And we don't want a cross Daddy."

"No."

"So no need to tell him?"

"All right."

"Our secret, then?"

"Yes, Mummy."

"Goodnight, sweetheart."

I kissed her goodnight and put out her bedroom light, leaving the door ajar, so that she would get just enough light from the landing to keep the bad dreams at bay.

*

Molly now turned and moaned gently in her sleep. She was clasping Charlie's hand and running through the tunnels of children. *Chip, chop, the last one's...* She was out of the tunnel and into the light. I leant over her and dropped the memory into the dream.

*

There is tinsel hanging up in the hallway, and in the living room, our own Christmas tree, decorated with silver baubles and coloured lights that flick on and off. Mummy is by the front door kissing a man who is not your daddy. He is wearing a padded beige jacket, so you can't see the butterfly-tiger tattoo on his arm. But you know that it's there. You know it's there because you saw it on his arm earlier, when he took off his jacket in the car. We had stopped at red lights. The car had warmed up, was getting too warm. He quickly undid his seat belt, took off the jacket, turned and threw it on the back seat next to where you were sitting. You saw the tattoo there on his forearm as he leaned over towards you. Its colours were bright and it fascinated you. A giant butterfly with a tiger's face at the centre, alight on his forearm. You saw it there, just for a moment. Just before you fell asleep...

28

Katie Clements was having a bath. She'd run bubble bath, lavender scented, into the stream of water from the hot tap, and it had foamed up into crescents that covered her body up to her breasts. She leant back in the bath, stretched out, her toes playing with the sprouts of the taps, and closed her eyes.

I knew she was thinking of Ben. She was thinking of the way he had kissed her on Saturday night. He had got out of the taxi to walk her to her door, and when she had turned to him and said, "Thank you for a lovely evening, Ben," before putting her key in the lock, he had kissed her. Quite lightly at first on her open surprised mouth, but then again, more lingeringly this time, his hand sliding under the fall of her hair and resting on the back of her neck. She had kissed him back.

I'd watched them. The house had a narrow blue-painted door and original sash windows. There was a small gravel forecourt with plants growing in a circle. It had reminded me of the terraced cottage in Brighton where I'd lived when

I first met Ben. I'd wondered if it had reminded him, too.

She hadn't asked him in. The taxi was waiting to take him back to the hotel, and anyway, she wasn't the kind of girl who would ask a man in after a first date. He knew that. He was glad of that. He didn't want to compromise her, or himself, or what might possibly develop between them.

Katie Clements sighed, remembering that kiss. And then her shoulders, showing above the water line, flinched slightly as the shrill ring of the phone from her study next door disturbed her. She moved to stand up and I left her to get out of the bath. I waited on the landing. She came out of the bathroom draped in a thick towelling dressing gown. I followed her into the small bedroom she used as a study where the ringing phone sat on top of a cupboard.

"Ben, how lovely to hear from you."

I could see a current of energy flicker through her body just at the sound of his voice. Then she went quiet and her face had a pensive thoughtful expression. Faint lines of consternation creased her forehead.

"Are you sure?" Katie said. "Rachel died in June. If this is the man who killed her, then she must have known him for a long time."

I don't know exactly what Ben said in reply. But I can imagine what it was. He would have told her about Molly's drawing earlier that evening.

*

It was after Molly's bath, when she would settle down with Ben for a while. I often liked to be with them at this time, when they were peaceful and relaxed. Ben would watch the regional news programme on the television, whilst Molly would take out her colouring pens and sketch pad and draw pictures about her day. I loved to see her drawings, to see what was important in my daughter's world.

She would draw her teacher, Miss Austin, a moon face on a tiny stick body, small pinpricked eyes behind glasses that were almost bigger than the head they were on. But it was clearly Miss Austin, because of the short curly hair and the glasses. She would draw pictures of herself and Chloe, skipping ropes revolving around their heads, or herself and Charlie running, above their heads an arch made of children's fat arms and banana fingers.

"That's me and Charlie playing Oranges and Lemons. We're trying not to be caught by the axe-man," she had told her father. And Ben had nodded seriously, respecting the otherness of his daughter's world, understanding the excitement and the terror that had stretched the mouths on the faces of the children in the drawing into a wide shrieked 'O'.

Ben was listening to the weather report. Gales were on the way. They would hit the Brecon Beacons quite severely later that night. I thought of the trees that bordered the rear of the garden, and knew he would be thinking of them too, and of the wooden playhouse that he'd built for Molly which the trees overlooked.

The news report finished. Ben reached forward and picked up the remote control from the coffee table. He looked down at Molly's drawing on the open sketch pad. She had drawn a man and a woman. They were standing close together, their faces pressed closely as if they were glued together. The woman wore a skirt and a red and blue striped jumper, and her hair, coloured red, stuck out from her head in a scribble of curls. Ben leaned forward to have a better look at the drawing. He was remembering the red and blue striped jumper I used to wear sometimes in the winter, with its high turtle neck.

"Who's that in the picture, Molls? Is it Mummy?"

"Yes," she said, calmly.

She picked up a yellow pen and coloured in the man's spiky hair.

"And that's me?" he said, pointing at the man. But he knew it wasn't. He knew it couldn't be. His own hair wasn't yellow, wasn't blond.

"No," she said. There was a trace of anxiety in her voice that he could not fail to detect.

"Who then, sweetie?"

"Mummy's friend."

"What's the friend's name, Molls?"

"I don't know, Daddy."

He stared at the drawing.

"What are they doing, darling?"

She didn't answer for a moment. She was busy drawing a green spiky object floating on the right side of the figures. She exchanged the green pen for a red one.

"I think they're kissing."

She drew a red box under the spiky umbrella shape, and he suddenly realised the spiky shape was a Christmas tree.

Molly turned then and looked at him. She had something veiled in her eyes. Something almost like fear.

"Mummies should only kiss daddies, shouldn't they? So maybe Mummy is naughty."

"Is that a Christmas tree, darling? Is it Christmas time?"

"Yes."

"Well, maybe Mummy is just giving her friend a Christmas kiss," he said. "That's not naughty."

She was colouring in a spidery star shape on the top of the tree.

"I think it is."

Ben said nothing. He sat there abjectly as his daughter finished the drawing, and I knew he was feeling a cold rain in his heart. The gale that was predicted had already started inside him, blowing his memories wide open.

*

Our cold war had lasted for several months more after that encounter I had with Nicholas Hedges at the station. If it hadn't been for Molly we surely would have parted: we would have given up. I could not get the images of his betrayal with Claire Bishop out of my head. I imagined that evening, that first evening when he had responded to her seduction, over and over. I saw them lying together on her cream damask sheets, I saw him making love to her whenever he was lying in bed next to me. Even though he did not attempt to touch me. Even though we both clung to our disparate edges of the bed, our backs coolly turned towards each other – except for that one time. Even though the inches between our bodies felt like acres of impenetrable space, even then, I saw them together, the sheets slipping off their writhing bodies to the floor. *Was she as good as me? Was she better?*

Eventually he stopped trying to compensate for his

guilt, treading carefully around my hostility as if he was walking on glass. He became laconic towards me, cool, indifferent. I knew that this was just another self-defence. He started working longer hours, and although we still occupied the same bed at night, we became like strangers that met in communal areas of the house, Molly most of the time being present and acting like a buffer. If we talked, which was not that often, our talk revolved around Molly and small routines. Who is able to drop by the supermarket today? Who will be able to take Molly to nursery, pick her up, take her to the dentist?

And Nicholas Hedges? What became of him? Did I slip his business card out of my purse with the phone number on it? *Phone me. Any time. If you need to talk...*

29

If we could spin ourselves backwards to that moment in time, to that window through which we step and by doing so change everything forever, we would do exactly the same things again.

I did phone him. But not to have a chat… not to use him as a shoulder to cry on. For something much more practical than that.

I was having a kitchen installed. The old one was looking dated. Dark oak-effect panelled doors to the units, boring white laminate work surfaces. Maybe I really wanted to update myself. To look less mumsy. To be slim, svelte, sophisticated. Like Claire Bishop. But that was much harder to do. The kitchen was easier. I wanted a cleaner contemporary look. I had decided to replace the oak-effect doors with cream Shaker-style ones, the laminate with real wood. All the parts that had been ordered from B&Q had arrived on time and were waiting in the garage, but the price quoted from the store for fitting the new kitchen was exorbitant.

"We could shop around for a local workman to do it," Ben said. "Could possibly save us a couple of thousand, at that price."

"I might know someone. Someone a colleague at work used recently."

"Well, if they can recommend him, that's a positive," Ben said.

*

It was about a week into the New Year. Ben was out visiting a client and Molly was in bed. I slid the card out of my purse and dialled the mobile number. He answered more or less straightaway.

"Nicholas? It's me. It's Rachel," I said, and I detected a very slight pause, a faint intake of breath before he spoke again.

"Rachel. Good to hear from you. How are you? Happy New Year, by the way."

I wished him a Happy New Year back. I said I was fine. I said I was phoning to see if kitchen installations were the kind of thing he often did. I needed a quote, I said. To install a new kitchen.

"I've done quite a few in my time. No problem. Can't touch the electrics though. You'll need to get a registered electrician in to do those. Plumbing's no problem, or tiling, I can manage that."

I said I'd got the layout plan if he wanted to drop by some time and look at that before quoting, and he said, yes, he would, but how would thirteen hundred sound? He worked on his own, he said, and that would be about nine or ten days' work for a kitchen my size. That worked out close to his normal daily rate, give or take a bit. I said that sounds great, considerably less than the contractors the store used were going to charge.

We ended the call and I put the phone down, and as I did so I noticed a very slight quiver in my hands. Was it fear or excitement? A man who had a conviction for rape, who I had worked with in a sex offenders' therapy group, would be in my house for about ten days, fitting my kitchen. I only worked two days a week then, so a lot of the time I would be in the house whilst the work was going on. Molly, perhaps not. If the kitchen was to be out of bounds, like a bomb-site, it might be best to take her to Wales to stay with my parents. I could drive over there to drop her off the weekend before Nicholas due to start, spend a little time with my parents. It wouldn't hurt her to miss nursery school for a while and my mother was always asking to have her; she loved having Molly to stay.

So I would be there on my own most of the time whilst he worked on the kitchen. Doing things upstairs in the bedroom, having a bath, working at the computer next door in the dining room. Or hovering around him, making cups of tea, plugging the kettle into any nearby available sockets, while he worked, leaning over, drilling, screwing units to walls. Showing perhaps a builder's crack as his jeans slid down his muscled backside.

What was I thinking?

But it was too late now to close the window. My foot was on the ledge. I was about to jump through.

*

Of course it happened. I had known all the time that it would. Wasn't that what I wanted? Hadn't there always been that frisson of attraction between him and me, perhaps from that very first moment I had seen him in the group?

And I wanted my revenge. I might not have cared to admit it, even to myself, but that was what I wanted. A way of getting back at Ben. A way of punishing him for planting that image in my mind that I hadn't been able to forget. He and Claire Bishop making love on her cream damask sheets.

Of course, it didn't happen the first day. Nicholas was professional then, and conscientious. He worked hard; he ripped out all the old units and threw them outside into the skip that had been hired. He scraped the old tiles off the walls. That was a messy and laborious job and I left him to it. I went out for some of the time to visit a friend, to get away from the noise and the mess, and whilst I sat making small talk, trying to take an interest in my friend's new baby's feeding routines, I fantasised about Nicholas Hedges. He and I making love on my white cotton sheets.

Of course it was only a fantasy. Fantasies mean little. People have them all the time with no intention of carrying them out. But wasn't it a temptation that lingered at the back of my mind? More than just a fantasy. What I wanted.

To do back to Ben what he'd done to me.

*

When I arrived home Nicholas was busy clearing broken tiling from the floor, sweeping them and the debris of wood and plaster into a heap.

"Nearly done now," he said, smiling at me. Plaster dust clouded his face, streaked into the creases of his smile. "I'll be able to get down to fitting the units in the morning. You'll need your flooring retiled, of course. There are gaps between some of the new units and the floor tiles. I didn't quote for this, but I could do that for you too, when I've finished the fitting of the units. Only cost you a couple of hundred more. "

"That'll be great," I said. 'I've seen some black and white tiles in the store that I like.'

I made him a cup of tea and we talked of careful neutral things. How his work was going, which he said was well, very well, never been busier. About my parents' recent move to Wales.

"I've been there. Well, not Talgarth itself, but the Brecon Beacons," he said. "My mum had a friend that moved to Wales. Somewhere near Swansea. I remember we drove over the Beacons once. It must have been winter. The main road had been cleared but there was snow everywhere else. You could hardly see the sheep they were camouflaged so well."

We didn't talk that day about my marriage, about Ben's affair and how it made me feel. But it floated somewhere in the air between us. Like something cautious, afraid of being touched.

*

It didn't happen the second day. I was working that day. When I got home Nicholas had already left, leaving me a note. He wouldn't be able to come on the Wednesday

– had an urgent job to attend to, but would be there on the Thursday. I was working on the Thursday too, and when I got home Ben was already back and was talking to Nicholas about the technical problems involved in fitting new plumbing under the sink. Nicholas had all the floor units in place. I admired them and felt a great relief that the kitchen was starting to look like a kitchen again and not a bomb-site.

After Nicholas had left I microwaved a ready-made lasagne for tea as the cooker wasn't wired in yet. Ben and I sat down and ate it in our usual 'not speaking unless necessities' way. Ben was the first to break that rule of silence.

"Seems a good worker, that guy. How did you say you met him?"

"Someone I know at work recommended him." My mind was quite good at ticking over, creating stories. I'd probably make a good criminal.

Ben looked at me expectantly.

"What?"

"The person you know. Who was it?"

"Oh, a social worker I've worked on a few cases with…"

"What did you say his name was? This kitchen-fitter guy. He didn't introduce himself to me. Should have asked him, really."

"Nicholas."

"Nicholas who?"

"Nicholas Hedges, I think."

"Oh, well, we're lucky to have found him, I suppose."

*

It happened on the fifth day, the Friday. Ben had left early that morning, to drive up to Scotland to see that client about the castle restoration project.. He would be away until the following Wednesday.

It happened at three o'clock precisely that Friday afternoon.

I'd opened a bottle of Chablis. I knew what I was doing. I knew what a bottle of wine might lead to. Wasn't that what I was planning all the time?

"You're entitled to knock off early today, especially after all the hard work you've done," I told him. Nicholas was busy with a dustpan and broom, tidying up. I'll give him his due. He never left the place untidy at the end of the day.

When he had finished he sat down at the kitchen table with me and we finished off the bottle of wine. Nicholas mumbled something about not drinking too much because he would be driving, but he allowed himself a second glass. He knew what was going to happen. That was what he'd wanted all along, as well.

I supposed I seduced him and not the other way around. Somewhere into my third glass of wine, and possibly getting a little half-cut as I'd not eaten for a while, I placed my fingers on his forearm and stretched taut the bright wings of the tiger-butterfly tattoo. Then I slid my fingers up and squeezed his biceps.

"You're very strong," I said. "What's it like to be so strong?"

*

Later, when we had sex in the king-sized bed upstairs, where Ben and I would cling to our separate edges like people lost in a desert, I wanted to stop, to reverse everything. To jump backwards through that window to the time when I could have said no, and caught the taxi instead of accepting that lift home from Redhill station.

He lay heavily on me. One arm, the tattooed one, was up under my jaw, constricting my breathing. I had to drag his arm away. He seemed reluctant to move it, but then he did. I tried to think that it was passion taking him over. But I had a flashback to what it had said in his case notes about that girl he was meant to have raped – *she had bruises on her neck* – and I felt very uneasy and wanted him to stop. But it was too late. I couldn't jump backwards through the window. I sobered up then, the effects of the wine suddenly clearing from my head.

He stayed for a while afterwards. I made him a black coffee to clear his head after the wine he'd drunk earlier. He'd only had two glasses to my three, and he'd said that if he left it a little while longer before driving home he'd be okay. It wasn't that long ago – what had happened upstairs hadn't taken long – but I wanted him to go. I wanted him to go right then. I didn't care how much he'd had to drink, whether he'd be over the limit or not. I just wanted him to leave. But I was afraid to say that.

What if he turns nasty, what if…?

So he sat in my kitchen and drank black coffee. He didn't notice at first my change of mood, my coolness. He tried to make conversation with me. What plans had I for the weekend? Did I fancy perhaps, doing something nice with him tomorrow? We could catch the train to London. Take in a show. Have a meal in China Town.

I told him I had a lot to get on with this weekend.

My parents were bringing Molly back on Sunday and then staying over for a few days. I wanted to go through the house, get it clean and tidy. Wash the bed-linen for the spare room. He picked up on my change of manner, then, and coolness. I felt the tension set in his body. His shoulders stiffened, his jaw clenched.

"Well, see you on Monday, then," he said when I showed him to the door. There were still a few finishing jobs to do to the kitchen. Corner shelving to put up. The plinths and the architrave trim. And then the new black and white tiled floor.

I didn't answer except to say goodbye. He didn't try to kiss me. I wouldn't have let him if he had done.

I closed the front door. I went into the living room and watched him get into his van and drive away. I went upstairs. I ran a hot shower and scrubbed my body all over with one of those friction gloves. I scrubbed so hard on my breasts and my belly and my thighs that I made myself sore. Tiny pinpricks of blood broke out on the surface of my skin.

*

I phoned him up later that evening. I made my voice sound indifferent to hide my fear. I told him that I was grateful for the work he'd done so far, and that I'd still pay him the amount that he had quoted for the kitchen fitting, but I wanted to find someone else now to finish the job. It was a mistake, what had happened, and it should not have happened.

He sounded very icy on the phone. I don't blame him

for that. But then he said something just before I hung up.

You won't get away with it as easily as that, he'd said.

I tried to put the words out of my mind. He was just hurt, angry; it meant nothing. When Ben came home the following Wednesday he was surprised to find the kitchen hadn't been finished yet. I told him that the guy who had been fitting it had to go away. His mother was ill, possibly dying. He wouldn't be able to finish the job and we had to look for someone else.

"That's a shame," Ben had said. "He was a good worker."

"We'll find someone else," I said. "Someone just as good."

*

That night, when we went to bed, Ben turned his back to me as usual to go to sleep, but I couldn't bear the distance; I couldn't bear this cold desert that was our marriage anymore. I moved close to him and hugged him tight.

"I'm sorry. I love you," I said.

"Don't," he said. "Don't be sorry. I'm the one who should be sorry."

I wanted him to make love to me. I wanted it so badly. As if the act might take away the memory of the earlier one. Might take away my guilt. He did. He made love to me, gently first and then more fiercely.

That was the beginning of the thawing.

After that we were all right. We were the same as we used to be. Perhaps even better. He had betrayed me and I had betrayed him back. The score was even. There was nothing now to keep us apart.

30

Ben sat at the kitchen table burning the midnight oil. The gale was working itself up. Rain battered the kitchen window. The table was strewn with pieces of card, hardboard, MDF, off-cuts of wood. He had been down the garden earlier, after he'd finished talking to Katie, and searched through the packing chest in the small shed next to Molly's playhouse, where he kept various bits and pieces of wood and stuff. He'd found a jigsaw in the shed. A file, chisels, a Stanley knife, hammer and nails. Some wood-glue and PVA. Small match-pots of paint that I had bought when we were trying out colour schemes in the old house. Pots of enamel paint that he had kept since he was a boy in his model-making phase. He had put the collection of things into a strong hemp bag and carried them up to the cottage. He had retrieved the kitchen scissors from a drawer and had settled himself down at the table.

The radio was on, some mellow jazz music with the sound turned down so that Molly's sleep wouldn't be disturbed. He had been working for hours. Sawing, cutting, gluing, and now before him on the table, amidst the assortment of wood and card and glue and tools, was the half-erected shape of a doll's house. The roof had yet to go on, and the front of the house was left open, but most of the rooms inside were in place. I stood over his shoulder and I watched him. *Yes, that's how it was, Ben. That's the way I remember it.*

He was working now on a piece of hardboard that had been carefully measured out to fit the size required for the kitchen floor. With a steel ruler and a pencil he was carefully drawing lines on the hardboard, first this way, and then the other, until it was measured out into small, pencilled squares. Then he carefully painted in the squares with the enamel paint, alternating black and white, until the hardboard was covered with a chequered pattern.

He put the paintbrush down on a saucer and yawned and stretched. He was tired. He looked at his watch. It was late, very late. One o'clock in the morning. He gathered up all the odd pieces of card, hardboard, MDF and wood. Tipping the house onto its back he put them inside it. He would finish it off tomorrow night. He needed to sleep now. He had Molly to see to in the morning. He lay the chequered piece of hardboard on a high shelf by the sink to dry. It would be out of Molly's reach there. He gathered up the tools and put them in the hemp bag. He took a black bin liner from out of one of the kitchen drawers and carefully slid the unfinished doll's house inside it. He picked it up. He didn't want to leave it in the kitchen. He didn't want Molly to be curious in the morning and look inside it and see what he was making. He didn't want her to know it was there. Not yet. What had Katie said on the phone? – *Make it at night if you can, whilst Molly is asleep. It would be best if she doesn't see it... not before the therapy session, at least...*

Ben opened the back door and holding the wrapped-up doll's house in his arms, looked out into the garden. The gale was at its highest pitch. He was concerned about the old elm tree, the one whose brittle overhanging branches reached over Molly's playhouse at the bottom of the garden. The tree was dead and should have been brought down by now; it wouldn't take much for the gale to snap off one of the branches. He stared up at the dark sky. The sky was often crystal clear and thick with stars up on the Beacons, like a designated Dark Sky. But tonight the stars were partially obscured by clouds. He saw the moon momentarily creep out from behind a cloud, a smudged bluish orb.

He was remembering something. I could feel it. Something was tugging like a kite in the wind at the edges of his memory. Something about a workman.

That man who had started to fit our kitchen and then had suddenly gone away. What had Rachel said the guy's name was – Nicholas something? That would have been about three months or so before Rachel died. Early in the New Year.

During that time when things had been bad between us, he was remembering, when he'd seriously wondered if we'd ever ride out the storm.

Didn't that Nicholas guy have a strange tattoo on his forearm? An orangey-yellowy-black one, in the shape of a butterfly?

He had taken little notice of it at the time, but was remembering that he'd glimpsed it when he'd stood talking to the guy one afternoon. The guy had been leaning nonchalantly against the kitchen unit wearing a dust-splattered black tee-shirt, the tattoo exposed on his forearm. And didn't that guy have blond hair too, strikingly pale blond hair? The man Rachel was kissing in Molly's drawing – Molly had drawn him with yellow hair.

Ben had a knot of tension in his stomach. I could feel it there, tightening and clenching and cutting short his breathing. *Had Rachel been having an affair? Having an affair with that Nicholas guy who had fitted the kitchen for us?*

He was remembering now the abrupt way the guy had suddenly left, leaving the kitchen unfinished. We'd had quite a job finding someone else to finish it off.

Maybe he hadn't left on his own accord? Maybe she'd got rid of him. Maybe she'd got scared? Wanted to end the affair? Maybe that's why he'd killed her? Out of vindictiveness, maybe. But why months later? Why would he wait months to do it?

I could feel all these questions spinning around in his head. He was remembering too, that after the guy had left suddenly without finishing the job, when Ben had got home from Scotland, I'd turned to him in bed and wanted him to make love to me.

Why then? Why suddenly then, after so long…

He couldn't bear his thoughts, he couldn't bear how they made him feel.

I wanted to go to him, to lean on his shoulder, to touch his face with my cold hand, and say – *It doesn't matter. None of that matters now. It's only ever been you that I loved. Only you that I still love now…*

But I knew he wouldn't hear me.

He turned away from the door and put the wrapped-up doll's house on the kitchen table again. He got a half-full bottle of Scotch out of a cupboard and poured himself a large one. He gulped it down quickly. It warmed and softened the knot of tension in his stomach. It settled his thoughts.

He would phone Katie in the morning, he was thinking. He would tell her that he thought he knew who the man with the tiger-butterfly tattoo was. He would ask Molly if he could give Katie the drawing. The one of me and the man kissing, the Christmas tree floating above us in the void of the paper. If Molly didn't mind, he would remove it from her sketch book and give it to Katie before the session, so that she had a little time to look at it before Molly came in. He would also bring the doll's house; it should be finished by then. He would wrap it in a bin liner again, put it in the boot of the car and try and make sure that Molly didn't see it before the session.

He put the empty glass by the sink and picked up the parcelled doll's house again. He struggled down the garden with it. The wind was very strong in his face. He kept his head down, bent over the doll's house. His body felt like it had become weighted with lead. I followed him. It was easy for me to glide against the wind; the wind passed through me like a breath. There was a sudden loud noise from the bottom of the garden that startled us both, a creaking crashing noise rising above the howl of the wind.

In the blink of an eye I was outside Molly's playhouse. I saw the great limb of the elm torn from the trunk. It reached down into the felted roof like some monstrous intruding arm. Ben reached the playhouse and struggled to open the door. It was sticking badly, perhaps because its frame has been knocked out of shape. Then it gave way.

We could not see much in the darkness. Just the huge limb of the tree filling the space. But then, as the moon brightened from under a scree of cloud and our vision adjusted to the dark, the pale waxy faces of Molly's dolls. They sat on the shelves at the back of the playhouse, peering out through the twigs of the dismembered branches like the ghosts of dead children.

31

When Nicholas Hedges answered the call on his mobile from Sharon, cancelling his appointment with her, I saw the expression on his face change rapidly, from the initial pleasure at hearing her voice, to disappointment and irritation.

"No, of course I understand," he said. But he didn't. A flush of anger spreading up his cheeks.

"Yeah, we'll make it Sunday, then. That'll be fine."

He put the phone down. He sat for a few moments on the kitchen chair as still as a statue, his chin jutting forward and his face immobile. Then he breathed deeply, got up and filled the sink with water. He washed up the dishes that were stacked on the drainer, took the cloth and wiped it furiously over all the work-surfaces.

"Damn her! Damn the bitch!" he muttered under his breath.

He walked into his bedroom, opened a drawer and pulled out a white shoe-box. He took it over to the bed and sat down. He opened up the shoe-box and emptied its contents over the bed. Photographs. Some large, some small. Some of them clearly had been taken in the distant past, being in sepia or black and white. Others were in colour. He picked up one of the sepia ones and stared at it long and hard. It was a photo of a woman, perhaps in her early thirties. Her hair was shoulder length; as the photo was in sepia it wasn't possible to discern its colour very clearly but it was several tones lighter than mine. She wore a long floral-patterned skirt and a white lacy chemise that revealed her bare arms. She was leaning against a railing that appeared to be on a promenade, as beyond the railing was a beach and beyond that, blue sea merging with blue sky. A small boy with white-blond hair, in shorts and a striped tee-shirt, was nestled into the front of her skirt. Her thin arms were draped over his shoulders, her hands folded over his chest. She was smiling broadly, as if entertained by the person taking the photograph, while the small boy's smile was tense and ambiguous, bordering on a frown.

His thumb stroked across the small boy's face. He was remembering the uncertainty and anxiety that had been his world then. This need to be constantly watchful and vigilant, in case his mother should disappear. He turned the photo over and put it down.

All the other photographs scattered on the bed were young women. Sometimes he was in the picture with them and sometimes they were on their own. They all had either reddish or blonde hair and there was something about the shape of their faces that was similar. There was one of me. That shocked me. He must have found the photo in my house, trawled through the drawers in my bedroom where

I kept the photo albums. No doubt when he was there fitting the kitchen and I was at work.

The photo was one of my favourites. It was taken on the promenade at Brighton just before Ben and I married and moved away. In the photo the sun is shining brightly. I am leaning against the pale green-blue Victorian railings. Over my shoulder the long arm of the Palace Pier reaches out into the sea. The coloured sails of dinghies break the blue, and in the far distance, on the horizon, there is the hazy grey shape of a ship. I am laughing at Ben who is taking the photo. My left arm is draped over the railings, and on the hand hanging free, a tiny pinprick of light as my diamond ring catches the sun.

I stared at that photo, feeling the weight of memories crowd the place where my heart used to be. This was before real life began. Before Molly and mortgages. Before broken nights and the weight of responsibilities. Before Ben's affair, and mine. When the future was just like that distant ship on the horizon. When everything and all things were possible.

I reached up my hand to brush away the ghost of a tear that was threatening to slide down my cold white cheek.

Nicholas Hedges gathered up the photographs, dropped them all back into the shoe-box and put it back in the drawer. Then something alerted him: the sound of a car drawing up outside. He walked over to the living-room window. It was that man's car again, Sharon's boyfriend's black Saab. So that was the reason why she'd cancelled tonight. I could feel the tension start up inside him, the flare of anger like a bright red flash behind his eyes. He stood there and watched as the man got out of the car. He was holding a bouquet of pink roses and something in his other hand that looked like a bottle of wine wrapped up in blue tissue paper. Sharon opened the door; she wore a short red skirt and a black satiny blouse that showed off her cleavage. She smiled warmly and tilted her face immediately up to the man's to kiss him. The man stepped inside and the door shut.

Nicholas' chest heaved with anger. I could feel his thoughts: *How dare she put me off just to see him! She'll be screwing him later. She's nothing but a tart, a whore. Just like my mother was.*

He paced the confines of the room, trying to calm himself down. I could sense his anger subsiding, but in its place was the cold, insidious spreading of contempt, a need for revenge.

Then he was aware that he was hungry; he hadn't eaten yet.

He'd been hoping that whilst he'd been across the road putting up the shelves she would have been in the kitchen cooking a meal for them both. He had planned to take across a bottle of wine in the expectation that this would happen. He had imagined himself sitting down at her kitchen table – the child hopefully ensconced at his father's place – and Sharon serving out a meal, leaning over him, showing more of her cleavage as she slid his plate down in front of him. He imagined her then, sitting opposite him, leaning towards him, smiling at him, laughing at his jokes. They would finish the first bottle of wine – the one he had brought – and then she would fetch another from her fridge, and halfway through that one – perhaps by now they would be sitting together on her sofa – he would drape his arm around her shoulders and pull her towards him and they would kiss, and then they'd end up, just as he and I had done, lying together naked in her bed, the one with the pink and mocha duvet cover. She wouldn't have changed her mind halfway through the act, as I had nearly done; not in his imagination anyway. She would have loved what he did to her. She would have wanted him to do it over and over again. And there would have been no other man in her thoughts and in her bed, not ever again. She would be his. She would belong to him entirely.

*

He walked over to the fridge and took out some chicken fillets, onions, peppers and mushrooms. He started to slice them up, cutting the chicken fillets and the vegetables into thin strips for a stir-fry. He tried to keep his mind on what he was doing, but I knew that despite his efforts he could not stop himself from imagining what she was doing with that man across the road. She would be sitting down, eating the meal with that other man that she should have cooked for him. She would be drinking the wine that the other man had brought her, instead of the bottle that *he* himself would have taken. She was smiling at that other man, laughing at *his* jokes. Later she would be screwing him in her bed.

He stopped slicing the vegetables and slid his thumb down the sharp blade of the knife, until a slim line of blood appeared.

She's nothing but a whore, that's all she is!

He put the knife down. He had a thought in his head. I

could sense its darkness, but I didn't know what it was. He calmly took a wok out from one of the kitchen cupboards and started to cook. When he'd finished, when he'd eaten and done the washing up – because he was very fastidious about mess, very tidy – he went to the window again. It was dark outside. The curtains in Sharon's bungalow were drawn. He could see the light was still on in her living room, which was at the front of the building. He stood there for some time. He was thinking, they would have finished eating the meal that she should have made for him. They would be making out on the sofa. They would have music on. Something romantic. Her boyfriend would be lying next to her, kissing her throat, perhaps unbuttoning her blouse and kissing her breasts, one hand feeling its way up under her short skirt that would now be rucked up.

He suddenly moved swiftly away from the window. He walked determinedly down his hallway to the door. He took his jacket from the peg by the door and went out, across the grass in front of the flats, across the road to her front gate. I followed him swiftly. He eased her gate open as quietly as he could and then walked quickly up the path, following it around to the side of the bungalow, where it led through the car port, and then around to the rear garden. A sensor light came on at the back of the car port and for a moment he froze, just in case they noticed the light from inside the bungalow and came out to investigate. But nothing happened. He relaxed a bit. The light enabled him to make out the three windows at the back of the building. The one nearest to him he knew was the kitchen window. The blind at the window was still up and the light was on. He hunkered down and moved past the window trying to ensure that his head would not show just in case Sharon was in the kitchen. When he had passed the window he stood upright and pressed himself against the brick wall of the bungalow and waited again. No sound. Nothing. She couldn't have seen him. Then he stood and looked towards the other two windows. I knew he was trying to work out which one was the window to her bedroom. The small spare room that she wanted to turn into an office, he knew was at the other side of the bungalow, next to the bathroom. So one of these two was her bedroom and one was Leon's room. Leon, he had already decided, probably wouldn't be there. He'd be at his father's most likely. She might be a whore but she was a good enough mother; she wouldn't want to be shagging that man with the child sleeping in the room next door. He moved closer to the first window. The light was on in the room and the curtains were only half-drawn. He was looking for two bodies moving on the bed. He didn't know what he would do if he saw them.

But he didn't see them. He saw a bedroom decorated in blue wallpaper with a motif of ships and waves. He saw a small boy with tousled blond hair in a yellow pyjama top, sitting up in bed looking at a picture book. The boy looked up and saw a strange face pass fleetingly in front of the window and he screamed.

When Sharon came rushing only moments later into the room, Nicholas Hedges was gone. If she'd had her son's gift, she would have seen only my face, white and cold and full of distress, looking through the gap in the curtains.

"What is it, darling! What's wrong?"

"A face, Mummy. A man."

He pointed to the window. Sharon walked over to it

and drew the curtains right back. But she could only see the dark garden, the night-sky full of stars. She couldn't see me.

"What face, darling?"

"It's gone, Mummy. Only that lady now. That lady back again."

"There's nobody there, Leon. Nobody at all. You must have imagined it, darling."

"No. Lady. Lady still there, see."

Sharon opened the clasp and pushed the window open to the night. It passed through my chest. It didn't hurt, nothing hurts me very much now except the fear of losing those I love. Sharon shook her head. Her son's imagination was beginning to go beyond the boundaries of normal now, she was thinking. Especially if it frightened him like this. Perhaps she should discuss it with the doctor.

Minutes later her boyfriend went out with a torch. He walked all the way around the bungalow and down to the bottom of the garden. He even opened the shed and shone his light in there. But of course he saw no one.

I knew that they were all right, now. I knew that they were safe.

So I left.

32

On the drive down to Cardiff I sat next to Molly in the back of the car. She was wearing a blue crew-neck jumper with a red appliqué heart on the front that Sylvia had made for her. It reminded me of a jumper my mother had once made for me when I was about Molly's age, except that mine had been yellow with a brown rabbit appliqué.

Ben drove in silence. It was a glorious autumnal afternoon. The sun was shining in a deeply blue sky and the hills and mountains around us glowed tawny and golden.

Ben was playing Bach Cello Suites on the CD player, and it seemed to suit so well the autumnal scenery, the richly burnished golds of the hills and mountains. Molly didn't seem to mind her dad being silent. Or that strangely sad and evocative music, which sounded almost painful, like something was dying.

Molly had her sketch book on her lap, the one in which she had drawn the picture of me kissing a strange man, our bodies floating in a void, a Christmas tree adrift in the far corner of the page. Now, where the drawing had been, there was a faintly ragged edge of paper near the stapled binding where Ben had carefully torn the drawing out, intending to give it to Katie Clements before Molly's session.

He had asked Molly first: – "Sweetheart, would you mind if I take this drawing to give to Miss Clements? She'd be interested to see this one you did of Mummy."

Molly had looked at him strangely and then gave a quick nod. She was now drawing something else. She was drawing a picture of herself and Charlie Craddock. In the drawing Charlie was holding her hand. She wore a pink triangular dress and her legs were splayed out like sticks, whilst Charlie's legs in blue jeans were as thick as tree trunks. Their faces were split from ear to ear with smiles that looked more like gashes or grimaces. They were running this time, not through that oppressive tunnel of arms, but through a field that was speckled by flowers. The flowers were red and purple, with big yellow eyes.

When we arrived at the clinic I couldn't help but notice the smile Katie gave Ben. It wasn't just the quick, cool smile of the professional greeting a client, but was a little coy this time, a little shy. She was wearing a short tartan skirt over aubergine tights and a black polo-neck jumper. She had nice legs, very nice legs. Better than mine, if I'm honest. Better than how mine used to be, I mean. Although mine had been longer. Molly was left with her sketch book and pens under the kindly eye of Saffron, who seemed to have added yet another colour to her already multi-coloured hair. Ben fetched the doll's house, which was wrapped in black bin liners, from the boot of the car. Molly was too busy laughing at one of Saffron's funny stories to notice him carry it in.

He followed Katie into her consulting room. I stayed outside with Saffron and Molly. He returned a few minutes later, this time minus the parcelled doll's house. Katie looked across at Molly, who was sipping a glass of lemonade that Saffron had given her.

"Molly, Daddy's going to wait for you outside. I'd like to see you on your own again, if that's all right."

Molly glanced at her father for confirmation.

"That's all right, Molls. I'm going for a walk now, but I'll be right here waiting for you when your session is over."

I didn't follow Molly into Katie's office straightaway. Instead, I wistfully watched Ben as he scrunched over the gravel driveway and turned left to walk down the road. He was probably walking down to the cafe. We had passed it in the car driving up to the clinic. In spite of it being late October, chairs and tables were set out on the pavement outside.

Ben and I used to love sitting outside cafes watching people go by. I remember that once I had told him that 'people watching' was my favourite pastime. Ben had laughed and called me a 'nosy-parker', and I had said, "No, not nosey. Just curious." Curious about people: their lives, their passions, their secrets. I would make up stories about people that passed by. *This elegantly dressed woman is on her way to meet her lover... This harassed middle-aged man has serious money worries...*

Today, in the autumn sunshine, I wanted to sit with Ben once more outside a cafe and watch people walk by.

But I must be with my daughter.

Molly sat in her usual chair, hugging Miss Moffat.

"She's better now," Molly said. She held Miss Moffat

out to show Katie the neat line of black stitching across the doll's belly. "My granny sewed her up and made her better."

"That's lovely, Molly. Your granny's done a good job."

"I can see her stitches. But it doesn't matter." Molly settled Miss Moffat back on her lap.

"And you, Molly. How are you now?"

Molly screwed up her face. "I haven't been poorly."

"No, but you do sometimes get upset, don't you? About what happened to Mummy. Do you have bad dreams anymore?"

Molly looked away, down at the top of Miss Moffat's yellow plaited head.

"No, not really. Just dreams where Mummy makes me remember."

"Mummy makes you remember?"

"Yes. The dead mummy. She comes when I'm sleeping sometimes."

Molly looked at Katie Clements a little guardedly, daring her not to believe her. But Katie kept her face neutral. She reached over to her desk and picked up a blue clipboard folder. She opened it up and unclipped the first sheet of paper. It was the picture Molly had drawn of the tiger-butterfly tattoo.

"Like perhaps when you drew this, Molly? Do you remember drawing this?"

Molly's eyes drifted rather reluctantly to the drawing, then looked away again. She nodded.

"Did Mummy bring you the dream you told Daddy about? The one about the man coming to the door. The man who had a tattoo that looked like this drawing on his arm."

Molly nodded.

Katie put the picture back in the folder and unclipped the other one. The one that Ben had just given her before the session. She held it out towards Molly.

"And this one, Molly? Do you remember having a dream about this one?"

Molly glanced at the picture. "Yes," she answered, in a small voice. She hadn't really wanted Ben to give Katie Clements that picture. She had felt a little embarrassed about it. But Ben had been so persuasive about wanting Katie to see it, so sure it was the right thing to do.

"Who is in the picture, Molly? Who is the lady?" Katie asked gently.

"That's Mummy."

"And who's the man?"

Molly didn't answer.

"Do you know, Molly?"

Molly shook her head.

"It's not your Daddy, is it?"

Still no answer. And then in a small voice, Molly replied, "I don't think Mummy would want me to tell."

"Didn't Mummy bring you that memory in a dream, too? Perhaps she did that because she doesn't want it to be a secret anymore."

Molly said nothing. The expression on her face was blank and inscrutable. Katie Clements put the drawing back in the clipboard. She sat quietly for a while, looking at the little girl's shuttered face.

"Molly, I know this is difficult. I know it's painful sometimes to remember. But we need to talk about that day Mummy died. We have to try and find out what happened."

Molly still said nothing. She slowly slid Miss Moffat up to her face and pressed the soft stitched belly of the doll against her cheek.

"I can't remember," she said in a voice that was barely audible.

"Perhaps there's something here that might help you to remember."

Katie Clements stood up and walked over to a trolley that stood against the wall against which I was leaning. On the trolley was the doll's house that Ben had made, the replica of the house where I had died. Slate tiles had been painted in on the pitch of the plywood roof. Ben had considered putting a hinged front piece to the house that could be easily opened up with a small latch. But in the end he had run out of time, so the doll's house had been left completely open at the front revealing all the rooms. The ceilings and floors were made of pieces of hardboard, with offcuts of carpet stuck over the hardboard in the bedrooms and living room. The walls of the rooms were made of thick card. The ceilings and walls were all painted white.

Ben and I had spent the first few months after moving in, when Molly was still a bump under my painting overalls, stripping off the old flock wallpaper and putting up lining paper, then rolling white paint everywhere. In every room. On the walls and on the ceiling. In Molly's room we had stuck transfers everywhere. Pink princesses, mainly. And fairies in little tutus with gossamer wings. In the 'Molly's room' of this replica house, which was the smallest bedroom, and next to the bathroom, Ben had carefully duplicated this decor by finding tiny stickers of princesses and fairies from inside Molly's comics and sticking them all over the white cardboard walls.

He had done very well. This replica model had been done with great attention to detail, in spite of the time constraint that he'd been under.

Katie Clements rolled the trolley over to where Katie was sitting in the chair.

"Do you know what this is, Molly?"

Molly nodded. "A doll's house."

"Is there anything special about the doll's house?"

Molly bent down and peered into the rooms. She could see the painted cardboard walls. The black and white chequered square of hardboard that was used for the kitchen floor. She could see the dancing princess stickers in the room that was made to resemble the one she'd had back in our old house.

"It's made of card and things. Bits of wood. It's like someone made it themselves. Not from a shop."

"That's right, Molly. Yes, it is. But does it remind you of any house you've ever lived in?"

Molly pulled a face. "Don't know."

"Think about it, Molly. Try to remember."

"Well, it doesn't look like the house we live in now. It looks bigger. Maybe it's a bit like the house… the old house… the one where Mummy…"

"Where Mummy died?"

"Yes, maybe."

"What do you remember about that house, Molly? Do you remember anything?"

Molly shrugged. She didn't really want to remember. I stood near her. I leant down over her. I breathed my cold breath into her ear. *Think of the black and white kitchen floor. The princess stickers in your bedroom. Look at the green carpet in the living room that your dad has so carefully matched...*

"Not really," she replied. She paused. Then she peered at the kitchen floor again. "I saw the kitchen floor in my dream once. It was black and white like that one."

"Do you remember living in that house, Molly? You were only little, I know, but is there anything about it that you remember? This room, for instance? The one that used to be your bedroom."

Molly stared inside the doll's house at the room. "I don't know," she said.

Katie reached over and lifted out some wooden boxes that had been sitting on the trolley shelf underneath the doll's house. Two of them contained small furniture, handmade from stiff card or sawn scraps of plywood. A third contained scraps of fabric that looked like tiny rugs for the floors, duvets or quilted covers for beds. Tiny pillows and cushions, made out of scraps of foam covered with cotton material in various colours. Tiny curtains in all manner of colours and patterns, with thin strips of Velcro along the tops of them that could be stuck quickly into place on similar sized scraps of Velcro glued on to the walls above the windows in the replica house. Molly leaned forward and stared at the contents of the boxes, her face now aglow with wonder.

"Why don't you choose some furniture and put it in your bedroom, Molly?"

Molly leant forward and dipped her hand into the box of furniture. She took out a little bed made from pieces of hardboard. A chest of drawers, made of stiff cardboard and painted pink. A bedside table. A small bookcase. A little white-painted hardboard chair. She took a white 'rug' from the fabric box and put it on the blue carpet. She took out pink curtains and pressed them up against the Velcro strip. A pink 'duvet' to go on the bed. And 'pillows' with pink covers on them. Then she sat back as if she was finished. *That's right, Molly, that's almost the same as it was.* The only thing that differed from Molly's room in the old house was the colour of the curtains. She had chosen pink ones whereas the real ones had been light blue.

"Is this how your bedroom used to look, Molly?"

"It should have teddies and books and things in it but there aren't any here."

"That's okay. Would you like to choose a doll now from the doll box that could look like you?"

Molly peered into the doll box. She picked out one of the 'little girl' dolls, but then probably decided that its hair wasn't right; it had thick fair hair that stuck out like wire from its little teardrop face. She put it back and chose another one, slightly bigger than the first with long dark hair.

"This one is a bit big, but her hair is like mine."

"Where do you want to put her, Molly?"

Molly seated the doll on the carpet of 'her bedroom'. The doll's two little wooden legs, with red blobby shoes on the feet, stuck out in front of her. Molly giggled.

"She looks silly. She's a bit big for the room."

"We can pretend that she is smaller. What is the Molly doll doing in her bedroom?"

"She's playing with her Barbie dolls. She's taking their clothes off and putting different ones on. She likes dressing her Barbie dolls. Except that you haven't got anything that looks like Barbie dolls in the boxes so we have to pretend the Molly doll is doing that."

"Yes, that's right. We'll have to pretend. Now, what about choosing dolls to take the parts of Mummy and Daddy?"

Molly chose a tall 'Daddy' doll to stand for Ben. He had short dark hair and wore a red and yellow check shirt. I remembered that Ben had once owned a shirt like that. He had called it his 'lumberjack' shirt. He would wear it when he was working in the garden or out on walks. She chose a 'Mummy' doll with long reddish hair. She was dressed in a white summer dress with pink polka-dots.

"Mummy had a dress like this. It had pink flowers on it, not dots."

"We can pretend they are flowers. They could be little flowers. Where would you like to put the dolls?"

"Well, Daddy is at work, so I won't put him inside the house. Mummy is in the kitchen."

There were cardboard kitchen units made out of thick cardboard taped to the walls of the kitchen, a little white sink, a cooker, fridge-freezer, washing machine, all made out of cardboard. Molly placed the Mummy doll in front of the sink.

"Is that where Mummy spends a lot of time, Molly? In the kitchen, whilst you are playing upstairs in your room."

Katie's voice is very soft, very low, as if she is almost afraid to speak too loudly, in case it breaks up the spell that has entered the room, that sense of time having slipped backwards. It is almost as if we are back there now, in that house where it happened. On that day when it happened. Molly is that little girl sitting on her bedroom carpet playing with her Barbie dolls. I am standing at the kitchen sink, looking out down the back garden, to where washing is hanging on the washing line. I am looking at the dark clouds massing low in the sky and wondering how long before it rains.

Katie Clements sat back and folded her hands in her lap. I knew what she wanted to do next. I knew that she wasn't sure if she should.

"Molly," she said, quietly, "I want to ask you to try and remember what happened on that day that Mummy died. I know how difficult this is for you, but I want you to try. For instance, do you remember what you were doing when Daddy came home?"

"Maybe," Molly said, in a small voice.

"Can you use the dolls to show me, Molly?"

Molly picked up the Mummy doll and laid her down on the black and white kitchen floor. Then she picked up the doll that was supposed to be herself from the bedroom floor and put it next to the Mummy doll in a seated position.

"You are sitting next to Mummy when Daddy comes home?"

"Yes."

"And what if we were to wind things backwards. To go back to the time before Mummy is lying on the floor and you are sitting next to her. What is happening then, Molly?"

Molly was quiet for some time.

"I don't know," she said at last.

"Well, you are sitting on your bedroom floor playing with your Barbie dolls before sitting next to Mummy. You get up from your bedroom floor, Molly. You walk downstairs. Do you see anything? Do you hear anything? Is that why you come downstairs?"

Molly reached forward slowly and picked up the Molly doll again and put her back in her bedroom. But this time she is not sitting on the bedroom floor. She is standing at the bedroom window, which is made of a cut-up rectangle of acetate to resemble the long sash window that had reached nearly to the floor.

"You look out of the window, Molly? Is that what you are doing?"

Molly nodded again.

"Why do you get up and look out of the window? Do you hear anything? Do you hear a noise in the garden, perhaps?"

Molly nodded.

"What do you hear, Molly?"

"I hear Mummy shouting. Mummy is shouting at someone."

"Do you see anything, Molly? Someone else with Mummy, perhaps?"

"Mummy is hurt. She is holding her head. She is walking funny. Like she is trying not to fall over. She's walking towards the house."

"Is anyone else there in the garden, Molly? A man? Perhaps the man with the tiger-butterfly tattoo?"

"Someone is going out of the gate."

"Do you see what he looks like, Molly?"

Molly shook her head vigorously. "I can't see his face."

"Is he tall or short? Fat or thin? What colour is his hair? Is he the man with the tiger-butterfly tattoo? The one you drew in the picture. The one who was kissing Mummy?"

"No, no, he isn't." She was almost shouting. "His hair is dark. Like mine. Nearly black. But I can't see his face. I can't. I can't see it. Only his hair."

The tears were falling now. I wanted to say – *Stop, please stop. Don't ask her anything else.* But who would have heard?

But Katie Clements knew she had gone far enough.

"It's all right, Molly. Don't try to remember any more. Come back now. You're in this room with me. Daddy will be coming soon to fetch you. You've done wonderfully well. It's all right now."

33

Gardiner sat in her car outside the block of flats where Nicholas Hedges lived. I waited around the corner of the flats, watching. She glanced up towards the second level, where she knew that he lived. She could see the light on behind the drawn curtains. He was at home.

She had just been to Sharon's house to answer a call that had been made to the station. A little boy had seen an intruder outside his bedroom window. Normally she would have sent a pair of uniformed constables to do this. But because she knew that Nicholas Hedges lived on the same road as the person who'd made the call, she'd felt a compulsion to go herself, and to go on her own. She didn't really know why.

I did. It had something to do with mothers and daughters. How much they need each other.

Abigail was staying with Gardiner's sister. The flu that she had come down with last week had turned into a real stinker, giving the poor child a really chesty cough and a temperature that kept threatening to go well over 100 degrees, especially at night-time. At first, Gardiner's father had come over to stay with Abigail, but then as time went on and the fluey symptoms worsened instead of getting better, it made more sense for Gardiner to let her sister, who also lived in Guildford, come over and take Abigail home with her. It was fairer on her father, who was getting on now, over seventy, and past the age where looking after sick children was something he could take in his stride. Gardiner's sister was married and had two children, both in their early teens. As she didn't work she would be at home to take care of Abigail.

Guildford was a good hour's drive away and, as Gardiner often worked till late in the evening, she hadn't seen her daughter for several days. She had talked to her of course, every night on the phone, but Abigail had been feeling too poorly to want to stay on the phone for long, and anyway, a phone call was no substitute at all for having Abigail at home with her every evening. She had missed Abigail so much at times it had been almost a physical pain in her chest, a difficulty breathing.

Mothers and daughters.

That little girl, Molly, who had lost her mother. Who was found sitting next to her mother's dead body…

Gardiner could never quite forgive herself for not solving that crime.

But the week hadn't been without its blessings. For instance, the girl who had gone missing had turned up unharmed after all. She had been with her father at his flat in Croydon.

The parents had divorced three years ago. Things had

become very acrimonious and the father had dropped out of touch with his daughter. It had been believed at the time of the initial investigations into the missing child that he was now living somewhere in Spain. But apparently he'd come back a few months ago. He'd lain in wait for the child, sitting in his grey Peugeot, on the route he knew she took walking home from school. He had enticed her to go into the car with him – it wasn't hard, he was her father and she was excited to see him again – and took her away to the flat in Croydon where he now lived. For days he had kept her there, preventing her from contacting her mother. She had become very distressed, wanted to go home. He had to lock her up in her room for much of the time as she kept trying to run away. But in the end he had given way to the tears and the pleadings and had turned up at the local police station with the child. The mother had been beside herself with joy when the child was returned to her.

Mothers and daughters. A complicated bond sometimes, but one that can never be broken. Fathers and daughters too, sometimes.

That was why Gardiner was here. Working overtime. Making this 'off-the-record' call. Because of that little girl who had seen her mother die. Because of her failure to solve that case. Because that little girl had been left to grow up without her mother. Because it could happen to another little girl and her mother.

Because there was the slightest possibility that one day it could even happen to Abigail. As it had indeed happened to herself when her own mother had been killed by a hit-and-run driver.

*

I was there when Gardiner had interviewed Sharon. They sat together in the living room, Gardiner in the armchair by the gas fire and Sharon on the sofa. Leon had sat on his mother's lap, sucking his thumb and regarding Gardiner with curiosity. I hadn't wanted him to know that I was there so I stayed behind the half-opened door and peeped through at them.

"You saw a man at the window, didn't you, Leon?" Sharon was saying. "Tell the lady what you saw, darling?"

"A face. A man's face. Then the lady's face?"

"You saw a lady's face, too?" Gardiner asked him, with a sharpening of interest.

Leon nodded enthusiastically.

Sharon laughed, a little embarrassed.

"Don't take any notice of the lady, Inspector Gardiner. She isn't important. I think she's some kind of imaginary friend. He's said he's seen her before. He's said he's seen her in the kitchen. She isn't real. Just something in his head."

Gardiner nodded. She knew about children's imagination. She remembered how her own imagination as a child would conjure up the feeling that her mother was with her in the room sometimes, after the accident, after her mother had died. She would have been only a little older than Abigail was now. She would be sitting quietly at the kitchen table doing her homework, and she'd sense her mother was there. She'd smell that orangey scent her mother would wear, feel her mother's cool hand slip on to her shoulder. Gardiner remembered how real it had felt at the time; she knew children's imaginations were not to be treated dismissively.

"Did the lady's face frighten you, Leon?"

The little boy shook his head. He didn't have to think about it. "No. The lady is nice. Her face is nice."

Sharon was making a grimace, mouthing the words – *She isn't real*. Gardiner ignored her.

"And you've seen the lady before?"

He nodded. "When the man was here. Man with funny butterfly on his arm."

I could sense the alarm bells ringing in Gardiner's head. "What man is this?"

"Oh, it's just this man who lives across the road. In the flats. He was outside the house one day when I came home from work. He helped me pick up some shopping when the carrier bags got torn coming through the gate. He said he's a handyman – does carpentry jobs, mainly. So I asked him for a quote for some shelving. He seems quite nice – I can't imagine it was him the other night."

"Did he say what his name was?"

"Nick, he said. Short for Nicholas I suppose."

"This butterfly on his arm that Leon says he had. A tattoo of some sort, I expect. Did you see it?"

"I think he did have one. He had a cut on his hand. He'd cut it on the broken glass when he cleared up the mess from a bottle of wine that broke. He came in and I put a plaster on it for him. I think I may have noticed a tattoo. Didn't take much notice of it, to be honest. Leon's amazing, sometimes. The details he notices!"

Gardiner turned her attention back to the boy. "This butterfly picture the man had on his arm, Leon. Can you tell me a little more about it? You said it was funny. Why was it 'funny', Leon?"

"It was like a butterfly," Leon said. "Like a tiger, too. Remember, Mummy? Like a tiger." He opened his mouth wide and made a roaring noise, clawing his chubby hands like a cat.

Sharon laughed. "Funny the things children remember."

"Leon, this man's face you saw at your window. Do you think it might have been the same man? The man with the funny butterfly on his arm."

I was so intent on wanting to hear what was being said that I moved forward, out of the hallway and through the door into the living room. Leon had screwed up his face as if he was thinking hard.

"Don't know. Don't remember. I remember the nice lady's face."

I had moved out into the open doorway. I was trying to glimpse the look on Gardiner's face. Leon suddenly looked up and saw me. "There she is, Mummy! The nice lady is over there."

I quickly stepped back again into the hallway.

"See what I mean," I could hear Sharon saying. "I don't know where he gets it from, this imagination!"

I didn't hear Gardiner reply. I don't think she had Leon's ability to see me: not ordinarily, anyway. But perhaps she had sensed something. A feeling of someone standing behind her, watching. Hadn't she herself, as a child, had that kind of 'imagination' too? Sensing her mother was there in the room with her, even after her mother was dead?

Sharon showed Gardiner to the door. I disappeared quickly into the kitchen. I could still hear them through the open door.

"Look, I don't wish to alarm you, but I think you should get another quote for that shelving," Gardiner said.

"Oh, but I've already agreed that he'll come and do the job on Sunday. I'm sure it's just a coincidence, this man Leon said he saw in the garden. He could even have imagined him as well." Sharon gave a short, ironic laugh.

"Phone him up and tell this Nick person you've got someone else to do the job. Don't have him in the house. I'm not saying that he's necessarily the man that Leon saw at the window – *if* he did see someone. But I think you should know that there is a man who lives in those flats across the road, with the kind of tattoo on his arm that your son has described, who has a police record for rape."

I didn't hear what Sharon said. Perhaps she said nothing. Perhaps she was too shocked to reply.

"Look, I really don't wish to alarm you," Gardiner continued, "and I'm probably not supposed to tell you this. Breach of confidentiality and all that, and we don't know that he's actually done anything wrong. But I just want you and your little boy to be safe. Cancel it. Please. Find someone else."

"Y-yes, of course. I'll do that. Thank God you told me that, Inspector Gardiner."

*

Gardiner got out of her car and walked up to the block of flats. There were two small blocks of them, each with two storeys. She believed that they had been originally built as private flats in the eighties but had since been taken over by a housing trust. She went into the entrance to the second block, to where it said 'Flats 12–24'. She knew Nicholas Hedges lived at number 21. She took the lift to the second level. I glided up the stairs. When I got up to the central area, where the front door to Nicholas' flat was, she was just coming out of the lift. She rang his doorbell. He answered the door almost immediately, looking startled for a brief moment when she flashed her police badge at him. He recovered quickly. He was good at hiding what he felt.

"Nicholas Hedges?"

"Yes."

'Detective Inspector Gardiner."

"What can I do for you, Inspector?"

"I've had a call about an intruder at the house over the road. I believe you know the lady that lives there with her son? A Mrs Sharon Tyler."

"Wouldn't say that I know her. Not well. She's more like a customer. She's asked me to do a carpentry job for her. Put up some shelving. That's my trade, carpentry."

"Perhaps you wouldn't mind answering some questions? Just routine enquiries. May I come in?"

"It's because of the police record, isn't it? I'm sure you're not making enquiries with every Tom, Dick or Harry who's ever given the lady an estimate." He sounded contemptuous although he kept a smile on his face.

"Well, you do live very close by, Mr Hedges."

"Or every geezer in this tenement building either."

Gardiner paused. "May I come in, Mr Hedges?"

He made a nonchalant gesture for her to come in. I waited outside for a while. I wanted to go in but I was concerned that she would be put off by sensing I was there. I wanted Gardiner to have her wits about her, for her keen discernment of the skewed and off-kilter versions of 'the truth' to be at full strength. But eventually my will power dissolved. I glided through the closed front door. I could hear voices from the living room. I waited out in the hallway again, watching them through the half-open door. Gardiner was perched on the end of the greasy black leather chair. Nicholas Hedges sat on the brown flock sofa opposite. He leant forward and flicked the end of a rolled-up cigarette towards the ashtray on the coffee table. Some of the ash missed and landed on the table.

"I believe you used to know a Rachel Vincent?" Gardiner was saying. "She was employed as a prison psychologist during the time you were serving a sentence in Wandsworth."

"You know I did. I was interviewed just after her murder. All the blokes who'd been in this sex offenders' group she ran were interviewed. You'll have that somewhere in the files. Anyway, I gave an alibi that checked out okay."

"Yes, I am aware of that, Mr Hedges. I just need to establish for myself a few facts regarding your relationship."

"What the hell's that got to do with the intruder over the road?"

"No direct connection, Mr Hedges. But obviously there is a need to rule you out of being a suspect to the intruder incident. You do have a record, unfortunately, of sex offences."

"One so-called sex offence, if you don't mind. One incident."

"Yes, perhaps so. But a serious one."

"Five years ago, that was. Give a dog a bad name and hang him, that's what you lot do, isn't it?"

"I have as much belief as anyone else in the importance of rehabilitation for offenders, Mr Hedges."

He looked at her, a little sullenly, as if he was trying to work out if she was being sarcastic or not. He must have decided to give her the benefit of the doubt.

"Okay, Inspector. What is it you want to ask me about Rachel Vincent?"

"In the interview that took place after Rachel's murder you stated that you didn't meet her again after your release from prison. That was a routine kind of interview, since every man that attended that sex offenders' group had to be questioned, and I could understand your reluctance to have any spotlight put upon you at that time, even if you were entirely innocent. But I'm asking you again. Did you ever meet Rachel Vincent again, or know her socially in any way?"

He stared unblinkingly back at Gardiner. I could feel his mind ticking over. *What should I tell her? Should I tell her the truth?* He gave a crooked half-hearted smile, a short dry laugh.

"Were we mates, or even lovers? Is that what you want to know? An ex-con and a prison psychologist. Not the kind of thing you lot would approve of, is it?"

Gardiner kept her voice even. She wasn't going to be provoked. "Did you ever meet her outside of the prison? Bump into her somewhere? Or go to her house?"

"Yes, I did."

I couldn't see Gardiner's face from where I was standing in the room, but I doubt if she would've completely concealed her look of surprise. She wouldn't have expected such frankness.

"I lied, when I was questioned back then. Didn't want it to get too heavy, too complicated. But I was innocent. I didn't kill her."

Gardiner gave a quick cursory nod. "Can you tell me when that was? When you met her again?"

"About Christmas time. Nearly two years ago now. I bumped into her in Victoria station. She was living near Reigate. I had already moved here to Redhill. We found ourselves catching the same train home. I'd been up to London to see a mate. Someone I'd met at Wandsworth. We'd had a few pints and then went back to his flat in Battersea to watch Arsenal play Aston Villa. I only remember that because of the surprise of meeting Rachel Vincent at Victoria station later."

"What happened when you met her? Did you sit together on the train?"

"Yeah, we did. She was going to get a taxi from the station to her place. But that seemed daft, especially as she had the little girl with her and it was beginning to rain. So I offered to give her a lift. It seemed the natural thing to do. And anyway, I liked her. She was good to me at Wandsworth. I had a lot of respect for her. Anyway, when we got to the house she asked me in. I had a cup of tea. We just talked. We talked about lots of things. Her marriage, for a start."

"Her marriage? Why would she talk to you about that?"

"I don't know. Maybe I'm easy to talk to. Anyway she got upset. Her husband apparently had been having an affair. She hadn't got over that. Things were very dodgy between them. Then about a couple of weeks later, after the New Year, she phoned me. I'd left my business card with her. In case she ever needed a handyman. She asked me if I could install her new kitchen and I did."

"When would that have been?"

"I started working on it about the middle of January. On a Monday. What happened between us was on the Friday."

"*What* happened between you, Mr Hedges?"

"When she came on to me. Seduced me, if you like. It only happened the one time. Maybe she just needed to get even, so to speak. Her husband had an affair, then she did. Squared things up. Then she dumped me."

"How did she 'dump' you?"

"She phoned me up. That evening. On the day it happened. The day we slept together, only we didn't sleep, if you get what I mean."

"How did that make you feel, Mr Hedges? Being dumped like that."

"I knew it wouldn't last. We weren't exactly in the same league, her and me."

"And that was the last time you had any contact with Rachel Vincent? When she phoned you that evening?"

"Well, there was one other time."

Gardiner waited for him to continue.

"It was the Sunday after she dumped me. I thought it was a bit callous, the way she'd done it over the phone. I was angry, I guess. I went over to the house to see if I could talk to her. I knew her husband wasn't there because she'd told me earlier that he was going up to Scotland for a few days. He was involved in some building project up there. Anyway, I rang her front door bell. She answered the door but she wouldn't let me in. There was a bit of shouting and I probably swore at her, called her a bitch – that sort of thing.

I was out of order, because her little girl was at home. That was the last time I saw Rachel Vincent. The next thing I ever knew about her, months later, was when I read in the paper that she was dead."

I couldn't stay any longer. I couldn't bear to. Something was making me feel uncomfortable, causing a pressure, a deep aching in my throat, if I had a throat to feel pain anymore. He is speaking the truth but not the whole truth.

But I wasn't ready for the whole truth yet.

*

Gardiner would have been completely taken back by his 'honesty', by his unexpected revelations. In the morning she'd go back to the office. She'd pull out the notes made on the interview with Ben that evening at the station on the day that I died. She'd read them again in the light of this new revelation. She'd be asking herself, is it true that Ben had an affair? That our marriage was not the unblemished relationship she'd imagined it to be? Is it true that I'd slept with Nicholas Hedges, and if so, did Ben ever find out? Did I ever confess it to Ben later, perhaps? To off-load my guilt. In anger or a desire for revenge.

She would even have felt a cold creeping of suspicion. What if Ben himself had murdered me, whilst his own daughter was in the house? What would something like that do to a child?

She would wish perhaps that the dead could talk.

She would also wish, as she had sometimes wished before, that she was just an ordinary mother. A mother at home looking after her child. Instead of feeling as she did this terrible responsibility. To try and rid the world of the horror of dead or missing children.

Or children growing up with murdered mothers.

34

I am unsettled. I don't know where I want to be, if I want to be anywhere at all. I am growing weary of being attached to this world that I no longer belong in. There is a sharp coldness in the air and on a high ground a frost at night, so that in the early morning, when the sun comes up, a mist drifts slowly down the hills and into the valleys where the rolling pastures are dotted with sheep.

The end of October. The time of the year when the veil between the worlds is at its thinnest.

I stand and watch my daughter at school. I watch her in the classroom, her head bent over her tasks. She forms her letters carefully on the lined paper the teacher gives her. She can write her own name. The 'L's are a little too long, and stretch up beyond the line above the writing, the 'Y' is a little too short. The 'M' is comforting and wide and the 'O' is an almost perfect circle. I watch her screw her thumb into clay and fashion a rudimentary pot, brush thick poster paint on to sheets of sugar paper. The colours she is using these days are brighter primary colours. She rarely uses black now.

She paints pictures of Charlie with a heart floating above his head. She colours the heart in red. I smile at my daughter's world, but strangely find that I don't want to belong to it anymore.

I stand behind Ben in his little office room in the cottage, watching him drawing out plans for the artist's eco-friendly house. I do not dip into his thoughts much these days, if I can help it. They are nearly always full of her... Katie. Her hair, her eyes, her smile. The memory of her mouth on his.

Sometimes I go and press my face up against the glass and watch the bright people at the party. Sometimes I imagine I see people that I know, or have known, or would have known perhaps if I had not died. Everyone smiles at me when they see me, and some of them beckon to me, but I shake my head at them. I cannot pass beyond the glass yet.

Sometimes I think I see Mr Jackson with his wife and little girl. The little girl is always the same age. She is always wearing a candy-striped dress and her strawberry blonde hair is always in pigtails. I mouth at Mr Jackson through the glass – "When can I join you?"

"When you let go."

"Am I nearly there?"

"You're getting closer. Be patient."

His voice comes back again, like an echo. I can hear the sound of laughter, like the peal of faraway bells.

35

My father stretched the net over the pond and fished out a dark and rotting clump of old leaves. *Be careful. Don't fall in.*

Ben was seeing Katie Clements that evening and would be dropping Molly off later. My father wanted the pond to be clean so Molly would be able to see the fish clearly.

It hadn't surprised my parents that Ben was going out with Katie Clements again. My father had taken the call. He had wanted to ask – *Is this serious? This Katie woman. Is she going to take the place of Rachel in my granddaughter's life? Is that what you are wanting to happen?*

But of course he hadn't. It was none of their business, Sylvia would say, and he knew that she was right. *My daughter is dead*, he would tell himself. *There is nothing that will bring her back*. Ben, of course, had to make another life for himself now, another life for Molly…

My father leant forward over the pond again with the net in his outstretched hand and scooped out some dead leaves that were floating on the surface. Two goldfish swam out from beyond the reeds at the edge.

He was remembering the other pond, the one we'd had in the garden of the cottage in Wilmington. I could see the image of it forming in his mind. It had been a smaller pond than this one. I'd stood and watched him digging it out when I was little, heaping the chalky soil to one side that would form the rockery later. Shallow shelves had been left around the edges for the baskets of reeds and other pond plants. Later, long weedy trails of plants that had no roots were thrown into the water that my father said would help the water to breathe. It took some time for the plants to do their work, for the brown sludgy water to clear to a transparency that reflected the sky. My father told me how to scoop out the green algae around the edges with a net to keep the pond clear. Water lilies were planted in baskets that sat in the deep centre. Then we'd bought some fish. That was my favourite part. In the summertime I would lay on my stomach, my chin resting on the crazy-paved edging, and I would watch the fish. I would watch them swim out from the foliage and disappear into the black depths, then break towards the surface, their tiny mouths nibbling on flies. I thought the fish were miraculous. My father told me that they always grow to the size that their environment allows. That's why, he said, the ones in the pond were bigger than the ones kept in a bowl indoors.

Here, in this much bigger pond, the fish were fat and bloated. I stepped behind him, leant over his shoulder to glimpse them, and for a moment my father imagined that he saw me, my reflection appearing as a hazy shimmer, my red hair the same colour as the fish. He called out in consternation and had to steady himself, to stop himself from falling. His hand flew to his chest, to the scarred wound over his heart.

He turned to see if I was there.

But I, too, can make myself vanish into black invisible depths.

36

Ben sat next to Katie on her sofa in the cottage. She had phoned him on the Wednesday to tell him that she would rather discuss what had occurred at Molly's last session in private than over the phone. Ben had said that he'd arrange to drop Molly off at my parents after school on Friday, then come over to her place, if that would suit her. He hadn't been sure if he should have made it sound like a date, but he had wanted to. He'd suggested bringing over a bottle of wine. *What do you prefer – red or white?* She said that she was rather partial to Pinot Grigio and then suggested that she cook supper for them. How did he like scallops? – they should go well with the wine.

By the time Ben put the phone down he was fairly sure that this was a date of sorts, although perhaps its content was somewhat more serious than the date on the previous weekend, when nothing more than a mild debate over the main themes in *Equus* had occurred. Then, he'd been happy to bow graciously to her superior knowledge.

*

They had finished the meal; the scallops in white wine had been good. Ben had been very circumspect in not allowing himself to have more than a single glass of wine, knowing if he had too much Katie would feel compromised and say – *You shouldn't drive; stay the night in the spare room.* How could he go then, with such an invitation, into the dark night and the long drive home alone over the bleak Beacons? But then again, how could he sleep a wink, lying in the spare room with her across the landing in her bed?

He leant forward and picked up the cup of coffee from the coffee table.

"So what are you saying, Katie? That you don't think this man – the man with the tattoo – you don't think he's the one who killed Rachel?"

"Well, I know that Molly's memories are not to be given too much weight – she wasn't even four at the time – and after such a long time delay there will always be the likelihood of fabrication – but Molly seemed clear about this one. She looked out of the window and saw someone go through the gate the day her mum died. She said he had dark hair. She seemed sure about that."

Katie sifted through the portfolio of Molly's drawings that she had on the table in front of her. She drew out the one that Molly had painted on her first day at school. The one of me lying on a black and white floor, a pool of red under my head. A man standing over me that has no face. Just a grey wash of paint where his face should be, and a yellow blob of hair.

"Look at the man's hair in this picture. He's blond." She shifted through the portfolio again and brought out the painting of Nicholas kissing me, the Christmas tree floating in the right-hand corner of the page.

"And this one. This man has yellow hair, too."

"Okay. But what are you saying, Katie? In the first one Rachel is dead on the floor and he's there, the yellow-haired man. So the memory you said she had of another man, one with dark hair, going out through the back garden gate on the day she died, well, that's just inaccurate. She got that one wrong."

"Or she is mixing memories up."

"Why should she be doing that?"

"On the previous session I had with her, the one before this last one, she indicated through her actions that she had hid with Miss Moffat under the stairs. Remember, I told you what happened? I thought that was on the day her mother died. But maybe not. Maybe it was on another occasion. She seemed so sure in what she was communicating to me through the doll's house. She'd heard shouting in the garden. Rachel shouting. She got up and looked through the window and her mother was staggering back towards the house and she saw a man, another man – not the blond one – going out through the garden gate into the lane."

"Well, maybe she came downstairs then and hid under the stairs."

"Why would she do that? The man had gone. And it's not where you found her two hours later, is it? She was sitting by her mother's dead body, wasn't she? That's what she told me, too. She came downstairs and her mother was lying on the floor and she sat down beside her."

"Well, I don't know. I don't know what to make of any of it, Katie."

Ben put his coffee cup back on the table. He sat with his head in his hands. Katie shuffled the pictures back into the portfolio. She touched him lightly on the shoulder.

"I know this is very difficult for you, Ben. Maybe it's time to let it go. I think Molly's remembered enough. She doesn't have the nightmares anymore, does she? Maybe she should just be allowed now to get on with it. To just be a little girl now, having a little girl's happy life."

I knew what Ben was thinking. He was thinking of Molly's drawing of me kissing a man with yellow hair. He was thinking of Gardiner's question – *Did your wife ever have an affair?* He was thinking of his own affair, and how much it had hurt me. He was thinking of all the unanswered questions – *What was the significance of the man with yellow hair and the tattoo on his arm? How well had Rachel really known him?*

"I understand what you're saying, Katie," he said, raising his head. "But I just want you to have one more session with Molly. I want you to try and take her back to the day she hid in the cupboard under the stairs. Why did she hide? What was she frightened of? I just feel that it had something to do with this man with the tattoo."

"I'm not sure that's a good idea, Ben…"

"Please, Katie. Just one more time. And then I'll let it go. *We'll* let it go…"

He placed his hand on her arm. She turned to look at him, and he kissed her.

She kissed him back. Then she suddenly pulled back

from him and looked over towards the shadows at the back of the room.

"Do you know, Ben, I have the strangest sensation sometimes…"

"What?"

"That I'm being watched sometimes. That there's someone in the room with me."

"Who?"

"I don't know. It's silly, really…"

The moment had passed now. Ben stood up. He picked up his jacket from the back of the sofa.

"I better go now. It's late. Think about it, Katie," he said.

37

Later that night, I stand next to Peter Bates' bed and watch him sleep. He doesn't sleep the sleep of the innocent. He tosses restlessly and sometimes he moans, queer clicking sounds in his throat. His breathing is rough and raspy from too much smoking.

I've been to his bedside several times whilst he slept and reached into his dreams. His dreams are dark and sticky and they never console him. There is his mother, always larger than life, like some solid impenetrable force. His mother always knows best. She speaks and he obeys. He dare not disobey. He dreams of the cornfield and a dark night, his terror and his mother's urgings. It rained heavily that night. He was soaked, his wet hair plastered to the thin bones of his skull.

He dreams sometimes of the prison and the beatings. The man he fears the most has a chip on his front tooth and very light blue eyes, so light they look almost colourless. He knows this because this man pokes his face right up close to him. He smells the sourness of the man's breath. Perv, the man calls him. *Dirty little perv.* And then the fist hitting him hard in the belly, taking away his breath.

I reach into his troubled dreams and give him another one. This is not a memory, but an imagining. The half-moon swings on its back like a hammock. He is carrying something heavy. He is walking like a man who knows where he's going. His mother sits at home, silent and unknowing. The stubble of the cornfield is rough under his boots. He dreams of leather shoes, size ten. He wonders if they will ever polish up again. He dreams of something hard. He will know its hardness when he finds it.

His body jerks under the bedclothes. Then he sits bolt upright in the bed. His eyes are staring right through me. He whimpers, like a child. He reaches up and touches his face with his cracked hands. He imagines that blood is pouring from the sores. He can't see the blood, but he knows it is there.

It drips down, large fat drops, staining red the white of his sheets.

38

Halloween. When the dead are supposed to walk the Earth, as I do.

*

I watched Nicholas Hedges receive a phone call from Sharon. I could guess what she was saying to him. She was telling him that she did not want him to fix the shelves for her the following day. She was making some excuse. She had changed her mind. She didn't want to turn the spare room into an office anymore.

He sat in the chair by the window, unmoving, for half an hour afterwards. He stared out towards the bungalow opposite. He saw the black Saab draw up. He saw Sharon come to the front door. He saw her tilt her face up towards the man's and kiss him. He noticed her glance over towards the flats apprehensively, as if she feared that he was watching. He moved his head backwards so that he was hidden by the curtain.

He stayed watching the bungalow in his chair by the window until he saw the lights go off in her living room. The Saab was still there. I could feel his memories clouding his head. He was a little boy lying in his narrow bed at home, listening to the sounds through the bedroom's thin wall of his mother being shagged by some stranger.

He got up suddenly and turned off the light and lay on his bed. He couldn't bear it anymore. She could not treat him like this, she could not be allowed to get away with it... Tomorrow night he would show her...

He imagined what she was doing with that man in her bed, under the mocha and cream duvet cover, with her son trying to sleep in his room next door. The dog-eared teddy bear from her childhood sitting in the wicker chair, staring out of its one glass eye.

*

In the blink of an eye I had left him, and I was outside Peter Bates' house again, where a group of small figures clustered outside the front door, the external light above the door illuminating the fluorescent skeletons, white masks shaped like teardrops.

They rang the doorbell. They were laughing, talking loudly, their voices rising with excitement. None of them noticed me; they were too vivid, too alive; too unlike the undead that they were impersonating.

Mrs Bates came to the door. She waved a fierce fist at them, shouted coarsely – *Get out of it, you little gits!* They turned, startled, stumbled through the gate, their white masked faces dipping and rising in the dark. One of them, the tallest boy, stayed at the door and cursed fearlessly back at Mrs Bates. She slammed the door shut. The boy threw something at the front bay window; it spread into a white mist upon the cold glass. She burst through the front door again, a walking stick clutched ferociously in her hand, thrashing the air to get at the boy. He leapt the gate, came running over the road towards me. As we collided I felt the shock pass through his body, chill his blood. But he carried on running after the others.

Mrs Bates cursed after them. Then she suddenly turned and stared over the road towards me. I don't think she could see me. But I disappeared. In the blink of an eye. Like a memory of white mist upon glass.

*

I am back. This time, waiting in the Bates' back garden.

Peter Bates comes through the kitchen door, walks towards the shed. He's dressed in black. His face shines waxy white in the moonlight. Now he belongs more to the dead than the living.

He fiddles with the padlock on the shed door. Opens it, goes inside. At first there's only darkness. Then I make out his shape, a shadow shuffling towards the back of the shed. He stands up straight. He is breathing hard. I hear him mutter – That'll do. He comes out of the shed. He is holding something under his left arm that is loosely wrapped in sacking. It is a long shape, and from the way he carries it, stooping slightly over it, it appears to be heavy. He carries it along the path that leads around the side of the house and down the front path to the gate. When he comes out of the gate he doesn't turn left this time, as he normally does, to walk down to the beginning of Gale Lane. He turns right, then right again. I realise that he's going down to the gap in the hedgerow that will lead him straight on to the cornfield.

He does.

The sky is clear tonight. The moon, swelling up to its second quarter, is slung like a hammock in the night sky, low on the horizon and a fiery orange. Peter Bates walks quickly, as quickly as he can in the limited light from the moon, stumbling now and then on the rutted frosted earth. I follow him, gliding over the rough ground like one who doesn't belong to the earth. He stops as usual at the oak tree and throws down the implement that he is carrying. The sacking falls loose and reveals the shiny metal of a spade. He rolls a cigarette, puts it to his mouth, flicks on his lighter. The flame wavers and goes out. He strikes the wheel again with his thumb, ducking his head towards the flame. His hand is shaking in agitation. He draws heavily on the cigarette, then holding it in his tight lips, he picks up the spade and begins to dig. I watch the red tip of the cigarette move up and down through the darkness like a glow-worm. Like something caught between the world of the living and the dead.

It carries on glowing, moving up and down as he bends and straightens, digging in the stiff earth. When the spade hits the hardness he is looking for, with a sharp clunk of sound, he stands up straight. He takes the cigarette from his lips, throws it down and stamps on it.

The light goes out as suddenly and as finally as life leaves the body when it dies.

39

Gardiner dropped into bed exhausted, after putting Abigail to bed.

They'd spent the evening at a friend's Halloween party. I went there after leaving Peter Bates alone in the cornfield.

The friend's house had a large garden and someone was entertaining the children down at its far end, where Jack o'lanterns hung from the trees, red lights glowing eerily through their jagged teeth and diamond-shaped eyes. The children were dressed as witches, ghosts, ghouls and goblins. They rushed around amidst the trees, shrieking, playing tag; the red light from the lanterns rippled strangely over their bodies.

Gardiner sat on the patio with the other adults. She was dressed as a Grey Lady ghost. Her face was whitened with face paint and she wore a late-Victorian tulle wedding dress that she'd found in a charity shop. She'd soaked it in pale grey dye. She thought it made her resemble some washed-out memory of herself.

She was uncomfortable with being here. She didn't like this casual flippant make-believe foray into the world of the dead. It seemed like making fun to her. She was uneasy about that, unless those more spiteful amongst the dead have a way of getting back at the living. She watched her daughter, a white-sheeted ghost, rushing amongst the trees and the glowing Jack o'lanterns at the bottom of the garden. She wanted to get Abigail home. Back to being a normal little girl who belonged firmly to the land of the living.

Gardiner knew, more than most people know, how easy it is to slip from one world to the next. She had seen enough dead bodies to know that. She often wished she didn't have such knowledge. That she could erase for ever the images that would sometimes seep unbidden into her mind.

Like the memory of me lying dead on those black and white tiles, red blood bathing my head.

Murdered mothers. Dead mothers. Daughters growing up without their mothers.

She thought of her own mother and how she had missed her when she'd died. She remembered now, almost as if it had only just happened, the bitter shock of that day.

Two policemen had called unexpectedly at the house. One, she remembered, had been burly and grey haired and reminded her of her grandfather. Her father had asked her to wait in her room whilst he talked to the policemen. He'd been trying to spare her, thinking perhaps that if it was bad news it would be better coming from him later than from the mouths of the policemen. But as she waited for him upstairs, sitting on her bed, idly twisting and turning a Rubik's cube in her hands, she already knew that her mother was dead. She didn't know how she knew or why she knew. But she knew.

She heard the front door close. She heard the sound of the police car starting up outside. She waited for the sound of her father's tread on the stairs. It didn't come straightaway. Ten, maybe fifteen minutes later. And all the time she sat quietly on the edge of the bed, twisting and turning the sections of the cube, looking at the colours on its faces build then fall away, the knowledge of the accident growing inside her. She could almost hear the screech of the car's brakes, the thud of her mother's body against the bonnet. She could almost see her mother, in that green woollen jacket that she had been wearing, lying on the road, one leg twisted awkwardly behind her. When her father came up later into her room, his eyes red rimmed from crying, she could've almost put the words into his mouth herself, so clear had the knowledge now formed inside her. *Your mother's had an accident. A hit and run driver. He didn't stop. Someone called an ambulance. It was too late. Your mother didn't make it. She died before the ambulance arrived…*

*

Dead. It sounded so final. Saying it was almost like breaking a taboo. Almost like a profanity.

*

She had made it her business now, dealing with the dead. And with those who bring about their deaths. How many dead bodies had she seen? But her own mother's? No, she had never seen that. She hadn't wanted to. She had only been nine at the time. Just a kid…

She thought of how she'd sometimes felt that she was being watched. It was usually when she was thinking of my murder. She glanced up and looked down the garden to where the children were playing, and just for a moment she imagined she could see me there, standing under a beech tree, the red candlelight from the Jack o'lanterns deepening the red of my hair, flowing over my face, over my light cotton dress. She shut her eyes, briefly, and when she opened them again the image had disappeared. It was just her over-active imagination, just like when she was a child imagining she'd felt her mother's cool hand on her shoulders…

Her eyes searched for Abigail amongst the rushing children. But she couldn't see her. She wasn't there. Abigail had run back into the house at the time to use the toilet, but Gardiner didn't know that. She stood up, full of fear, like a Grey Lady ghost haunted by the death of a child.

*

But now she was sleeping. Abigail was sleeping too.

Gardiner had seen Abigail to bed. She had taken off the grey tulle wedding dress, roughly cleaned the white face-paint from her face with an exfoliating face cleanser and had gone straight to bed herself. She was dreaming now of ghosts rushing amongst trees. Abigail was lost again; she couldn't see Abigail. Gardiner tossed restlessly, moaned in her sleep with a strange anxiety. She was looking for Abigail, she was searching again amongst the rushing children and the trees. I stood over her, I leant down, my cold breath on her cheek. *It's all right. Abigail is safe, she is sleeping...*

The moaning stopped. She slept peacefully again. And then I bring back a memory in another dream...

*

Peter Bates is in the small interview room at the police station. The tape whirs softly on the desk. His thin cheeks flinch nervously when she asks him questions. He glances up every now and then to the CCTV camera on the wall.

She is asking him about the knickers he admitted stealing from Rachel Vincent's washing line.

"How many times did you take them?"

"I don't know – maybe a couple of times."

"Can you tell me when that was, approximately?"

"I don't know – could be two weeks ago."

"Can you describe the knickers you took on that occasion?"

"Red ones."

"And the other time? You said there were a couple of times."

"I don't remember. Maybe only once. Yeah. Only once from her garden. Christ, I don't always remember. I steal knickers sometimes from women's washing. I know it's wrong, I shouldn't do, but it's what I do. Not often. Just sometimes. I can't 'elp it."

She is jumping back to the day of my murder. I am lying on the black and white tiles. The forensic men in their white snowsuits are taking samples of blood and hair. She steps out on to the patio through the open back door. Sergeant

Williams follows. They quickly take in the scene. They see bloodstains on the flagstone patio that haven't been washed off by the rain. They see the gate at the bottom of the garden that has been left open. They see the sodden washing hanging on the line. They walk down the garden to the red plastic washing basket that has been left there. They see a pair of black lace knickers lying on their own at the bottom. Several feet away lying on the grass are two clothes pegs.

"Looks like she'd just started taking down the washing when it happened," Williams said. "Whoever it was must have come in through that garden gate and surprised her."

In her dream now, she can see the black lace knickers lying on their own in the plastic basket. They look wet, because of the rain. And hanging on the line, soaked through, are two pairs of Ben's trousers, sheets and pillow cases, several shirts, Molly's tops and jeans, a bath towel, a dressing gown.

Her dream jumps back to the interview room. She notices how Peter Bates wrings his hands nervously as he speaks. It doesn't mean much in so far as indicating guilt goes. He's a bag of nerves. A simpleton really. Didn't have much of a chance in life. She almost pities him. She looks down at his hands and sees that they are covered with a rash.

"Dermatitis," he tells her. "Need to wear cotton gloves for most things I do round the house."

In her dream now, there is blood leaking from the sores on his hands. She stares and stares at the blood. It will not stop flowing. It flows in a thin river across her desk. Falls over the edge and on to the floor.

*

Gardiner woke suddenly. She thought for a moment she had heard Abigail calling her. That it was Abigail that had woken her. But the house was silent. She thought that she could sense someone there watching her in the darkness of the room, but she didn't feel disturbed by this sensation, not in the way the dream had disturbed her. Nevertheless, she reached over and switched on the bedside light. There was no one there, although the sensation of being watched remained.

She sat upright. She was trying to recall the details of the dream. Why had she chosen tonight, she wondered, to dream of that interview with Peter Bates? The rash on his hands. Those knickers lying alone in the basket in the garden.

If I had eyes to close, I would close them now. I would close them so that I could concentrate better. I was trying to plant the thought in her head, trying as hard as I could: *Why would someone take down the small things first, the lighter things – underwear, for instance – when they think it is going to rain? Why not start with the heavier things? The things that are harder to dry. The trousers, the sheets, the towels.*

40

My father was raking leaves in the garden. He started at the top tier of lawn, the one that was immediately outside the French windows that led out from the dining room. Molly was outside with him, throwing a ball for Goldie.

He was feeling tired. He'd gone to bed early last night and had slept in till past nine. He'd slept well and deeply, yet had woken up still feeling tired. It was an odd sort of tiredness. Not like the tiredness caused by lack of sleep or by over-activity, but a sort of weary sluggishness that made him feel that his blood was moving slowly around his body. All his muscles seemed to ache, and his head was foggy. He hadn't said anything to Sylvia about it; he hadn't wanted to worry her. And he hadn't wanted to spoil their weekend with Molly. It was important to them both, this time at the weekend when Molly came to stay. He didn't know how long it might continue now that her father had another woman in his life. He didn't know for sure how serious the relationship was, but he suspected that if Ben had anything to do with it, then soon it would be. Ben didn't do things in half measures, not where relationships were concerned; he'd give him credit where it was due.

He didn't know how he would feel, seeing another woman in the role of Molly's mum. In my place.

And if Ben and this Katie woman ended up getting married, they might move away. Down to Cardiff where she worked. Or even further afield. Anywhere really. Then he and Sylvia might be lucky if they got to see Molly more than once or twice a year, if that.

There was no telling what the future would bring.

It made him uneasy. It made him almost feel that he was losing me again.

He carried on raking the leaves. He glanced over towards Molly. She was running around the lawn in her little red hooded coat, the dog running after her. He loved seeing the two of them together like this. We hadn't had a dog when I was Molly's age. Probably because my mother was expecting John, and it hadn't been a good time to bring a dog into the family, who might possibly get jealous when a new baby arrived. Even the most good-natured of dogs can get jealous in circumstances like that.

Molly came running up to my father.

"Granddad, can Goldie and I go down and look at the fish?"

He'd told her earlier he had cleared out the pond so that she could see the fish more clearly.

"Well now, I'll be finished here soon…" he said.

He never felt comfortable letting her go down to the pond by herself. Sylvia didn't like it, although sometimes he wondered if she didn't fuss too much. After all, Molly was getting a big girl now, she was at school, and Ben had told them she was almost swimming without armbands when he last took her to the local pool.

"I'll wait for you by the pond, Granddad. I'll be careful," Molly said.

"Now, you mind you are," he said. "Just stand on the edge. Don't lean over."

She was running off already, in the direction of the pond, Goldie barking at her heels. He raked the leaves into a pile. That evening he'd burn them in the garden incinerator.

He was remembering how I used to help him do this, in the big garden we had when we lived in Brighton. I used to help him do lots of things in the garden whilst my mother was busy with John in his infant years in the house. My father would stake out furrows for the seed and I'd squat by the furrow and pinch in the seed. We would try out all kinds of things: onions, radishes, carrots, turnips, lettuce and beetroot.

I stepped close to him. I felt the memories blowing through his heart. This weariness was making him sad. He held a hand up to his chest and felt an ache there.

Molly. Don't forget Molly.

He sighed deeply, and then walked over to the shed to put the garden rake away.

Molly. She's down by the pond.

He turned and walked down to the lower lawn, then through the wooden trellis to the stone steps that led to the lowest tier where the pond lay under the shelter of some elm trees. He saw Molly's red coat by the water. Goldie was standing by her side. This pain in his chest. This heartache.

He suddenly felt incredibly tired, like it was an effort to move his legs. Molly was standing at the edge of the pond, leaning over, holding out the net that he'd left there several days ago. He felt a flash of irritation. Hadn't he warned her about that?

"Molly," he called out, "be careful. Don't lean out like that." His voice sounded far away, as if he was hearing himself through a cloak, a veil. Neither Molly nor the dog seemed to have heard him; both were too intent at staring at something they could see in the water. Out there, towards the centre of the pond, nudging itself under a water lily, a goldfish, a dead goldfish, floating belly-up, its fat distended underbelly white and parched. Molly had seen dead goldfish before. Smaller ones, in the tank we used to keep in the living room in the house in Reigate. They had frightened her, the dead goldfish. They looked so unnatural, so *un-fishlike*, bobbing helplessly on the surface of the tank. I remember the first time she'd found a dead one floating belly-up I told her we needed to get it out quickly, because it would start to decay, which meant to go rotten, like food goes rotten if it's left in the bin. And that would not be good for the water or the other fish. I'd put on my Marigolds, fished it out by the tail and wrapped it in kitchen roll. I was going to chuck it in the bin or even down the toilet, but Molly stopped me. She said it deserved to be buried so it could go to heaven properly and live in God's goldfish bowl up there in the sky. I'd felt a warm rush of love for her then, for the wonderful image she'd placed in my mind of a giant goldfish bowl in heaven where all the dead goldfish can go and swim in peace.

We had gone down to the bottom of the garden where

I kept a small vegetable patch, so that I could teach Molly about growing things like my father had taught me. We dug a small hole amidst the runner bean stakes, planted the dead goldfish, and asked God to look after it for us.

Goldie had noticed him now. She started excitedly towards him, jolting into Molly's legs. Molly was leaning far out by now and the dog caught her off-balance. With a small scream of fear she tumbled forward into the water.

"Molly, Molly…!"

My father started forward into a run, but Goldie was galloping towards him, entangling herself with his legs, getting in his way.

"Goldie, not now…!"

He could see Molly struggling at the edge of the pond. She was grasping the reeds, trying to pull herself forward, trying to find a foothold amidst the root-filled baskets on the pond's perimeter shelf. The pond wasn't that deep, not even at its centre, but my father had heard of children getting drowned in bathwater. If she panicked, if she got tired…

He pushed the dog out of his way. He tried to run again, but his legs seemed to have given up working altogether. He fell down to his knees. There was a tight squeezing in his chest, a deep ache down his arms. He wasn't sure if he could see Molly anymore. Everything was merging into a haze of colour. He could see blue, green, brown, a blob of red in the centre of the colours. He thought he could hear a sound but wasn't sure what it was or where it came from.

He was lying on the ground now, his hand clutched to his chest.

There is a point, just before the light goes out of the body, when the two worlds collide together, the veil between them thinning and melting. I saw my father slide free of his body. He stood there, shaking his head, looking disorientated. He could see Molly still struggling at the edge of the water, still trying her best to find a foothold on to the shelf. She was screaming, crying, and her efforts were getting more frantic and more ineffectual. He wanted to go and help her, but he knew he was beyond that now. He looked over towards me.

"Rachel…"

"You can't stay. You have to go back."

"I miss you…"

"There are others who need you more. You can't stay. It isn't your time yet."

"You were so young… was it your time then?"

"Yes."

"Why?"

"I can't explain. One day it will be clear. Go back."

I knew he was seeing me, not as the age I appeared now – which was only a mask really, a projection, but as I was as a child, in that time when he and I were closest.

*

I am seven. My mother has tried to tame my unruly red hair into pigtails but they don't really work. They stick out like corkscrews from the side of my head. My nose is speckled with freckles. I am wearing blue corduroy jeans and my favourite jumper. The yellow one with the brown rabbit appliqué that my mother had knitted…

*

In the blink of an eye the decision had been made. My father was back.

He groaned as he lay on the grass. His lips were blue but he was breathing. I had to act fast. I was running out of time.

I was in the water, heaving Molly up on to the shelf. She could not feel anything, except perhaps this sudden, fresh surge of energy. Her knees were slipping on the algae covering the shelf. She was grasping at the reeds, at the marsh marigolds in their containers. She was pulling herself over the crazy-paved edging stones. She was lying on her belly on the grass, her little body heaving with effort. She was on her feet and running up to my father. She was on her knees, tugging at him, calling his name. Then she was running fast up to the house, Goldie at her heels, screaming at the top of her lungs for my mother.

41

My father woke up in intensive care. Sylvia had been sitting by his bedside for hours but had just gone out for a cup of coffee and a break. He lay there feeling like he used to feel as a child, waking at his grandparents' house in Torquay on the first morning of a holiday and not quite knowing where he was. He could see several other beds half-curtained from view. He looked over to his right. He could see the heart monitor screen, its thin blue line rising and falling in shallow peaks and troughs.

Is this all there is to life, this faltering pulse that could be extinguished at any time? he thought.

He lay there listening to the occasional blips and whirrs from the electrical equipment around him. His body felt light and spacious and incredibly at ease.

There's nothing really to fear. Dying doesn't hurt. It's easy. It's natural.

Images floated back to him, seemingly disconnected. A pile of leaves; Goldie running after a ball; Molly's red coat by the pond. He remembered calling out to her, and then the dog knocking her off balance; he had seen her tumble into the pond. He remembered feeling incredibly tired, the pain in his chest. His failure to reach her.

He remembered all these elements as if he had dreamt them, and yet he knew that he hadn't.

Molly! How is Molly?

He glanced around him. He could see a bleep button over his head. He reached up and pressed it, and within moments a nurse appeared.

"Mr Brooks? How are you feeling?"

"My wife," he said. "Is she here? I need to speak to her..."

Just at that moment my mother returned, bearing coffee in a takeaway cup.

"Sylvia... Molly... how is she... is she all right?"

My mother sat down beside him, put the coffee on the locker and held his hand. "She's fine, Ted. She's been wonderful. She came running up to the house to fetch me. You had a heart attack... you would have died if she hadn't."

Another memory was coming back to him. He remembered seeing himself lying on the ground. He was lying perfectly motionless. There was no sound of his breathing. All the colours around him – the green grass and blue sky, the elm trees turning rich golds and oranges, the vibrant yellow flowers of the Marsh Marigolds – were intensified. He imagined that it was a little like the experience of someone who'd been on hallucinatory drugs – although he himself had never been. He remembered seeing me. At first he'd seen me as I'd been on the day that I died; he thought it strange that I was wearing summer clothes – that light cotton dress with the tiny rosebuds and sandals on my feet – on a briskly cold day at the beginning of November. Then I seemed to metamorphose in his gaze to the way I'd been as a child. I was wearing that yellow jumper with the brown rabbit appliqué on the front that Sylvia had once made for me. My hair was in pigtails. He had the strangest feeling that he could at will make me any age he wanted to make me. This was the one he seemed to prefer.

When he'd heard me speak to him though, I had sounded the way he last remembered me. It was the adult voice that had spoken, not the child's.

Go home. It isn't your time. Others need you more than I do.

He looked over at Sylvia. She had tears in her eyes. He was suddenly overcome by a wave of tender love for her. He wanted to take all the feelings that she had – the sadness, the fear and anxiety – and change them into joy. He had the strangest feeling that it was possible to do this. That joy was something you come upon turning a corner from sadness. That the two were much closer than he'd ever thought before. That you could even stumble upon this joy after the pain of losing a child.

I died. I died, and then I returned again.

"I've been so scared, Ted. So scared I might have lost you."

At first he thought that the words sounded meaningless. That losing someone you love was never really possible. He squeezed her hand.

"You'll never do that," he said.

He wondered if he should tell her that he had died and then come back again. He wondered if he should tell her that he had seen me, and that I'd been all right.

"The strangest thing, Ted," Sylvia was saying. "Molly said that her mother was there by the pond. She didn't see her but she felt her, she said. She said that her mother helped her, gave her the strength to get out of the water. Do you think Ted, do you think it could be true?"

A tear was sliding out from Sylvia's eye and over her cheek. He reached up a hand and stopped it with his thumb before it could reach her mouth.

"Yes, I do," my father said. "I'm sure it's true. We never lose those that we love. They're with us always. They always will be."

I was standing at the foot of my father's bed but now I made myself disappear. I had another place I needed to be. They would be all right now. They didn't need me to stay.

42

It was Abigail's birthday. Gardiner sat in the cafe at the children's zoo with Abigail and her friend, Alice, stirring the foam on her latte. They had trooped around the zoo for hours and now they were all tired. It was time, soon, to go home.

Abigail's father was supposed to have spent the day with them, but he had phoned that morning to say that 'something had come up' and he couldn't make it. He'd pop in later that evening with Abigail's present before she went to bed, he'd said.

Abigail had been disappointed, of course; in fact, she had cried non-stop for twenty minutes, lying face down on her bed, which of course was a horrible thing for anyone to be doing on their birthday. I watched whilst Gardiner sat on the edge of Abigail's bed, her hand on her daughter's thin shaking shoulders, waiting for the sobs to subside. She hadn't tried to cajole Abigail out of her tears. She'd understood that grief was something that had to be endured and got through, and if she was totally honest with herself, she was slightly relieved that Abigail's father wasn't coming, which made her feel a little guilty. She would have put up with it, of course, the tension that would have sat in her stomach all afternoon, trailing around the zoo with her ex-husband by her side, as if they were just a normal family out with their daughter on her birthday. She would have put up with anything for her daughter's happiness. But it wouldn't have been easy. Bob would probably have been on good form, holding up well his veneer of jollity and amiability for this half a day on his daughter's birthday, but all the time she would have known that he was waiting for the excursion to come to an end so that he could rush back to his life and the young woman that now shared it with him. Chelsea. Aged twenty-four.

No doubt the important thing that had cropped up had a lot to do with Chelsea, who was very good at sabotaging these rare and precious visits with his daughter. *Even on her birthday, even then,* Gardiner thought fiercely.

She wasn't that good at hating. In her job, despite the despicable things that people did, she had learnt not to hate. Hating clouded issues, clouded decisions. She had learnt to remain calm, detached, dispassionate. Her job was to solve crimes, to bring the right people to justice. Judgements belonged to the courts. *And to God,* she thought. If you believed that sort of thing.

But sitting beside her daughter's sobbing body that morning she had hated the two of them intensely. Bob and his precious Chelsea.

*

They sat in the Lemon Tree Cafe. The girls were eating chocolate ice-cream sundaes, with plump cherries and those whirly cigar-shaped biscuits on the top. They were arguing good-naturedly about what animals they had found the most interesting. Abigail said the capuchin whilst Alice preferred the meerkats.

They were tired. Everyone was tired. The day was over. Gardiner thought about Bob's visit that evening. He would call around seven, knowing that, as Abigail was back at school in the morning, her bedtime was around eight, so he wouldn't have to stay long. He would be all smiles and hugs. He would say the nicest sweetest things to Abigail, which is easy to do when you're only a very occasional parent. He would give her an expensive present. A laptop perhaps, a new bike, a portable television for her bedroom.

And then he'd leave and go back to Chelsea, who would be excellent no doubt at massaging his ego, at vanquishing the small kernel of guilt he might feel at not having been there for his daughter's birthday outing.

Gardiner glanced around the cafe. There was a young mother trying to placate her bickering sons sitting across at another table. A young couple with a baby in a high chair. A middle-aged woman sitting on her own. She had that odd sensation again of being watched. *I was sitting as far away from her as I could, but even so she felt uneasy. No wonder. Despite the fact I was sitting at a distance, I was trying as hard as I could to plant thoughts in her head. Nicholas Hedges. Had he been telling the truth? It seemed so unlikely. It seemed such a misjudgement on Rachel Vincent's part, a professional woman, a psychologist, married with a child, having an affair with an ex-prisoner who had served time for a sex offence crime. It couldn't be true. Perhaps it had all been just part of his fantasy – something he had wanted to happen but hadn't really happened. Something he had made up.*

And yet she had to rule him out for the murder. His alibi had worked out back in June last year when he had been interviewed, as had all the other men in the group. And the timing was wrong. He'd said the affair had happened at the end of January; it was brief, nothing more really than a one-night stand. The murder had taken place in June. If revenge was his motivation why wait months?

She glanced at her watch. It was half-past four. The cafe was closing at five. It would take about half an hour or so to get home, perhaps a little more after she had dropped Alice off. She couldn't just rush away without having a chat with Alice's mother.

She was remembering what that Sharon Tyler had said. Nicholas Hedges was supposed to be coming at seven-thirty that evening to put up the shelves. She hoped with all her heart that the appointment had been cancelled, that Sharon Tyler had heeded what she'd told her about Hedges. She thought of that little boy, Leon. He was such a cute child, with that odd sense of knowing about him. She thought about the woman he'd said he'd seen at his bedroom window, the one with the long red hair that his mother had dismissed so readily as being 'just his imaginary friend'. Rachel Vincent's hair had been long and red. And hadn't she herself thought she had seen, ever so briefly, a woman with long red hair on Halloween night, standing down the garden close to where the children were rushing around?

And in spite of the weather, which had been cold and frosty, the woman seemed to be wearing a skimpy dress, exposing tanned arms and legs.

She dismissed the thought immediately. She was a police inspector. She wasn't given to such fanciful notions. She had only imagined it. Like she imagined that feeling of being watched sometimes. Like she'd imagined that sensation of her mother's hands on her shoulders when she was a child…

She finished her coffee and carrot cake. The two girls were giggling stupidly, probably over the fact that they each had a thick creamy moustache of chocolate ice-cream above their upper lips. She glanced at her watch. If she left now and drove home quickly, and if she dropped Alice off with some excuse about needing to get home for Abigail's father to visit, then she'd have plenty of time to get to Redhill easily before half-seven. Her own father would come over and babysit Abigail. He would be better than she was at putting on social niceties for Bob. And she'd have to arrange for Sergeant Williams to come with her to Redhill. Something told her she shouldn't go alone.

She got her mobile out of her pocket and began to dial the number for her father's house…

43

The time was half-past seven. Nicholas Hedges sat in his usual chair by the window. He was watching Sharon's house. Waiting for the boyfriend to arrive in the black Saab. I stood behind him, looking over his shoulder. He shivered after a while, as if he was cold.

Half an hour went by. Still no sign of the boyfriend's car. He wouldn't be coming tonight.

Nicholas got up abruptly and went to the wardrobe. He took out the box of photographs again. He tipped them on to the bed. Some fell face up and some face down. He rifled through them quickly. His face looked agitated. There was a tense energy about his movements, snatching up photos, peering at them sharply, then slapping them down again. Then he found the one he was looking for. It was the one of himself as a small boy standing with his mother on Southend promenade. She is smiling into the camera and he is frowning. He stared at it hard. His thoughts fell like shadows in the room. He was thinking what a bitch she looked in the photo, what a tart. He could see the dark roots coming through her bleached hair, the heavy black eyeliner she was wearing. The hardness around her mouth. She had her arms crossed over his chest as if she was a loving mother but he knew that was only a show put on for whoever was behind the camera taking the picture. Some man, of course. Some man she wanted to impress.

I felt his feelings as if they were my own. The knot of tension that had been in his stomach all day was rising now into his throat. It was hard and painful and could only be dissolved if he could find some way to turn it into tears. But he couldn't do that; he could never do that. He wasn't a wimp, a ninny, a gay. He had a flashback to the children's home where he'd been sent on a few occasions between the ages of ten and fourteen, when his mother would take off for weeks at a time with the latest man that she'd attracted. The other kids had laughed at him when he'd broken down and cried – which he had done a few times on the earlier visits until he soon learnt not to show tears. Never to show tears. To only cry on the inside.

And then, after a while, not even then. All that was left, this cold hard stone that used to be his heart.

Stone hearts don't hurt. They never hurt. He preferred it that way.

He got to his feet and fetched a pair of nail scissors from a small pot on the dresser. He sat down again on the bed. He picked up the photo and carefully, very carefully, cut around the image of the boy with the ambiguous smile and blond mop of hair. He enjoyed the way he could cut through the woman's arms just above the wrists, leaving her slender hands crossed over the boy's chest. He reached into the back pocket of his jeans for his wallet and slipped the little boy inside it. Then he picked up the rest of the photo, showing only a childless woman now, with hands severed just above the wrists. He scrunched it up slowly and put it in the bin.

He left the rest of the photos on the bed.

He was ready. I knew he was ready. He pulled out another drawer in the dresser. This one had scarves in it, and gloves, and a black woollen balaclava that for some reason he had kept since those days in the children's home, when long hikes in the countryside in all weathers had been mandatory. A member of the staff had knitted it for him, to keep the winter wind from chilling his face. Her name had been Josie; she had been plump and warm and motherly. Everything really that his own mother hadn't been, which was probably the reason he had kept it all these years. Sometimes in the winter when he had a job to do outside – repairing someone's fencing, putting up a shed, laying a patio – he would put on the balaclava. He enjoyed the feeling of anonymity it gave him. He put it on now. It could be worn different ways and usually he pulled the bottom section down so that both his eyes and his nose were revealed and breathing was easier. But this time he pulled it up so only his eyes showed through the gap. He wrapped a scarf around his neck and put on a donkey jacket. He pulled on his work boots, laced them up. He looked tough. He wanted to look tough. He wanted to frighten her. *Serves her right. She's a slag. All women are slags…*

He walked into the kitchen and slid the largest knife out from the knife block. He hid it inside the jacket, keeping his hand pressed to his chest to stop it falling through.

He picked up his keys from the hallway and quickly

went out of the flat and down the two flights of stairs to the lobby area below. I followed him down. He met no one on the way, which was a relief. He walked quickly across the lawned area at the front of the flats, and crossed the road over to the bungalow. He took no notice of the dark Ford Focus that was coming down the road towards him, slowing down, as if the driver was getting ready to park near the flats. He glanced at his watch under the light of a street lamp. *Nearly half-past eight.* The little boy should be in bed. He would leave him there. If he woke up, then he'd have to deal with him, he was thinking. I sensed the thought and it chilled my blood, or would have done, if I'd still had blood to chill.

He lifted the latch on the garden gate. The gate squeaked a bit when he let himself through it. He looked up quickly towards the front living-room window where he could see, around the edges of the curtains, that a light was on. Nobody tweaked the curtain, nobody looked out; he was all right. He walked gingerly around to the side of the bungalow. He passed the shed, and tried the shed door. It was unlocked. He went inside.

I knew what he was looking for. He was looking for a tool in case he had to break the window. They were all double-glazed windows; it would take a hefty weight to break one but he would be willing to go that far. He came out with a club hammer. It made me draw back for a while, the sight of the club hammer. I still remembered what that had felt like, the sudden blow on the back of my head.

He held the knife now in one hand and the club hammer in the other. He walked around to the back of the bungalow. The garden light came on automatically when he reached the patio at the back. He could see now what he was hoping for. A window had been left slightly open to let in some fresh night air. And because he had been here before, he knew immediately which bedroom the window belonged to. Leon's room. The little boy's room.

He stooped down and placed the club hammer on the patio flagstones. He wouldn't need it now. He walked up to Leon's window. The curtain was drawn and there was no light on inside the room. He slid his hand through the gap in the casements and caught hold of the window lever. He half pulled, half pushed the window wide open, wedging the top half of his body through to manage it. He held back the curtain with his arm and looked inside. The little boy was sleeping. Sleeping on his stomach with his head turned sideways onto the pillow, a small curled fist near his mouth. On his bedside cabinet there was a white cylinder-shaped night-light with little blue space rockets zooming over its surface. Nicholas Hedges put the handle of the knife in his mouth and gripped it with his teeth. He hauled himself up with his hands onto the window-ledge; he swung his legs over and into the room. The child stirred but didn't wake. I entered the room the usual way, walking through the wall. The rough brick didn't touch me.

Nicholas Hedges started out across the carpet towards the bedroom door. He hesitated by the pillow with the child's sleeping head upon it… He looked down at him. Little, sleeping, blond-haired boys can almost look like angels. And Leon did. He looked like an angel. Perhaps he was an angel. Nicholas Hedges stared down at that angelic face and I knew what he was thinking. He himself had been that young once, that beautiful, that angelic. How come his own mother hadn't loved him for it, or hadn't loved him more? Why did this mother love her child and his mother hadn't loved him? The knot of tension was back in his belly. No. This woman, this Sharon, didn't love the boy properly. She couldn't do. She was no better than his own mother had been. She was a slag, a whore – like his mother had been. She let men friends stay the night whilst the child was sleeping. She shagged them in her bedroom next door, not caring a damn whether the child woke and heard them.

He gripped the knife tightly in his right hand. He opened the bedroom door and crept out into the hallway. He could hear sounds from the television leaking through the living-room door. He closed Leon's bedroom door, leaving me behind.

I leaned over Leon's sleeping head. I breathed my cold breath on his cheek. *Leon. Wake up Leon.* He didn't wake. He was deep in his dream-world. I entered his dreams.

*

He is running through a field after a dog. He doesn't know what kind of dog it is, other than it is golden haired and large. But most dogs are large to him, and beautiful. He hasn't got a dog but his mother said to him the other day that when he is bigger he can have one, and he said, how big would he need to be? His mother said, big enough to look after it and take it for walks. He wondered how big he would have to be to do that. He decided, probably very big. So until then he had his dream dog, this golden one with the flamboyantly waving tail, rushing on over the green grass with him rushing after it. Then all of a sudden, into the dream comes the lady with flame-coloured hair, wearing a dress with tiny roses upon it. She is smiling at him and calling his name. He is turning now from the dog, the dog is lost to him. His warm hand is held by the lady's cool one. He is getting up now from the bed. He is pushing his feet into his slippers. The lady is leading him quickly out of his room and across the hallway towards the front door. He can hear noises coming from the living room. It frightens him because it sounds like his mother screaming. Then the screams are being muffled and he can hear the grim angry voice of a man. He wants to tell the lady who is leading him that he can't follow her – he must go in there and help his mother. But the lady is opening the front door. She half pushes him through it, half tugs him down the garden path towards the gate. Outside the air is sharp and cold and it snatches at his breath. The moon floats on its back before him like a melon that has been cut in half. There is a car parked across the road. Two people are getting out of it and running towards him. One is a man in a policeman's uniform. The other is a lady he thinks he has seen before.

"You all right, son?" the policeman says. But he hardly stops to find out. The policeman can hear the muffled screams too, and rushes past him into the house. He finds himself scooped up into the arms of the lady. He is not frightened of her; he recognises her. She is a sort of police lady. She came to visit the other day. He had liked her because she believed him when he had told her about the lady that he sometimes sees when his mother doesn't.

"She's here," he is saying to the police lady. "She's here with me now." He squirms around in her arms trying to look back at me, as the police lady carries him across the road to *the car. She turns to glance back towards the bungalow but in the blink of an eye, I am gone.*

"I know, I believe you, Leon," I hear Gardiner telling him before I go.

44

Sharon Tyler, thank God, was unhurt. Other than the mental trauma she had suffered having someone wearing a black balaclava break into her house, threaten her with a knife and attempt to rape her.

*

She had jumped immediately to her feet when the man had entered the room, her heart in her throat. Then she'd recognised the clothes the man was wearing. The donkey jacket, the jeans, the leather boots, the blue scarf knotted against his throat. She saw him wearing those clothes sometimes on a Saturday morning when he walked down to the garages to fetch his van.

"That doesn't fool me at all, that thing you're wearing on your face. It's Nick, isn't it?"

"Take off your blouse."

"Why are you doing this?"

"I said, take it off."

He brandished the knife towards her pointing it towards her chest. She undid the blouse and let it fall to the carpet. She stood there on the rug in her jeans and a black satin bra. He walked up to her, touched the blade of the knife against the skin of her neck.

"Where's your boyfriend tonight, Sharon?" His voice was cold, edged with mockery.

"I'm not seeing him tonight. It's over between us." She tried to make her voice sound strong and confident. She'd gone out with a policeman once who told her that psychopathic types feed off other people's fear.

"I don't believe you."

His left hand was undoing the top button of her jeans, his right still holding the knife close to her throat.

She struggled to pull away from him. "Stop it, please… stop it!" She wasn't able now to keep the fear out of her voice.

He thrust his hand down the half unbuttoned jeans. She screamed, pulled away, tried to yank his hand out of her knickers.

"Don't you like that, Sharon. Bet you like it when lover boy does it."

She put her hands up against his chest and tried to push him off. He took his hand out of her jeans and grabbed her right arm. His grip was hard, he was hurting her. She yelled out in pain.

"Take them off." His voice was icy.

She shook her head furiously.

He pushed the knife up against the skin of her neck again. This time it left a faint line of blood. She screamed.

"Shut it, bitch. Do you want to wake your kid?"

She thought of Leon waking up, coming out of his

room, walking in to confront this scene. She shuddered. She couldn't bear the thought of that.

"Are you going to do it? Or do I have to do it for you?"

She pulled down the jeans, slipped out of them, stood before him in her underwear, shaking with anger or fear, or both.

"Lie down there," he said. He indicated the sofa with a movement of the knife.

She lay down on it. The leather was cold against her back.

He placed the knife on the coffee table and lay on top of her, but before anything else could happen she suddenly came out of whatever deep-freeze state she was in. She bit him, she kicked and screamed. He tried to ram his arm up under her throat to restrain her, but it wasn't easy. She was strong. Strong on hate and fear.

And that's when Williams had burst in upon them. Hedges had tried to leap to his feet, tried to reach for the knife again, but the sergeant was a large hefty man, armed with a truncheon and pepper spray. He overpowered Hedges, handcuffed him, and pinned him to the floor.

*

I knew all this because I was there with Sharon, watching from the back of the room, when Gardiner returned later to take down her statement, having safely delivered Leon into the care of his father for the night.

I was also there when Nicholas Hedges was charged with attempted rape and assault, and locked up in a cell down at the station.

What did I feel? The sweet taste of vengeance?

I thought I would feel that. But what I really felt was sad. That a little boy was once so damaged that he'd grown up not knowing anything about love.

I didn't think I would ever feel that.

45

Katie had arranged with Ben that Molly's last session would take place at her own home rather than at the clinic. "I want her to feel relaxed," she'd said.

Ben had agreed. He was feeling in a different mood now about the whole thing. On Monday, Gardiner had phoned him and told him that Nicholas Hedges had been arrested for attempted rape and assault of a neighbour, but had been ruled out completely as a suspect to my murder. She hadn't mentioned Nicholas Hedges' revelation about my having had consensual sex because by now she was beginning to think that it was highly unlikely. That if anything had happened it was more probable that he had forced himself on me too, but as there was no likelihood of proving it why rock the boat after all this time? Why take away from Ben the beliefs that had sustained him about our marriage? That I had always loved him, always been faithful. Even though he hadn't been.

She didn't, of course, know about Molly's drawing, and the unsettling doubt it had planted in Ben's mind.

"What will happen to him now?" Ben had asked.

By his response, I can assume that she told him it was very probable that Hedges would be assessed as having a very serious personality disorder and sent to a high security hospital.

"Broadmoor – that kind of place, do you mean?" Ben had said. "It's supposed to be virtually impossible to get out of those kind of places, isn't it?"

He sat now on Katie's worn leather sofa. Molly sat on a small tub chair next to Katie's armchair, clasping Miss Moffat on her lap. The doll's house that Ben had made, the one that resembled our old house, was on the coffee table in front of them. Katie stood up and drew the curtains in the bay window. The clocks had gone back now and, although it was barely four o'clock, it was already dusk. She turned the dimmer switch down and softened the light in the room. A fire burnt in the grate and the room had a cosy, warm atmosphere that made Ben feel more relaxed. He had wondered, all the way over here in the car, if he really should be doing this, putting Molly through this one last time. Didn't he know the truth now, not about who had murdered me, but about whether or not I'd had an affair. But maybe this session would help Molly – help her to exorcise the last of her demons. If there were demons still to be exorcised.

Anyway, now he was here it seemed churlish to entertain doubts. He reached over and squeezed Molly's hand reassuringly. Katie sat down again.

"Tell me, Molly," she said. "How have you been? The last time we met you said you weren't getting the bad dreams anymore. Are you still not getting them?"

Molly looked over towards Ben for reassurance. He smiled encouragingly at her.

"No, I don't think so. Do I, Daddy?"

"I don't think so, Molls. But you're the best one to say."

"Well, I don't," she said more firmly.

"Are you getting on well at school? Are you making friends?"

I could see Chloe and Charlie in her thoughts, her teacher, Miss Austin.

"Yes. School is nice."

"That's good, Molly. Now, can you think back to the last time we met? Can you remember what we did?"

Molly glanced over, a little anxiously, towards her father again. "Yes. We played with the doll's house. That one, the one Daddy made."

She indicated with a movement of her head the doll's house on the coffee table.

"That's right, Molly."

Katie took out the box of little wooden peg dolls. The furniture and furnishings that Molly had chosen were still in the doll's house.

"Do you remember what dolls you chose for yourself and Mummy and Daddy? Would you like to choose the same ones again? Or maybe different ones if you prefer?"

Molly reached over and picked out the same dolls again. She placed them on their backs on the coffee table next to the doll's house. She glanced up at Katie expectantly.

"Molly, I want you to look at these drawings that you did again." Katie took them out from the portfolio and showed them to Molly. There was the tiger-butterfly tattoo drawing and the one of me kissing a man with blond hair.

"Do you still remember drawing the tiger-butterfly tattoo Molly? You said that you dreamt about the time when a man with a tattoo like this on his arm came to the front door. You said he was cross and he shouted at Mummy."

Molly nodded. She grasped Miss Moffat closer to her chest.

"And do you remember when you drew the other picture, Molly? We talked about it the last time we met. Daddy asked you about it and you said it was a man kissing Mummy. You said the man wasn't Daddy; it was another man. You gave him yellow hair because his hair was blond. Do you remember that, Molly?"

Molly glanced a little fearfully over towards her father.

"It doesn't matter, darling. You just tell Katie what you remember. I don't mind, whatever it is," Ben told her gently.

"Was it the same man, Molly? This man who was kissing Mummy? Was he also the man with the tiger-butterfly tattoo?"

"I think so. I think I saw it in the car."

"In the car? Mummy gave him a lift?"

"He was driving the car, not Mummy. We'd been to see the big Christmas tree."

"In London, Molly? The one at Trafalgar Square?" Ben asked her. He turned to Katie. "Rachel took Molly up to see it just before that Christmas. I think that was the weekend I went up to see my sister in York…"

Katie gave him a very slight shake of her head to indicate she'd rather he didn't interrupt. He gave an apologetic gesture. Katie turned back to Molly.

"Molly, can you find a doll in the box that looks like the man with the tattoo?"

Molly reached over. She picked up several of the 'man dolls' and then put them down again. She returned to one that had blue jeans on and a red tee-shirt. His hair was yellow.

"This one," she said.

"Did you ever see him again, Molly? After that time when he came to the house and was cross. Do you remember ever seeing him again?"

"I don't know."

Molly sat there for a moment, a closed-up expression clouding her face again. She pressed Miss Moffat's lumpy tummy against her cheek. Then she suddenly reached forward and picked up the Mummy doll from the coffee table, bent back her jointed little wooden legs and placed her in a kneeling position on the black and white tiles in the kitchen of the doll's house. She picked up the Molly doll and stood it in front of the Mummy one.

"It's too big," Molly said. "I was very little then. Mummy should be bigger than me even if she is kneeling down."

"Mummy is kneeling down in front of you in the kitchen, Molly?"

"Yes. Mummy always kneels down in front of me when she has something very important to say. She kneels so that I can see her better, I think."

"What does she say that's important, Molly?"

I could sense the tension in the room. I could hear Ben's heart beating.

"She says that was a bad man who came to the door and if he ever comes again I must hide."

"Mummy tells you that you must hide? Where does she tell you to hide?"

Molly opened up the hardboard door under the stairs. There was a space here that extended back the length of the staircase, just as it did on the real house we used to live in. The house where I died. Molly picked up the Molly doll and bent her into a sitting position and squashed her inside the space. Because the doll was too big the top of her head pushed up the cardboard stairway and made a hump in it.

"Under the stairs. That's where Mummy wants me to hide."

"And did the bad man come again, Molly?"

Molly nodded.

"Where were you when the bad man came?"

She took the Molly doll out from her hiding place and put her in her bedroom upstairs.

"So you were playing in your room, Molly? What were you playing?"

"I wasn't playing. Mummy had sent me to my room."

"Why did she send you to your room, Molly?"

"I don't remember. I was naughty and Mummy was cross."

"When do you come downstairs, Molly? What makes you come downstairs?"

"I can hear noises. Scary noises."

"What kind of noises, Molly? Who is making them?"

I stood behind my daughter and I placed my two cold hands lightly on her small shoulders. I leant down and I kissed the top of her dark head.

It's all right, darling. You mustn't be frightened now. It's all over now. You're safe.

"Mummy screaming. I can hear Mummy screaming."

Tears were rolling down her cheeks. Ben leant over

towards her and tried to hug her but her body was tense and rigid. She struggled away from his grasp.

"It's all right, Ben. Let her finish her story. Molly, what did you do? Show me with the doll what you did?"

She picked up the Molly doll and placed her in the hallway by the open kitchen door.

"What do you see, Molly? Is there someone there, besides Mummy?"

She nods.

"Do you know who it is?"

Molly picked up the doll with the yellow hair. She stood him in the kitchen near the door that led out into the garden.

"It's the man that came to the house earlier, isn't it? The man with the tattoo on his arm?"

Molly nodded.

"You can see the man in the kitchen with Mummy. What is he doing there, Molly?"

Molly picked up the Mummy doll from her kneeling position, straightened her legs, and placed her with her back against a cardboard kitchen cupboard. She picked up the yellow-haired man doll, and pressed him up against her. She pressed the doll with so much force against the other one that the cardboard cupboard and work-surface bowed with the pressure. When Molly released her grasp the two dolls toppled towards the floor. I looked at Ben's face. It was whitened with anger. His jaw was fixed and tense. I wanted to slide my cool hand into his warm one.

It's all right, Ben. I'm over it. It doesn't hurt anymore. Nothing hurts anymore.

"And where are you, Molly?"

She opened the hardboard door again to the space under the stairs. She squashed the Molly doll back inside.

"Are you frightened, Molly, hiding under the stairs?"

"A little," she answered. Her voice sounded very small and timid, like a younger child. "But I have Miss Moffat with me. Miss Moffat is keeping me safe."

"What happens next, Molly?"

Molly picked up the yellow-haired man doll and put him back in the wooden box that contained all the different dolls. She picked up the Mummy doll from the kitchen floor, bent her legs forward so that she was sitting, and shoved her inside the cupboard next to the Molly doll. Now two heads bumped up against the cardboard staircase and, instead of stairs, it looked like a humped bridge.

"Mummy's crying," Molly said. "'Don't tell Daddy,' she says. 'Don't tell Daddy the bad man came back.'"

"Okay, that's enough, Katie." Ben leapt to his feet. He crossed over the room to Molly. He picked her up and hugged her tight. Miss Moffat slipped out of her arms and fell softly to the floor.

"No more memories. No more." Ben's voice was thick with emotion. "Let's bury the past now. Let's leave it alone."

*

I slipped away then, leaving them together, Molly and Ben and Katie. I slipped out of that cosy fire-lit room into the cold November evening. I longed for that other warm welcoming room full of people waiting for me. The one I've glimpsed beyond the glass. I longed to see their smiles, feel their tender hands upon me.

It wouldn't be long now. It was almost over.

46

My father's small suitcase was repacked with the items that had been brought in for him by my mother. His pyjamas, toiletries bag, paperback books, a small radio with earphones. He said goodbye to all the nurses and told them how wonderful they had been – those that were on duty at the time – and then he and my mother linked arms and walked slowly out of the ward and down to the lifts.

Outside it was already dark, although it was only half-past four. My father stood just outside the entrance to the reception area and breathed in the cool November air, felt the breath enter his body, and with it the smell of dying leaves. Car doors slammed and opened, voices rang out greetings. A middle-aged man supported an older man who walked very slowly back into the building. A young woman pushed an older woman in a wheelchair over towards a waiting car. My father felt the thickness and throb of humanity around him and was so glad to be alive.

I stood watching him. Standing next to me was a young,

very thin man. Little more than a teenager really. He was clad in pyjamas and dressing gown and was smoking, despite being linked up to a drip trolley. I could sense the cancer cells dividing and multiplying throughout his body and I knew that he hadn't long to live. I lay my cool hand very gently on the young man's back. He shuddered slightly, as if he could feel death standing close by.

I watched until my parents had disappeared into the trees that ringed the car park and into the gathering darkness.

*

Molly lay her crayon down on the coffee table next to the open sketch book.

"What's it like in heaven, Daddy?"

Ben looked up at her, startled, from over the top of the newspaper.

"Why do you ask, darling?"

"Because Mummy's there, isn't she? Is it nice there? Will we all go to heaven when we die?"

"It's very nice there," he said, gently. "It's everything you want it to be."

"Will I be able to do my drawing there? And play games with my friends? And eat ice-cream?"

"Yes, darling. All those things. Everything you want. But you won't go there until you're a very old lady. That's a very very long time away."

"But Mummy wasn't a very old lady and she went there. And if I'm very old I won't want to eat ice-cream and play games, will I?"

"Well, if you want to you'll be able to." He sounded a little unsure of himself now. What do very old ladies do in heaven?

"Will we all be together one day in heaven? Mummy and you and me."

"Yes, darling. Yes, I think so."

"But what if you get married again Daddy, and I have a new mummy? Will she be in heaven with us, too?"

"I don't know, sweetheart." He was being honest now. He was floundering in the apparent lack of logic. "Is that what's bothering you, Molly? That I might get married again? Won't you like it if I do?"

She wrinkled her nose. "I don't think I will mind if you do. It's just that I want us all to be in heaven one day when we die, and if you marry another lady then you might have to be with her instead."

He smiled at her. "I think we'll work it all out, darling. I think people who love each other can all be together in heaven and nobody minds. Nobody gets jealous, or anything like that."

"That's all right, then, Daddy. You can get married again if you want to one day. And anyway, I might grow up and marry Charlie Craddock. Then he'll have to be in heaven with us too, won't he?"

He laughed. "Yes, I expect he will, darling." He was beginning to think this heaven sounded a bit crowded and wanted to change the subject. He put the newspaper down on the floor and leaned forward to look at her drawing.

"What are you drawing, Molls?"

She held up her sketch book for him to see. There were three people floating in a blue space under a big yellow sun. In the middle was a small figure, a child perhaps, in a blue jumper with a red heart on her chest and long dark hair streaming behind her, which no doubt was meant to be Molly herself. On her left, holding her hand, a man with dark hair who could have been Ben, and on her right, a woman with a mass of flame-red curls in a dress with red dots on it. All the figures had wide pink mouths curved up into big smiles and under their feet were flowers. Pink and purple flowers, with golden eyes at their centres.

"That's lovely, Molly."

"It's a picture of us in heaven. But I've left out Goldie."

At the sound of her name, Goldie stirred herself as she slept before the fire. Ben and Molly had been looking after her whilst my father had been in hospital, so my mother had been free to visit him as often as she wanted.

"I haven't done Granny and Granddad yet, but I will. Granddad nearly got to heaven to see Mummy, didn't he? But now he'll have to wait until later."

"Yes, darling," Ben said softly. I felt his heart swell. He was touched by the strangeness of life. I had been murdered, and yet he and Molly had survived and now good things had entered their world. Molly had saved her Granddad from dying. Some strange force had helped her that day, too, given her the energy to get out of the pond. She had told him her mummy had helped her; he had put that thought to the back of his mind as one of life's insolvable mysteries. He was in love with Katie Clements and Molly was in love with Charlie Craddock. Perhaps he and I had both lost faith in each other for a while back then, in a time that no longer belonged to the present and could no longer be understood.

How much did it really matter now, and how easy was it to forgive?

*

How easy is it to forgive?

47

Gardiner knocked on the door of Peter Bates' house. Mrs Bates opened the door, just wide enough to peer antagonistically through the opening.

"Yes?"

"Inspector Gardiner." She flashed her ID badge. "And this is Sergeant Williams. You might remember me, Mrs Bates? I interviewed your son, Peter, in connection with the murder of Rachel Vincent in June last year."

"What do you want?" The tone was hostile.

"Is Peter in?"

"What's it to do with you?"

"I'd like to ask him a few questions. May we come in?"

The door stayed partially closed. "What's it to do with?"

"It's just a few enquiries in relation to Rachel Vincent's murder. It won't take long."

"Thought you'd finished with him. He didn't do it. You might as well clear off. You're wasting your time."

"It won't take long, Mrs Bates. May we come in, please?"

The door was grudgingly opened. Gardiner and the

sergeant stepped into the hallway, with its clutter and greasy carpets. The door closed again. But of course doors are no problem to me, and neither are walls. In the blink of an eye I stood in Peter's room. He sat on the bed, smoking one of his roll-ups. He heard his mother calling for him up the stairs. He went to the bedroom door and opened it.

"What is it, Mum?"

"Two coppers here to talk to you, Pete. You'd better come down."

I heard him take a sharp intake of breath. His thin cheeks started working nervously. He took a hard drag on the roll-up.

"What do they want?"

"How do I know? You better get down here and find out."

He shut the door. *Oh my God! Oh my God.*

The time has come, now. The time has come when you can be free. You only need to tell the truth.

But he didn't hear me. He started to pace the room in agitation. He stopped before the wardrobe door. He opened it and reached up to the top shelf to fumble amongst the bedding that was stored there. His hand seemed to find what it was looking for. He closed the wardrobe door again.

Oh my God! Oh my God!

He stubbed the roll-up out on an overspilling ashtray on a cabinet by the bed.

The time has come, Peter. The time always comes.

He picked up a comb from the top of his dresser and raked it through his thin dark hair. He peered at his face in the mirror.

What do they want?

"Pete! You coming down, or what?" The sound of his mother again, calling from the bottom of the stairs.

He took a deep breath. He opened the bedroom door and went downstairs.

They were in the living room waiting for him. Gardiner and Sergeant Williams were seated on the grubby washed-out pink velour sofa. His mother stood in the middle of the room with a face like thunder.

"Took your time, Pete."

"Sit down, Mr Bates. We're just here to ask you a few more questions about Rachel Vincent's murder. It won't take long," Gardiner said.

Peter sat down awkwardly on the edge of an armchair. He had to move a scattering of his mum's women's magazines to the floor to make room for himself. He fumbled in his pocket for his tobacco and papers and started to roll another cigarette. His hands were shaking. Only very slightly but enough for me to notice. And Gardiner.

"He didn't do it," his mother said.

"No one is saying he did," Gardiner replied.

"What you here for, then?"

"Mrs Bates, I think it would be better if we saw your son on his own. Would you mind leaving the room for a while."

"Don't see why I have to. My house, ain't it?"

"Please, Mrs Bates. If you don't, then we might have to ask Peter to accompany us to the station to help us with our enquiries. I'm sure you would rather that was avoided. It would obviously be more stressful for your son."

Mrs Bates glared at her. "Well, this better not take long. You said it wouldn't."

"I don't anticipate it necessarily taking long, Mrs Bates. Now, if you don't mind…"

"I'll be in the kitchen, Pete. Don't let them bully you. Just remember, you ain't done nothing wrong."

He shook his head. "Be all right, Mum."

With a final parting glare at Gardiner, Mrs Bates left the room. Gardiner turned her attention fully now to Peter Bates.

"Now, Mr Bates, I just want to try and think back to some of the things you said when you were interviewed in June last year, in regard to Rachel Vincent's murder. If you can bear with me for a moment, I've got the transcript of the interview here in my briefcase…" She opened up the briefcase and fumbled amongst its contents. She drew out the sheaf of papers. "Now let me see… Ah yes, here it is. You were asked at what time you walked your dog that morning and what was the route that you had taken."

"I can't remember what was said. But if you're saying that you asked me that, then you did, I suppose."

"Yes, well we did. You replied that you had left the house about twelve noon. You said you had turned right into the main road and walked down to the entrance to Gale Lane. You had walked up Gale Lane to where the road divides and had taken the right turn. You had proceeded up the lane, past Rachel Vincent's house, and then continued to the end of Gale Lane to where it joins the main road again. I have a statement here made by one of Rachel Vincent's neighbours just before the time of your interview. She confirmed that you were on Gale Lane at about the time you said you were. She's a retired lady, was often at home."

"Yeah well, so what?"

"I want you to try and remember walking past Rachel Vincent's back garden that day."

"It was a long time ago. How am I supposed to remember...?"

"Mr Bates, did you try the back garden gate as you walked past? Did you try and find out if it was open or not?"

"No, 'course not. What do you take me for?"

"Well, by your own admission at that interview I take you for a man who has an occasional compulsion to steal women's knickers from their washing line. Washing was out on Rachel Vincent's washing line that day. You told us in your interview back then that you had stolen knickers from Rachel's garden several times."

"Once. I said once."

"Well, in this transcript here you admitted to taking them several times."

"Well, I don't know. Maybe. I only remember the one time now."

"Can you remember what colour knickers you took that one time, Mr Bates?"

"Black. Could be black."

"In your interview you stated that the last time you stole knickers from Rachel's washing line they were red satin ones. You were quite specific. Your room was searched later on and red ones were found that Rachel's husband identified as looking like a missing pair of his wife's."

"Well, what you asking me for if you've got it all there written down. How am I supposed to remember what I said all that time ago?"

Gardiner ignored the irritability building in his voice.

"That morning when you took your walk. The neighbour's statement said that she saw you about quarter-past twelve. She could be quite accurate about the time because she said she always had her lunch at twelve-thirty and it was just before that. She said she was in the back garden taking in the washing because it had started to spot with rain."

"Yeah well, what if she did?"

"Do you remember it raining that day, Mr Bates?"

"I dunno."

"When you walked past Rachel's back garden, can you recall whether you could see if she had any washing on the line?"

All the time he had been speaking his right hand had been plucking nervously on the material of his trousers just above his knee. Now his foot was tapping too, and his mouth working strangely; he was sucking in, then relaxing, his pock-marked cheeks. I almost felt sorry for him. (*How easy is it to forgive?*) He had stubbed out his roll-up and now he began to roll another. A man rolling a cigarette cannot disguise his shaking hands.

"No, don't think so. No, no washing. She must have taken it in. Because of the rain, I suppose…"

"Are you sure…?"

"Yeah, sure. Sure as I can be now."

"Mr Bates, I think you should know that I have sent Sergeant Williams over to Rachel Vincent's back garden gate. The people who live there have not changed it; it is the same gate as it was on the day in question. Sergeant Williams is clearly a little taller than you, yet he has stated that when he stands in the lane behind the gate and the fence – that are approximately the same height – he cannot see anything at all in the garden. He can't look over the gate or the fence, Mr Bates. So you wouldn't have been able to see if washing was on the line…"

"Well, I thought I did. I thought I could see… Now you're telling me different. Why you asking then? Why are you asking if you know the answers?" His agitation was rising, he was almost shouting.

If you tell the truth you'll be free. That's all it takes…

"Because I would rather hear the answers from you, Mr Bates." Gardiner stayed calm.

"Well then. No, I couldn't have, could I? Must have been mistaken."

"So are you still saying there was no washing on the line?"

"How would I know if there was or not? I wouldn't have been able to see it, you said."

"Well, you might if you had opened the gate and gone into the garden."

"Why should I bloody well do that?"

"May I put it to you, Mr Bates, because you intended to steal another pair of knickers from Rachel Vincent's line?"

"No, I didn't, I didn't do that…" The anger was turning to fear now. His whole body seemed to be shaking.

"You took black ones from the line. But Rachel Vincent saw you do it. She came out into the garden and had some words with you. And then you gave them back. You dropped them into the washing basket that was on the grass."

Tell the truth and you will be free now.

He started to sob. Deep choking sobs that racked his body.

"I didn't mean to do it. I tried to give them back to her. But she was still angry. She said she was going to phone the police. Have them send me back to prison again. I just wanted to stop her phoning. Didn't want to go back there. You don't know what it's like there, what they did to me before…"

His words were swallowed up in the sobs. Mrs Bates burst into the room. Perhaps she'd been listening outside the door.

"Are you bloody satisfied, now? Look at the state of him! Look what you've done with your questions…"

"Mr Bates," Gardiner continued, her voice still calm and controlled, "did you pick up the club hammer that lay on top of the rabbit hutch in the garden? Did you strike Rachel Vincent with it?"

"Pete, don't say a word, don't answer…!"

But he didn't seem to hear his mother, didn't seem to care anymore. "I didn't mean to hurt her. I just wanted to stop her phoning the police. I couldn't go back there to prison, you see. I couldn't go back."

"Did you strike her with the club hammer, Peter?" Gardiner's voice was almost gentle.

"Yes, yes I did. I hit her. I picked up the club hammer and hit her on the back of the head. I only hit her once. I didn't mean to kill her. I just wanted to stop her…"

I stood behind him and lay my cool hands on his shoulders. His sobs subsided. *It's all right, Peter. Well done. You've told the truth now. You're free now.*

"Don't listen to him," his mother was saying now to Gardiner. "He's simple, he is. Doesn't know what he's saying half the time—"

"Shut up, Mum. I ain't that simple. I ain't a kid anymore."

"Do you know where the club hammer is now, Peter? What did you do with it? Did you hide it somewhere?"

"I brought it home at first," he said. The agitation had left him now; he was almost calm. "I was going to confess. And then my mum, she told me not to. She said they'll send me back to prison. She said they'll do bad things to me again, the other prisoners. Beat me up, like they did the last time. She told me we had to hide the hammer, bury it. My mum went out later with me after it was dark and we buried it in the cornfield 'longside Gale Lane. Not near Rachel Vincent's house. Further along than that."

"Is that where it is now?"

He looked over at his mother. A concerned look, as if he wanted to say he was sorry. Her face was buried in her hands. He looked back at Gardiner.

"No, it ain't. I dug it up last week. I was thinking of turning myself in. It's been worrying me, been giving me nightmares."

"Where is it, Peter?"

"It's upstairs. It's in my wardrobe now."

48

It was muddy and brown with rust and it had my blood upon it still. Forensics confirmed that conclusively. The blood was dried and brown and looked like rust spots. The shoes were still buried in the cornfield. The size 10 Clarks brown lace-ups that he had been wearing on the day that I died. He took the two police constables along to the cornfield and showed them the spot. They dug them up. The leather was hard and stiff and caked with mud.

Peter Bates was taken to the station where the duty solicitor was summoned and he made a statement. He was practically illiterate, so someone had to transcribe it as he said it. Then it was read back to him and he signed it. Everything he said was the way it had happened…

*

I hadn't seen him enter the garden as I'd been busy upstairs putting away ironing. Molly was in her room. I popped my head in there, to check that she was okay. I'd been cross with her earlier; she'd had a silly tantrum about something and nothing and threw her cup of milk across the kitchen, so I'd sent her to her room.

I wanted to show her she was forgiven. She had her back to me when I came in the room. She was sitting on the bedroom floor playing with her Barbie dolls.

"Molls, you can come downstairs if you want. Shall I make you some lunch? What would you like?"

"Not hungry."

"Well, you can come down if you want."

No answer. I decided not to push her. She'd come around when she was ready. I came downstairs and into the kitchen. I walked over to the sink. That's when I saw him through the window. Peter Bates. He was in the garden, reaching up to the washing line, pulling my black knickers free from the pegs. A sudden fury overwhelmed me. I rushed out into the garden and screamed at him – "What are you doing! What in hell's name do you think you're doing!"

He turned and stared at me, his face white with panic. "I'm sorry, I'm so sorry. I'll put them back." He stepped forward towards the plastic basket on the grass and dropped the knickers down into it.

"You think that makes any difference? I've caught you in the act this time. I'm going to phone the police."

He stepped towards me and started groping at my arm. "No, please Missus. Please don't. I won't do it again…"

"You've done this before, haven't you? Red ones, last time. How many times have you done this? It's disgusting. I'll see what the police have to say about this—"

"No, please…" He was whining at me, pleading. "Don't

phone the police. They'll send me back to prison... I can't go back there..."

"Not my problem," I said, coldly, contemptuously. "Maybe your sort belong there."

I meant perverts, sex offenders, men who prey on women.

I turned icily and started towards the back door. I don't know what I would have done if I'd got inside the house, whether I really would have phoned the police or not. I wanted to frighten him mainly. Why should he get away with it? Others get away with nothing.

"STOP!" He shouted. "Stop, or else."

There was something in his voice I couldn't ignore. I turned around. He was standing only a few yards away from me, holding our club hammer in his hands. He must have picked it up from the top of the rabbit hutch. Ben had left it there the other day when he had used it to put up new fence panels down the bottom of the garden.

"Don't phone them," he said. "Don't phone the police."

I might have sneered, pulled a disgusted face, shrugged my shoulders. I thought he was bluffing. I thought he was too simple to actually do anything. I turned away again and started walking determinedly towards the back door. And then he struck me. There was a sudden firecracker bolt of pain. I clutched my head. I felt the blood immediately, sticky and warm. I started staggering towards the door. If I could make it inside, if I could only make it to the phone... I glanced up towards Molly's bedroom window. Her small white face was staring down at me. Then the whole window was full of Molly's faces, lots of them, a multitude...

Colours burnt on my eyes: green grass, a pink striped

paddling pool on the patio, Molly's red tricycle. The colours swirled into a mist, and then were compressed into a bright light. I felt myself sucked towards the light. Then the light disappeared and the darkness softened into a grey mist of shapes and colours again. Ben was calling my name. My parents were calling my name. I was a child again in the garden of the cottage in Wilmington: the taste of sherbet on my tongue; Mr Jackson's smiling face over the fence; smells of my mother's baking drifting from the kitchen door. I was spinning round and round under the skylights in my little house in Brighton, whilst Ben was taking a bath upstairs. I was making love to him, drowning in his kisses, smelling the musk of his skin. I linked my father's arm as I walked towards the altar. Smelt lilies, heard organ music, saw a throng of familiar faces shining like soft petals in a dim light. I was lying on a rack of pain under bright lights, the faces of nurses murmuring down at me. My daughter cried and the pain was broken.

I was lying on the black and white tiles of the kitchen floor.

Molly stood in the kitchen doorway. Her white face like a teardrop Halloween mask.

Molly, it's all right, Molly. Don't be afraid.

She didn't hear me. She started to whimper.

Molly, please don't cry. I'm all right.

There was a point at which I had a choice. I could have let go right then. I could have gone towards the bright light, that welcoming, warm room beyond the glass, or I could have stayed, cast adrift in the gloom at the edges of my daughter's life but never part of it again. I chose to stay. I saw the sadness and the fear enter my daughter, like a shadow she was swallowing. How could I have left her? She sat beside my body for hours. At first she rocked as she sat, moaning softly, and then she sat still and silent. I stayed with her. I laid my cold hand on her shoulder but I couldn't reach her anymore. Ben came home and I saw the shock enter him, too. He swept Molly into his arms and he wept over her silent face.

How could I leave them?

*

How easy is it to forgive?

49

I never hated him. I never hated Peter Bates.
I hated Nicholas Hedges though. I could not forgive him.

*

The Sunday after I had allowed Hedges to do what he did – I can't say *make love* because it doesn't describe at all what happened – he had come knocking on my door. Ben was in Scotland. Molly had been in her room but she'd come out and I saw her halfway down the stairs, listening to me arguing with Hedges. I panicked then. I said I'd meet him at his flat on Tuesday just to get him to go, to leave me alone. I hadn't intended to go. I'd been lying.

I didn't turn up. I dropped Molly off at her nursery and then went around the shops and had lunch out in a little bistro. All the time I was eating my pasta carbonara I was thinking of Nicholas Hedges pacing the floor in his flat, watching the clock. He would be realising by now that I wasn't coming. I felt a glow of satisfaction that I was causing him pain, but I also felt fear. What if he should seek some kind of revenge? Retaliation?

What if he should hurt Molly?

No, surely he wasn't capable of that.

*

It was several days after that. He must have entered from Gale Lane, letting himself into the garden through the back gate. I was in the kitchen doing the ironing. The ironing board was set up so that I had my back to the kitchen window and didn't see him coming until he burst through the back door that led into the kitchen. It wasn't locked. It is rarely locked when Molly and I are both at home on my days off. He gave me such a fright I nearly dropped the iron on my foot. He called me names at first. *Prick teaser, whore, slut.* All sorts of names. Ugly names. He didn't notice Molly standing at the door that opens to the hallway. He was facing away from her. I signalled to her with my eyes. I think she understood. He pushed me up against the kitchen work-surface. It dug into my lower back. Then he dragged me to the floor. He was strong; I didn't stand a chance. He had one arm wedged up against my throat. I couldn't breathe. I thought I was choking, I thought I was going to die. It is a complete fallacy to think that women can prevent being raped if they fight back and struggle. The best thing to do, the only thing, is to go limp, to make out as if you are already dead. I stepped outside my body so that I couldn't feel him do it.

It was almost like already being dead.

I'm not sure exactly when Molly hid in the cupboard under the stairs, or how much she had seen, but that was where she was when it was over. She sat there in the darkness, rocking, holding Miss Moffat. I crawled in beside her.

"It's all right, Molly. Mummy's all right."

She didn't answer.

"Don't worry, Molly. He won't come again. Never again."

We both started crying, rocking together, hugging each other. I didn't know who was comforting who.

Later that evening I made her promise never to tell anyone, never to tell her father.

It was the second time I had made my daughter keep a secret to protect me. It was wrong of me, and I shouldn't have done it. I was a psychologist. I, more than most people, knew the damage that is inflicted when an adult entreats a child to keep a dark secret. But I had so much to lose. I had nearly lost Ben, then found him again. If he knew about the rape, then he would've insisted I called the police and prosecuted. Then eventually it would've had to be revealed that I had previously willingly slept with Hedges.

Molly kept my secret. She lost the words for the memory, lost the comfort of the words. The memory was swallowed down in some deep place inside her and was sealed up. She went very quiet for a while. Preferred solitary games. Developed food fads. Went through a phase of wetting the bed. Ben was concerned about her. *She'll grow out of it*, I said. *All children go through funny phases at this age.*

I would make love to Ben sometimes and odd fragments of memory would jump into my mind. The edge of the kitchen work-surface digging into my back as

Hedges pressed up against me. Molly's shocked face in the doorway. Being dragged to the floor. Hedges' arm wedged up against my throat.

I would cling to Ben like someone who is drowning and force the memories to go away.

*

We live our lives as if we have choices, but it is our lives that live us, that pass through us. A window opens and we jump through it and in that moment all other possibilities are closed to us. We say – *If only I hadn't done such and such, then this wouldn't have happened.* Not realising that the choices we think we had weren't really there.

If only I had responded differently when Peter Bates came into my garden to steal a pair of black knickers from the washing line. If only I hadn't confronted him but had just let him do it. Or been more gentle with him, more understanding. Then he wouldn't have picked up the club hammer and struck me. Then I'd be alive and my daughter would still have a mother.

*

I could go back a step further. If only I had been out when the gas man called. Or not invited him to have a cup of tea. Or if it had been another gas man that day that came to read my meter. Then he might not have lunged at me, cornering me against the wall, touching my breasts. *Housewives like you, you're gagging for it, aren't you?* – he'd said. Some women would have found him attractive – and no doubt many did – with his green eyes and Irish looks. But all I noticed was his small teeth like a ferret and the smile that missed his eyes.

I pushed him away, slapped his face, shouted – *Get off me you creep! Get out of my house.*

He swore at me. *Bloody frigid bitch.* I told him I would report him to the gas board if he didn't go right now.

But he was just trying it on. Like a lot of men do. He wasn't a rapist.

*

Let me go still further back, to a few days before the day the gas man called. I'd been into Redhill to the Saturday market with Joanne. I rarely went into Redhill, except sometimes to catch the train to London. I rarely went because Nicholas Hedges lived there and I didn't want to risk bumping into him. But Joanne wanted to go. The Saturday market was a good one, lots of fresh food produce, and she was planning a party for her husband's thirtieth and asked if I'd go with her. We'll have lunch out together, she said. Try the new Thai restaurant. Make a nice outing of it. I thought, why not? The chances of seeing Nicholas Hedges there were negligible, I decided. It was time, anyway, that I put it behind me. Lived my life the way I wanted to. Why let him make me a victim a second time by fearing him like this?

We were in the queue at the greengrocery stall. Joanne was asking for asparagus and strawberries. I felt someone pressing up close to me from behind. I turned and there he was. Nicholas Hedges. The shock of seeing him again was like being punched in the solar plexus. He was leering at me, gloating at my discomfort. He said nothing; he didn't need to. I started to shake. Joanne had what she wanted and we moved away.

"You okay, Rachel? You've gone very pale."

"I'm fine," I said. But I wasn't. Seeing him, having him standing so close to me, his groin almost pressing up against my hip, had opened the wound again. I felt the humiliation, the fear, that I'd felt on the day when he'd raped me.

*

So when only days later the gas man made that loafish clumsy pass at me, the wound was still raw, still bleeding.

After the gas man left I picked up the phone and tried to call the gas board to report him. I thought it would make me feel better if I did that – less of a victim. But I had that awful mechanical voice in my ear, telling me to press this button and then that one. Then I was left hanging on the line for minutes, irritating music being played into my ear. In the end I got frustrated and gave up. I went upstairs to check on Molly. She was still sulking; she wasn't ready to forgive me. I came downstairs.

The weather that morning had been glorious. The day had started with clear blue skies and I had hung the washing out early. But showers were predicted later on. I went to the sink and looked out the window to look at the sky for signs of rain. I saw Peter Bates in the garden, snatching my black knickers from the washing line, and something in me jumped up white and hot and searing.

It wasn't about Peter Bates. It wasn't even about the gas man.

It was about Nicholas Hedges, and what he had done to me back in January.

*

All the *if onlys* can rack up to nothing. Once that window has been jumped through, the way I jumped through it when I accepted the lift he offered from the station, that day Molly and I went up to London to see the Trafalgar tree, all the options and choices I thought I had about my life had disappeared.

We are free. We are not free.
Another paradox, Ben.
How easy is it to forgive?

Not easy. I am getting there. I can see the brightly lit room beyond the glass. Faces turned towards me, smiling warmly.

I'm nearly ready, I tell them. *I'm almost there.*

50

Ben took Katie with him when he took Molly to visit my parents the following Sunday morning. She had been there in the kitchen with Ben, who was making pancakes for breakfast, when Molly came downstairs. Molly may have been a little surprised, but didn't seem to mind seeing Katie in her silk dressing gown in the kitchen with her father that morning.

"Come on, Molls, let's show Katie how it's done." Molly placed her hands on the handle of the frying pan and Ben covered them with his. They tossed the pancake together, landing it perfectly on the other side.

"Bravo!" Katie clapped. I noticed her shiny eyes, the bloom in her cheeks, how happy she looked.

"And again!" Ben shouted. This time it landed on the edge of the pan. Half of it broke off and fell to the floor. Goldie rushed forward and gobbled it up.

Molly laughed. She laughed so loud she could not stop. She slid down to her knees, grasped the greedy dog and buried her laughing face into Goldie's side.

"Bloody hound!" But Ben was laughing too. "Thank God we're getting rid of you this afternoon."

*

My parents were waiting out in the driveway when Ben's car drew up. They were ready for this. Ben had phoned to ask if he could bring Katie to meet them.

"Of course! Love to meet her," Sylvia had said. But when she put the phone down she went over to my father who was sitting in his chair pretending to be reading the newspaper.

"Ben's bringing Katie," she said.

"Ahh, yes," my father said.

"She'll be good for him. Good for Molly, too."

"I know."

Sylvia stood behind the chair and leant down over him, her arms cradling him.

"We've got to let go now."

"I have done. But Rachel's always with us, you know. Nothing changes that."

My mother straightened up and moved over to the sideboard. There was a framed photograph on it of John smiling broadly in black gown and mortar, taken when he'd graduated in engineering from Surrey University. My mother considered it; I could feel her heart warm, as it always did. She stroked his face softly with her thumb. There was also a framed photograph of Ben and me on our wedding day. She gazed at that one for a while. Then she picked it up, kissed my blurred smiling face in it, slid it into one of the drawers of the sideboard.

And now here they were. Ben and Katie. They were laughing, looking happy, as people recently in love always do. Molly was looking happy too. Happier than they had seen her for a long time.

After the introductions, the perfunctory kisses and hugs, they all trooped into the kitchen. Sylvia made a big pot of tea and put out the batch of cherry scones she had baked that morning. Molly sat on my father's knee. She laid her small hand on his chest.

"I can feel your heart beating," she said. "Is it better now, Granddad?"

"I think so," he said. "Better than it was."

Ben took Molly's sketch book out of a bag. "Molly's got a picture here that she wants to show you, haven't you, Molls?"

"Oh yes," Molly said gleefully, remembering. She slid from my father's knee. She took the sketch book from Ben and laid it on the kitchen table. She turned to the right page. It was the picture she'd drawn where Ben, Molly and me floated together in a blue space under a brilliant sun, bright flowers under our feet.

"It's a picture of all of us in heaven," she said.

She had added to the picture now. There wasn't just the three of us anymore. Katie was there, on the other side of Ben, with long dark hair fanning out around her head and spiked red shoes on her feet. And Sylvia and my father on the other side of me, Sylvia with a maze of curly hair and earrings that dangled to her knees, and my father, balding with goggle-glasses bigger than the face they were on. And Goldie too, solid and rectangular with little stick legs, snuffling amongst the flowers under Molly's floating feet.

And up high, in the left-hand corner, a round bowl-shape crowded with orange fish.

"It's beautiful, Molly," Sylvia said.

"And I haven't left out Mummy. Look, there she is!" Molly pointed to the figure on the right side of herself in the picture, the one with the mane of red hair and the dress with little dots on it.

"I can see that," my father said. "That's good. Your mummy shouldn't be left out."

*

And in the blink of an eye I am gone.

ABOUT THE AUTHOR

Elizabeth Diamond has been widely been published in poetry journals, and has a collection entitled *Windfalls Weighing Down the Heart,* which was written as part of her MA in Creative Writing from Glamorgan University, Wales, where her private tutor was the renowned Welsh poet, Gillian Clarke After the MA she switched her focus to writing prose, and had two novels published by Picador, *An Accidental Light* and *Underwater. An Accidental Light* was also sold in the US and Germany, and was translated into German as . Elizabeth would describe herself, amongst other things, as being a survivor. She has overcome a difficult childhood, poverty as a young single mother of two sons and has battled with a stammer and depression. Now in her sixties, she is happy and comfortable in her own skin, and uses her life experience in writing about characters 'on the edge' of their lives. She lives in Devon, only a short walk from the sea. She enjoys painting seascapes and animals in acrylics, and has sold a number of her 'fish paintings' in her local town.